Marriage Can Be Murder

(Dr. Benjamin Bones Mysteries #1)

By

Emma Jameson

Marriage Can Be Murder
(Dr Benjamin Bones Mysteries #1)

Edited by: Jenx Byron & Theo Fenraven
Cover design by J. David Peterson
Formatted by PyperPress

DEDICATION

For Mom, Dad, Jim, and Barbara

Chapter 1: A Fresh Start
1 September 1939

Things will get worse before they get better, Dr. Benjamin Bones told himself, as much by reflex as conviction. The phrase was a maxim his grandfather often spouted, particularly at grim moments: funerals, bankruptcies, and elections which ended in another Tory victory. A firebrand reformer and socialist, Granddad had written and crudely published his own hand-folded, ink-smeared political tracts, passing them out on street corners until his mortified wife dragged him home. Of all the futures Granddad had imagined for Ben, who was his only grandson, marrying into a highly respectable Tory family like the Eubanks hadn't figured. And if Granddad, who'd been cold in his grave these last five years, had been alive to learn of Ben's marital troubles, the old agitator would have received such scandalous news—the possibility of the Bones family's first-ever divorce— by cracking open a bottle of Glenlivet.

Not Mum. She'll cry into her pinafore, Ben thought. *And Dad might turn me out of the house. After finishing his one-thousandth speech about men upholding their obligations, that is.*

It was a speech Ben knew well; he'd assaulted himself with it every day for the last six months. Divorce was dishonorable. Divorce was shameful. Divorce was a lifelong black mark that would haunt his future prospects to the end of his days. A divorced man was, after all, either a cad, a bounder, or weak-willed, unable to keep his house in order. And a divorced woman? With the exception of cinema stars, who existed in some silk-clad, diamond-encrusted alternate universe, a divorced woman was thought damaged goods. Even in cosmopolitan

London, Penny would be called a reject and presumed a slut. After a suitable interval, Ben would have the opportunity to win back the confidence of his community by remarrying. Penny would not.

Unless Albie follows her to Cornwall and sweeps her off her feet.

But no. Albie Sanderson was married with two small children. He also enjoyed a munitions factory supervisor job supplied by his father-in-law. Ben, who'd disliked Albie even before his suspicions were aroused, could easily imagine the man abandoning his wife and kiddies. But the employment his rival's father-in-law provided? That was a "reserved occupation," immune from conscription in the British Army. Even if Albie truly loved Penny, which Ben did not believe, would he cast aside a guarantee of never being sent to Poland or France on the eve of near-certain war? Not likely.

He stole a glance across the car seat at Penny. Only three feet of black leather upholstery stretched between them, but the distance felt far greater. She'd insisted on making the journey with him, saying it must be fate. A fresh start, a chance to mend their marriage. Was she right?

As a twenty-seven-year-old male in good health, Ben had expected to be called into service as an Army doctor. Instead, he'd received notification that he, like Albie, held a "reserved occupation"—a job critical to the preservation of the homeland during wartime, and one that could not be filled by a hastily trained woman. But London was full of physicians, many retired but willing to return to practice. So the Ministry of Labor was relocating Ben to a needier segment of the country. Instead of the Harley Street practice he'd aspired to, he was driving down to Cornwall, to a village west of the port city,

Plymouth. Like London, Plymouth boasted a small network of physicians too old for conscription, but Plymouth's surrounding villages, all with suitably bucolic names like Birdswing and Barking, did not. Ben had been ordered to take up residence in Birdswing, which had recently buried its elderly doctor. From there, he would take patients from a twenty-mile radius and assist Plymouth with disaster relief, should the city be bombed. To say these government orders represented a sharp departure from Ben's career hopes was a towering example of British understatement. Still, a few months or years in the country was his duty, and he meant to see it through. For a woman like Penny, even a few days in the country would be excruciating.

And Birdswing? Ben stole another glance. She was curled against the passenger door of their Austin Ten-Four, navy Chanel peacoat rolled up beneath one cheek. Though Cornwall, land of castles, coasts, and moors, was reputedly beautiful, there would be no *haute couture* in Birdswing, population 1,221 souls. Penny knew that better than anyone; she'd been born there, escaping to London around age seventeen. Perhaps the fact her husband had been sent back now, by government order, was truly fate in the form of a choice: remain in London, rendering divorce inevitable, or accompany him to a place she loathed in the spirit of sacrifice.

Sacrifice didn't come naturally to Penny. Last night, she'd stayed up till almost dawn playing Guy Lombardo records on the gramophone and drinking with friends. Irritated by the hen chatter and the music, which was far from his taste, Ben had gone to bed early, plugging his ears with cotton wool so he could sleep. Now he understood her plan: to sleep the day away rather than sit beside him in what amounted to a wheeled cell, with nothing to do but stare at the moving English countryside and answer "yes" or "no" when he tried to initiate a conversation.

Yet she's here. And I should be grateful she doesn't want a row, Ben told himself. *Even when she was awake, she kept her nose in a book.*

Penny had fallen asleep clutching it, a slender volume of Shakespeare's sonnets. Lately, she carried it everywhere, in her hands or tucked in her purse. Did some verse in it remind her of Albie? Ben felt his upper lip curl. The idea didn't infuriate him, only struck him as nauseating. He wasn't sure if that response boded well for the restoration of their marriage.

Once his knowledge of the affair had become obvious, Penny had tried to explain, and Ben found himself unable to listen. That first rupture of trust, now more than three years ago, had cut too deeply, severing his awareness of certain beliefs, certain feelings. Sometimes he wanted to transcend that, to heal. Other times he preferred to just carry on, blindly if need be. Often he had no idea what went on inside his own heart, but he knew this: if their marriage was to be saved, hearing the gory details about Penny and Albie's affair had to be avoided at all costs.

Surely that isn't so strange, Ben thought, seeing the countryside unspool beside him without really taking in the swaying grasses or gentle green hills. *Easier to forgive when one has no specific facts to forget.* Besides, Penny's transgression aside, Ben's hands weren't spotless. He hadn't broken his wedding vows or even been seriously tempted. *But.* He'd given his burgeoning medical practice the bulk of his attention, reserving his deepest passion and enthusiasm for his patients. He'd worked late when he could have gone home; made routine house calls instead of taking Penny to the smart clubs and Bond Street shops she adored; read medical journals into the wee hours instead of going to bed when she did. In short, he'd done his best to live like a bachelor rather than face the wife who'd become a stranger after….

He cut off that line of thought. His father's pedantic voice came to him: *Marry in haste, repent in leisure. Many an ill-suited union has splintered on the rocks of that first year. But marriage isn't about pleasure or self-indulgence. It's about duty. That's why it arrives clothed in solemn vows and prayer. To signal the grave nature of the commitment you undertook when you repeated, "Till death us do part."*

How much of that speech did Ben believe? It varied from minute to minute, but his old dad was right on one count: people made mistakes. Ben, who'd fallen for Penny during his second year of medical training, had proposed marriage on their third date and been accepted on the sixth. Equating infatuation with love, he'd been over the moon when she said yes, unable to believe his luck. Barely five foot-eight and compactly built, he'd been unbearably wet behind the ears, unaware of how his wide blue eyes, mussed brown hair, and lopsided smile went over with the female set. His top marks in the classroom were balanced by gross ineptitude elsewhere, especially those spots where dance music blared and glasses clinked. In Ben's early attempts to meet girls, he'd missed tentative advances, ignored crushes, and squandered opportunities, all without the slightest clue.

Then came that evening in the quad.

Ben had been studying beneath a hornbeam tree since his final class let out, getting deeper into *Gray's Anatomy* as the sun disappeared, leaving sweeps of orange, purple, and red in its wake. He might not have noticed except for the gathering gloom; only a scrap of reading light remained. Overhead, the hornbeam had sighed, releasing a fresh volley of dry yellow leaves, and Ben pulled his nose out of the textbook.

Penny had been standing over him, dressed in a light blue frock and matching sweater. Her expression, slightly scornful, set off her prettiness, transforming it into near-beauty. And her light blue frock pulled tight where it should, revealing generous curves and perfect legs.

"That cow by the fountain," Penny said, indicating another girl sitting yards away, "called you a bloodless bookworm. I didn't appreciate her cheek, so I told her you were my boyfriend. Not to mention the best kisser on campus. Now why don't you stow that doorstop and prove it before she decides I'm a bald-faced liar?"

Ben had goggled at her. Hours later, it struck him that his ideal reply would have been, "Sure. And while I'm about it, why don't I buy you a drink?" But in those days, timely comebacks were beyond his powers. And asking out a girl of Penny's caliber had seemed a delicate, treacherous business, like spying on the Japanese or defusing bombs. So he'd actually said, "Terribly sorry. Must be some mistake."

She'd laughed at him, but sweetly, emboldening him to ask, "Have we, er, met?"

"Of course we have. Just now, silly." She'd poked Ben in the chest, just wide of his heart. "I'm Penelope Eubanks. You're Benjamin Bones. I've been watching you for ages, every time I come to visit my brother George. Working up the nerve to say hello." As he gave a weak, disbelieving chuckle, she glanced over her shoulder. "Oh! Little Miss Fountain is frowning. Quick, pretend to kiss me."

With enviable grace, she eased down beside him, seating herself on a hornbeam root as comfortably as on a satin pillow. Then she brought her face in, near enough for him to inhale her sweet breath.

Those perfectly painted lips didn't touch his. But they were so close, he felt as if something intimate passed between them. The singularity of that faux-kiss was like the first time he tasted a gin and tonic. Bright and tart, bracing as juniper buds submerged in snow; a little bit wrong and all the more desirable for it.

And comparing Penny to a cocktail was fitting, because in those days, everything about her was intoxicating. Her blonde curls, smart frocks, black patent heels, and tortoiseshell hair combs. The way she smoked unapologetically, holding the fag between her fingers like a man, declaring a skinny black holder too twee as she blew smoke in his direction. Her red lipstick called "Carnage," the whiff of *Sous le Vent* behind her ears, the way she laughed off a snag in her silk stockings while other girls moaned.

He'd loved her. And if it hadn't been love, the distinction was too narrow for Ben, just twenty three years old, to know the difference.

Penny hadn't wanted a long engagement or even a society wedding, which suited Ben just fine. Less than a month after she said yes, they eloped to Greta Green, like wayward lovers in a Jane Austen novel. Nowadays Scotland's "anvil priests" required twenty-one days of residence prior to nuptials, but Ben didn't chafe under the restriction. Especially since Penny, content with only a simple gold band, suggested they consider themselves as good as married.

Their holiday in Scotland was everything he'd hoped for. When Ben and Penny returned to England, they were congratulated all around, even by her wealthy father, who'd looked pale and shocked, yet forgiving. Much was made over the romance of it all—a business magnate's daughter and a promising young physician, too wildly in love to wait. A home was found for them while Ben completed his medical training, the first year's rent paid by Mr. Eubanks as a wedding present. In that house, a half-timbered mock Tudor with a stained glass rose on the front door, Ben and Penny began to know one another. All too well, it seemed.

It will get worse before it gets better, Ben repeated, passing a hand over his face. The hum of the Austin Ten-Four was almost hypnotic. Golden afternoon was dissolving into twilight, and still the road stretched on, nothing but farmland on either side. *But it* can *get better. War may still be averted. We could be back in London in six months. And perhaps seeing Penny in Birdswing, in the village she grew up in, will remind me of how I felt in the quad.*

***

"Ben?" Penny sounded groggy, but looked lovelier than ever in the half-light. "Are we in Birdswing?"

"I hate to admit it, but I'm not sure. According to this, we should be on Stafford Road. Problem is, all the signs are painted over." He'd pulled over a few minutes before, unfolding his map across the steering wheel and studying it by torchlight.

"Painted over?" Sitting up, she opened the glove box and slipped her book of sonnets inside. "Some sort of prank?"

"No, I think it's deliberate. A rural effort to keep the fifth column confused." Ben had heard that segments of the country took the notion of invasion very much to heart. Convinced that enemy agents might parachute into England, many citizens proposed eliminating the sort of information that might assist invaders in making their way to towns or cities, such as church and cemetery names, iconic pub signs, and all road markers. He had no idea what a freshly-dropped German spy, perhaps still in harness with a collapsed parachute in tow, might make of their position, but as a natural-born Englishman in possession of a decent map, Ben was well and truly confused. Either the buildings looming ahead marked the outskirts of Birdswing, or they'd wandered east, perhaps into Barking or another hamlet.

Feeling around in her bag, Penny located her compact mirror, opened it to check her hair, repositioned a few curls, and snapped it shut. "I look a fright. A drink and a fag wouldn't go amiss. That building over there…." She gestured. "Does it say Daley's?"

"I can't tell."

"If this is Birdswing, that should be Daley's Co-op, and *that*"—she pointed at a shape almost indistinguishable from the tall trees in front of it—"should be the Sheared Sheep. Our destination for the evening, and *très chic*."

"I'll bet." He squinted against the deepening dark. A few stars were appearing overhead, but not enough. The blackout, as the government called it, had only just gone into effect, but like most of the country, this community had long been compliant. As a result, the windows of both buildings were painted black, or else covered with opaque fabric and paper. Entryway lamps were doused, and streetlights were dark. The goal was to make even the most dense segments of England look uninhabited, to appear as strategically meaningless as cow pastures to enemy bombers.

"I see a sign hanging out front," Ben continued, indicating the shape Penny had called Daley's Co-op. "Are you sure that isn't the boarding house? Perhaps you have them reversed."

"Anything's possible. Even when I come back, I stick to Plymouth." Exiting the car, Penny yawned and stretched. "Still, if memory serves, the Sheared Sheep is behind those trees. And 'boarding house' is too metropolitan a term. It's a pub with a room to let. Here, wave your torch that way. The Fuhrer's watching."

"Very funny." Feeling a twinge of guilt for using it past twilight, Ben switched off the device, tossing it and his map inside the Austin Ten-Four. For the blackout to succeed, it was supposed to be absolute. That meant more than dark houses and businesses. It meant no lamps on cars or bicycles, much less a hand-held torch. Blackness helped Britain; so much as a lit fag-end aided Hitler. Back in London, Ben had assumed he'd grow accustomed to the necessity. But here, in the heart of the country, the darkness was dense and unnerving.

"Perhaps I should go check. We'll leave the car here overnight," Ben said. Its tires were scarcely off the road, but there wasn't much grass to park on, only a steep drop-off between the thoroughfare and an unplowed field.

"I hope no one careens into it." Putting on her coat, Penny buttoned it up to her chin as the wind kicked up. The light was fading so fast, the navy wool looked black, and her blonde hair, silver. "Folks drive rather recklessly in the long stretches between villages."

"Can't imagine they'll be driving now. I really think that building must be the Sheared Sheep." As he squinted at the sign, which appeared to be wound with rags to obscure the name, something glinted on the roof. For a moment, he imagined a human form, but then a crow cawed, flapping away.

"I promise you, it's behind those trees." Penny started toward the dark, swaying shapes, her pace elegant and unhurried, heels clicking as she walked. "Go on, try and prove me wrong. I can practically hear a pint of cider calling my name."

He let her go, taking long strides toward the building with the hidden sign. Surely the entryway of a village co-op would look more inviting, with… well… what? Sacks of flour? Bits of farm machinery? Rolls of chicken wire? It occurred to Ben as he closed the distance that he had no idea whatsoever what a provincial co-op should look like. And it was those moments as he lingered near the door, not quite resolved to knock, that saved his life, though he wouldn't realize it for some time.

"Who's there?" a heavily accented voice, female, called from inside. "I hear your footsteps." She sounded frightened.

"Is this the Sheared Sheep?"

"Across the road. Behind the trees!"

Smiling at his own pigheadedness, Ben turned to find himself in near-complete darkness. As he crossed the thoroughfare, he didn't look either way—there was nothing to see, and so deeply ingrained was his expectations of headlamps at night, the darkness seemed to guarantee his safety. He'd only just reached Penny when he heard it, something huge and fast rumbling toward them. Too startled to cry out, he tried to pull her behind him, and then….

SMACK

Then….

Falling, falling, and a *crack* like the earth had punched him in the back of the head. He smelled rubber and petrol, tasted blood, and heard another slow, wet creak as flesh and bone was pulverized. Half of him thought this was a nightmare, that it couldn't be happening. The other side—the physician side—realized that sound must be tires rolling over a human being. Then shock turned into pain, and pain transmuted into a deeper darkness, spiraling into the unknown.

***

"I am speaking to you from the cabinet room at 10 Downing Street…."

Ben realized he'd been awake for some time. Where was he? He didn't hurt, precisely, but had the odd certainty that if he moved or spoke, the pain would come and perhaps never leave. As for this scrupulous, upper-crust voice, he knew it; he didn't like it, but he knew it. Prime Minister Neville Chamberlain.

"… and that consequently, this country is at war with Germany…."

War? Yes, when he was a child, but that was the Great War, the War to End All Wars. Confused, Ben tried to crack open gummy eyelids. His mouth was dry, and his skin felt heavy, as if turned to lead. Morphine? Had someone administered morphine? Eyes half-opened, he registered a lumpy mattress beneath him and the smell of carbolic soap.

"You can imagine," Chamberlain went on, "what a bitter blow it is to me…."

The pain was gathering itself, threatening to break through. His right leg throbbed. His left… was it even there?

"… but Hitler would not have it…."

Ben tried to sit up, but nothing happened. "My leg," he mumbled, tongue almost too thick to move.

"Hush now," a soft female voice said.

"… his actions show convincingly that there is no chance of expecting this man ever giving up his practice of using force to gain his will…."

"My leg? Was it—crushed?"

"We have a clear conscience." Chamberlain's voice issued from a wireless on the bureau, Ben saw through filmy vision. "We have done all any country could do…."

"Hush," the woman said again.

"Penny?"

"Doctor," the woman whispered urgently. Only as Ben tried to form a reply did he realize she wasn't speaking to him, but over his head, to someone else. "Doctor, he's thrashing about."

"Dr. Bones." The voice, male and cool, was not unlike Prime Minister Chamberlain's, politely apologizing for a second world war, though he clearly held himself blameless. "Calm yourself, or you'll get another injection."

"Where's Penny? I heard—heard—" He broke off, remembering the sound of heavy tires pulverizing something—someone—and knew. Beyond all doubt, he knew.

"And now that we have resolved to finish it," Chamberlain went on inexorably, those plummy tones made tinny by the wireless. "I know you will do your part with courage and calmness."

"You heard the man. Courage and calmness." The physician pressed a hypodermic needle against Ben's upper arm, the prick infinitesimal against an ever-expanding universe of pain. "The world is at war. Count yourself lucky to sleep."

Chapter 2: The Lady of the Manor
10 October, 1939

Ben didn't need to leave his room over the Sheared Sheep to know it was getting colder; he felt it every time a southeaster blew through, penetrating the late Victorian heap as easily as a torn mack. Downstairs, raucous laughter and pint-fueled rows started in midafternoon and carried straight through till closing. After the issuing of the Call-Up Proclamation, it seemed most of the village's young men were heading into the pub a little earlier each day, either to drown their fears or enjoy what might be a final pint with friends. Ben often overheard long snatches of conversation, provincial and circular in nature, that did nothing to entice him downstairs. And if not for the insistence of his nurse, a curt sister with very definite views on the curative power of sunlight, he would have kept his blackout screens in place night and day. What difference did it make?

The words of the publican, Angus Foss, floated up from the barroom. That is, if the perpetually aggrieved tones of a perpetually aggrieved Scot can ever be said to "float."

"Aye, I'll fetch him for ye. Just what my poor spine needs, another wee traipse down the stairs with a full-grown man in my arms. Devil of a way to start the day. And me due to unlock the doors in a quarter hour…."

Ben checked the alarm clock beside his bed. Was it really not yet three o'clock? Dawn was trundling toward dusk even slower than usual.

"… but ye know my temperament. Man o' the people. Live to serve," Foss continued morosely. "Still, martyrs and saints have their limits. The Council—meaning your ladyship's mother, ye ken—had best make restitution for all I'm out in lost rent. That includes meals, housekeeping, and electric current. If I'm not assured payment by tomorrow morning, I'll put him out, I swear by God I will."

Foss's threat didn't trouble Ben. He'd overheard it many times during his slow convalescence, though never attached to a twenty-four hour deadline. The insistence of some unseen visitor to have him brought downstairs was what bothered him. Foss found the process inconvenient; Ben found it downright humiliating. As for whatever the visitor wished to discuss, it didn't matter. Unless the person asking represented the British army, Ben would say what he always said: no.

Easing his Edwardian wheelchair, a ghastly contraption fashioned of blond wood and rattan, out of his room, Ben maneuvered onto the landing. There, near the top of the stairs, he couldn't see the bar, where Foss and his visitor were standing, but he could hear her voice quite clearly.

"I understand he's lodged here six weeks. So lost rent is fair enough," she said in the flowing tones of an educated woman. "But surely you customarily provide meals to your guests? I've always pitied those souls unfortunate enough to squat in this hovel, but I refuse to believe even you would bill them separately for electric lights. Or what you call housekeeping, which amounts to Edith Hoovering twice a month and linens changed once per solstice?"

Foss cleared his throat. "Now, that's verra hard—"

"Nonsense. I was being kind to Edith. If I were the sort of woman who engaged in gossip, and I assure you I am not, I would add that outside Birdswing, 'Hoovering' is not the common term for Edith's primary occupation. I might also remark that you virtually never let that room upstairs, except for the sort of exchange that doesn't require a hot meal to sizzle."

"That's a lie!" Foss thundered. "No immoral congress takes place within these walls."

"Of course there's no immoral congress. A physician with two broken legs occupies the requisite space." As the woman laughed, Ben leaned forward, trying to get a look at her. "Mind you, I make no accusations. I never repeat gossip and would prefer not to hear the rumors about poor Edith and your tawdry little room. No doubt she's a nearly adequate maid, and it's a nearly bearable cell. So please believe me, my dear Mr. Foss, when I say I perceive your discontent. My mother perceives your discontent. Far away, nestled amongst the most distant stars, advanced life forms perceive your—"

"Dinna ken what you're on about," Foss said peevishly.

"Of course not. Being met with slack jaws and faintly suspicious eyes is both my blessing and my curse. But if you could just sublimate your habitual disgruntlement long enough to fetch down—"

"Blessing?" Foss cut in again. "How the deuce is it a blessing that regular folk can't make heads nor tails o' what ye say?"

"It reduces the volume of complaints directed toward my mother." The visitor sounded cheerful. "She's not a well woman, you know, and heaven knows my childhood travails contributed to her condition. How fortuitous that as I matured, I acquired sufficient vocabulary to speak my mind without ruining her day. Now. Mr. Foss. I've very much enjoyed our little talk, but the time draws nigh for you to ply your unsavory trade, and Edith to ply hers. So will you fetch down Dr. Bones, please?"

"Aye, Lady Juliet." The cantankerous Scot sounded defeated.

Ben wheeled back into his room. Somewhere in the midst of listening to that acid-tongued woman, he'd lost his resolve to say no, at least without hearing her out. But what could she possibly want? Everyone in Birdswing knew of his injuries. His right leg, broken below the knee, was mostly healed, but his left leg had been shattered. During that titanic *smack* of impact, the moment his torso struck the lorry's bonnet, his legs had connected with its iron grille, breaking the tibia and fibula in two places each. Moreover, his femur had snapped, either when the lorry hit him or when he struck the ground. Now Ben knew firsthand the truth of the medical school saying: a broken femur was the worst pain a man could experience. Its corollary, that childbirth was the worst pain a human being could experience, made him devoutly glad to be male.

Hearing the stairs creak under Foss's heavy tread, Ben gripped the arms of his chair and slowly, carefully, tried to rise. His right leg trembled. It had grown weak during the long recuperation. Two seconds later, his left buckled, dropping him back in the wheelchair with a stab of agony.

Perspiration broke out across his forehead. Sighing, he wiped it away. There was no more morphine for him: since the declaration of war, narcotics and other essential medications were strictly rationed. As a result, he'd been undermedicated, at least by London hospital standards, but that was probably a blessing. Morphine didn't eliminate pain, it just created detachment, placing the patient on a billowy cloud from which discomfort could be ignored. No other substance came close; not even single malt whiskey could compete with an injectable opioid. And Ben, who during his internship had struggled to comprehend the nature of morphine addiction, understood it now all too well. He'd survived the accident. Penny had not. The chance for them to repair their union, or at least face its dissolution together, had been snuffed out without amends or even goodbyes. When real physical pain was entwined with amorphous demons like heartbreak, guilt, or misery, and a substance existed that artificially detached the sufferer for a few precious hours, who on earth wouldn't be tempted?

He looked around the little room. The books and magazines his mum and dad had brought were long read; the condolence cards and letters from the extended Bones family were tucked away. His last visitor had been an aunt on holiday who'd dropped by out of morbid curiosity; his last telegram, from Penny's brother George, asking if Penny had any life insurance money due. A fresh distraction might be worth the price of venturing downstairs.

"Dr. Bones! Are ye decent?" Foss bellowed outside the door.

"Yes." Only due to the efforts of his nurse, who insisted her patients be fully dressed by breakfast, no lazing about in pajamas or dressing gown. Most days, Ben didn't see the point, any more than he saw the point of looking out the window at this sad little village he refused to call home. But defying such a grimly resolved sister wasn't worth the wear and tear on his vocal cords. So not only was he decent, he was properly attired to meet this backwater aristocrat, from his silk necktie to his Oxford dress shoes. "Do come in."

"Do come in," Foss mimicked. As usual, his hair was wild, his shirt was stained, and a bit of egg clung to his bushy mustache. "I've not come to take tea with ye. Here to break me back again in service to her ladyship."

"You sound like you don't fancy the task. Shame. Being carried by you is the highlight of my week." Ben kept his tone light. "So tomorrow morning I'm out on my ear, is that right?"

Foss had the decency to look abashed. "Ye heard?"

"As my mystery visitor put it, beings on faraway planets heard. Never mind, Foss, think nothing of it. If the government hasn't paid you yet for my room and board, I don't blame you for feeling ill-used. Tell me about that woman. What does she want?"

"Like anyone kens the answer to that. Beat down me door while I was at lunch and prattled on till I gave in. Her and her mother, Lady Victoria, come from people who once owned every acre of Birdswing. Reckon they still do, or near as makes no difference. I told her you're fit for nowt, but she wouldn't listen. That's how she wound up married to a bounder—not listening."

"Married to a bounder?" The revelation didn't surprise Ben; Birdswing brimmed with gossip. Everyone, even his nurse, seemed incapable of simple discourse without tossing in a few nuggets of personal information about someone not present to defend themselves.

"Aye, and not just any bounder, the prince o' the lot. As flamboyant as Valentino and as phony as they come, stuffed with lies and promises. Made off with half the family fortune, from what I hear. Course Lady Juliet and her mum are close-mouthed about it, but care to wager how it ended?" Foss lifted his eyebrows so high, small eyes gleamed within their narrow sockets. "The 'd' word."

Ben knew he was supposed to respond with disapproval and chose to depart from the script. "Good on her."

"There's no call for sarcasm." Foss adopted a tone of virtuous sorrow. "It's a stain on Birdswing. All the manor staff deny it—high-minded and high-handed, the lot o' them. But he's gone, isn't he, and Lady Juliet only wears her ring on formal occasions. Still, she's Mrs. Bolivar, not Miss Linton. Remember that." Taking a deep breath, he bent over the wheelchair. "Ready?"

"Ready." Ben steeled himself. Foss, stringy but remarkably strong, slid one arm around his shoulders and another beneath his knees, lifting him out of the chair. Bad enough to be held close by another man, particularly one like Foss, but the mere experience of being carried downstairs set Ben's left knee on fire. His thigh ached, too. By the time Foss deposited him on the pub's lone sofa, a red velvet affair long past its prime, fresh perspiration stood out on Ben's forehead and tears stung his eyes. Fortunately, Foss was too occupied with his own resentment to notice.

"You look like a slender wee lad, but you weigh more than a keg o' me best. At least when I shift one o' those, I'm padding me pocket while I strain me back." Foss sighed theatrically. "Let me fill my lungs and I'll fetch down your bloody chair."

It was a bumpy transit via wheelchair down the pub's front steps, beneath two elms, and into the dazzling afternoon sun. Parked by the curb was a Crossley 20/30, gleaming ebony and clean as a whistle. Its driver leaned against the bonnet, six foot two if she stood an inch, clad in what looked like waterproof trousers, a man's green

Macintosh, and galoshes. Dull brown hair was scraped back in a bun, exposing what seemed like too much face: a vast expanse of forehead and chin and cheeks, all of it sunburned. Ben, aware that during the war, unmarried women would temporarily fill the positions vacated by able-bodied men, thought this she-behemoth was better suited to farm or factory labor. Perhaps when it came to hiring drivers, Lady Juliet's judgment was as questionable as her taste in men.

"Good heavens, it's the man himself!" she called. "After such a long wait, I'd nearly succumbed to despair."

Ben gaped at her. He hadn't expected that smooth, educated voice to issue from those lips.

His expression must have amused the woman, who laughed. "Don't look so frightened, Dr. Bones. I don't eat injured men for lunch. Nor do I dress for dinner, as it were, to run midday errands. Unlike you." She eyed him critically, as if his London wardrobe were wildly inappropriate. "If my arrival had been foretold, would you have received me in top hat and tails? Mr. Foss, I fear our new village physician is the achingly formal sort. Introduce us properly, would you please?"

Slightly overwhelmed by the torrent of words, Ben tried to frame a rebuttal, but Foss was already speaking.

"Lady Juliet Bolivar, this is—"

"Linton. I've taken back my family name," she cut across him.

Foss's bushy eyebrows lifted, tiny eyes gleaming again. That new kernel of information would soon take root in his pub's fertile ground. "Lady Juliet Linton, this is Dr. Benjamin Bones. Old Sully says we ought to call him 'Broken Bones' on account of the accident."

"Ah, yes. An accident which killed his wife." Lady Juliet's smile disappeared. "Has Old Sully produced a clever nickname for that aspect of the tragedy, too? 'Wrecked Widower'? 'Heartsick Husband'?"

"Come now, Lady Juliet. The lads were just having a bit o' fun. No need to—"

"Dr. Bones, I see once again why it's folly to rely on others for introductions or, indeed, almost anything else," she said. "They omit what you care about, sprinkle in what you don't, and tie up the package with a ribbon of indifference. Best speak for yourself. I'm Juliet. It's a terrible name—curse of my life, next to my height—but there it is." Looming over the chair, she stuck a large hand in his face. The thumbnail was torn off to the quick; the palm was crisscrossed with scratches.

"I'm Ben." Quickly, aware he might be cut off if he gave her an opening, he continued, "You should know, my knee hurts like the devil and I have no idea why you insisted I come down to meet you. I don't suppose you've received a message from the Army?" More hopefully, he asked, "Are they ready to transfer me to a small hospital or sanatorium where I can continue my convalescence?"

She gave an unladylike snort. "No. I did hear from the Army a week ago—or my mother heard, which is the same thing. They're under the impression you're fit to begin work in the village. Still, the Council elected to give you a bit more recuperation time, what with the magnitude of your loss." She fixed him with light brown eyes. "My deepest condolences." For the first time, the words weren't tinged with acid.

"Thank you. But *fit*? I can't even walk."

"Must you walk to attend the sick?" From her great height, Lady Juliet studied him like a blue heron surveying a fish. "Old Dr. Egon was seventy-four. In the end he couldn't hear, couldn't see, and most assuredly couldn't walk, at least more than a few yards, without assistance. Also, he was drunk by eight o'clock every night. Nevertheless, in his final year he delivered eight babies, set eleven broken limbs, and treated any number of fevers and coughs. If the scotch hadn't killed him, he'd be staggering toward me now, peering through his thick specs and asking me to repeat every third word." She sighed. "Surely you can do better, even from a wheelchair. I have a—well, a delicate case, a situation that calls for a physician. Someone with *discretion* and a glimmer of *human empathy*," she added, pitching her voice toward Foss. "Are you willing, Dr. Bones?"

It was on his lips to say no. The sun beat down with summer-like intensity, his knee throbbed, and even if Foss helped him into Lady Juliet's car, heaven knew how much more pain a drive over rutted country roads would bring.

She stared at him, arms folded across her chest.

"Very well." He heaved a great sigh calculated to let this bossy, ill-dressed woman know how far she'd overstepped. It was drowned out by her crow of delight.

"Capital! Mr. Foss, please help the good doctor into my car before he changes his mind. Yes, there's room for his chair in back. This heap seats seven, don't you know."

"Wheels are a wee bit muddy," Foss warned after depositing Ben on the front passenger seat's threadbare upholstery.

"Never mind that." Climbing behind the wheel, Lady Juliet slammed her door with gusto. "Do I look like the sort who's afraid of a little mud?"

He struggled to come up with an answer. From this close, he noticed two things: her brown eyes were surprisingly soft, and there was a slender twig in her hair. It stood up, just atop her severe bun, like an intrepid climber who'd scaled a mountain.

"Oh, Dr. Bones, don't be so taken aback. I wasn't fishing for a compliment."

"I know, it's only… you have a stick in your hair. Now that I mention it—a walking stick. Insect, I mean."

He expected a shriek. Instead, Lady Juliet looked mildly intrigued. "Do I? It's a wonder I can't feel it. Relieve me of this uninvited passenger, there's a good man."

Gently, he plucked the stick-insect from her hair. Lady Juliet grinned at it. "I suppose you think you're terribly clever, catching a ride with me. Come on, then. Step this way," she ordered the bug, linking her finger with Ben's until the insect obeyed. "Let's get you sorted."

Ben watched her climb out of the Crossley, stride across the meadow opposite the pub, and deposit the insect on a tree stump. He heard her telling it something—parting advice, no doubt—and then she returned to the 20/30, leaving a swath of trampled grass in her wake.

"Now. Keys. Front pocket? Right," she muttered as she got behind the wheel again. Apparently even she wasn't exempt from her own constant stream of commands. "Sorry for the delay, Dr. Bones, but I couldn't drop him too close to the pub. Wouldn't that be a terribly ignominious end, flattened by Mr. Foss's heel?"

"I suppose. But my wife, Penny, would have squashed that bug without a second thought."

"Wrong. She would have screamed for you to do it."

Ben chuckled. It was his first genuine laugh in ages. "You knew her?"

"Oh, my dear Dr. Bones." Those soft brown eyes veered away as the car's engine roared to life. "Everyone in this village knew Penny."

"Yes, of course. I should have realized." Ben groped for something more. Penny had mentioned Birdswing many times; she'd relied on it as a punchline while entertaining their metropolitan friends. Her only fond memory of the village, she'd often said, was watching it shrink into oblivion as the train chugged away. "Were you friends?"

For once, Lady Juliet didn't soliloquize. She shook her head.

They were probably about the same age, Ben thought. *They must have been thrown together constantly, at least at school.*

"Did you have a falling out?"

"Oh. Well. You know what they say." Another sidelong glance, quicker this time. "Nothing but good of the dead." And to Ben's surprise, she spoke not another word the entire way to Belsham Manor.

***

It wasn't what Ben expected. During his medical training, he'd visited the country homes of wealthy classmates, most of which put him in mind of a Regency romance: square and somewhat austere, with box sash windows, classical columns, and a circular drive out front. Belsham Manor, with its turrets, oriels, pinnacles, gables, and gargoyles, looked like the love child of a Tudor palace and Dracula's castle. Nothing about it was symmetric, or even to proper scale. The windows were too narrow, the doors too wide, with a long, barracks-style east wing that looked about as graceful as a third arm grafted on a man's hip. Ben thought it must have been added decades after the original architect gave up, doubtless to seek work for which he was actually suited.

"Don't stare directly at the manor, you'll bring on a migraine." From a quarter mile away, Lady Juliet let the car idle, allowing him time and distance to take it all in. "Looking at our house is rather like observing an eclipse: proceed obliquely or not at all. Still, it's a grand old monstrosity." She smiled fondly. "I rather pity those who grow up in tasteful homes. Until I was eight, I assumed we were secretly vampires."

"It's certainly, well. Unique. What style of architecture is that?"

"Nouveau-riche." She winked. "Round about 1840, Mr. Thaddeus Linton, who made his fortune in railroads, was given a hereditary knighthood. Soon after, Sir Thaddeus set about building a country house of his own design, intended to impress the Peerage with its sheer magnificence. It failed to do so, of course, but in the ten years it took to raise it, Crow's Wing village transformed from a miserable blot to a thriving community called Birdswing. By the time Sir Thaddeus died, he was a great hero in these parts. A man who never forgot his origins, as they say—because the circles above him wouldn't permit it."

"And your father is his... great-grandson?"

"Great-great grandson. Dead these ten years. We Lintons tend to be delicate and short-lived, I fear. Well, except me, I'm strong as an ox. Nature's not-so-little joke on Mother. Now let's get you up to the house to meet her." Lady Juliet slipped the clutch into gear so smoothly, Ben's knee barely felt the acceleration.

The closer they came, Ben found the house progressively less ugly. Belsham Manor's gardener had been working overtime, it seemed, to mitigate architectural sins with horticultural beauty. Yellow marigolds, Bells of Ireland, and white chrysanthemums—or were those dahlias?—blossomed around what would otherwise have been a gloomy stone porch. White roses climbed the Gothic pillars, softening the entrance's pinnacle with masses of snowy blooms.

"I overheard you tell Mr. Foss she's not a well woman. I presume she's my patient?" he asked as Lady Juliet parked beside the obligatory granite fountain. It did indeed look like the sort of lawn ornament creatures of the night might favor.

"You presume wrong. At least for this visit. I have a troublesome maid and an exasperated housekeeper. But I'll say no more. I wouldn't want to prejudice your professional judgment." Lady Juliet leapt out of the driver's seat with the energy of a small boy. "But yes, Mother's been ill since Father died, so I expect you'll see her from time to time in the course of your duties. Besides, she's head of the village Council—every matter, great or small, comes before her sooner or later. You're of high importance to Birdswing, so you might as well be ushered into her presence without delay."

"Judging by all those flowers and hedges, your gardener's a capable man," Ben said. "Might we call upon him to help me down?"

Lady Juliet opened the Crossley's rear door, pulling out the heavy wheelchair as if it weighed no more than a frilly parasol, then Ben's black leather doctor's bag. "Since Thomas was called up for service, *I* am the gardener. And I've no intention of leaving you in the lurch."

"I don't think—that is to say, I believe a man would be more capable of—"

Lady Juliet would have none of that. "I told you: strong as an ox. Sing out if I hurt you."

She didn't. Ben suffered a moment's humiliation as Lady Juliet gathered him into her arms—what a smallish weakling he must be, for a female to handle him so—before his bedrock of good sense returned.

It's not that I'm a featherweight. It's just that she's extraordinary.

Settling him gently into the wheelchair, Lady Juliet let out a pant of relief. "You're a deal heavier than I expected. Was that as appalling as you feared?"

It wasn't, but surely a bit of gallantry was called for, to reassert himself as a man. "Of course not. I'm simply accustoming to being jostled by Foss. A sweet-smelling woman is quite an improvement. What scent are you wearing?"

"Stick-insect. Or cow manure. Don't compliment me, Dr. Bones." Gripping the handles of his wheelchair, Lady Juliet propelled him forward rather more forcefully than necessary. "Nothing ruins my day faster than a man with delusions of charm."

By clinging to the armrests with both hands, he was able to keep from tumbling forward out of the wheelchair as she maneuvered him up the steps, then over the threshold. His black bag, not so lucky, had to be retrieved and returned to his lap.

"I had it from Mary at the greengrocer's—cousin to your nurse—that you've been asked to practice walking on crutches," Lady Juliet said as she pushed him through the marble-tiled foyer. "How's that coming along?"

"Not well." He'd spent too much time sitting, brooding over things that could never be changed. "Perhaps I should have tried harder."

"From this moment on, you shall. *Mother*," Lady Juliet called as they entered the front parlor. Despite the undersized, diamond-paned windows, the room was surprisingly bright. Lemon yellow paint, wallpaper with a delicate buttercup print, and fresh cut chrysanthemums harmonized well, transforming a low-ceilinged chamber without much natural light into a cheerful, inviting space. "I've fetched the doctor as promised."

Beneath a brass lamp with attached magnifying glass, a blonde woman looked up from her needlework. Putting aside the embroidery hoop, she stood and smoothed her dress, although it was already flawless.

"Dr. Benjamin Bones, I'd like you to meet my mother, Lady Victoria Linton."

"It's a pleasure, Lady Victoria," Ben said, hoping his surprise didn't show. The hand which accepted his was light, gentle, and perfectly feminine, just like the woman herself. She must have been a great beauty once, or else middle age had been unusually kind. With her high cheekbones, rose petal lips, and dimpled chin, she looked more ingénue than mater, and no kin to Lady Juliet whatsoever.

"No, indeed, the pleasure is all mine," Lady Victoria said. "I apologize for calling you to duty perhaps ahead of schedule, but Juliet feels the need is great. And if it isn't too presumptuous"—she flashed a smile—"allow me to welcome you to Birdswing. I know your arrival was marred by the worst possible circumstances. Please accept our condolences for the loss of Penny. She made quite an impression on our village. We shall not see her like again."

This last was spoken so warmly, and with such evident kindness, Ben almost didn't realize that neither statement was necessarily positive. Lady Victoria's brown eyes, paler than Lady Juliet's but just as soft, glowed with sympathy, but not sadness. Had Penny run afoul of both Lintons during her time in Birdswing?

"Thank you." He cleared his throat. "I, ah, understand you're in charge of the Council. Should I mention that Mr. Foss intends to turn me out tomorrow unless he receives compensation for my room and board? I assumed the government might ship me elsewhere to finish convalescing, but Lady Juliet assures me otherwise."

"Oh, she's quite right. You're a hot commodity, Dr. Bones," Lady Victoria said. "A man over fifteen and under sixty, and a physician, no less. Our village would march on London before it gave you up. As for Mr. Foss, his wish shall be granted. If you don't mine a slightly imperfect abode, we'll move you into Fenton House a few days ahead of schedule."

"Fenton House?"

"Yes. It's to be yours while you reside in Birdswing. A lovely cottage just off the high street, and quite modern—completely redone. Ten electric points, a fenced garden out back, and a coke-burning boiler to keep it all toasty. No refrigerator, alas, but a cool larder. And a brand new gas stove."

"I suppose there are stairs?"

"Yes, of course, but we'll convert the sitting room into a temporary bedroom until you're strong enough to manage them." Lady Victoria was still smiling; in fact, her bright smile was beginning to look a trifle forced. "You might prefer sleeping downstairs, anyway. Get a feel for your new home from the ground up. And being close to the exit means when air raid sirens go off in the dead of night, you can—"

"Oh, for heaven's sake, Mother," Lady Juliet interrupted. "Tell him why Fenton House is empty. And has a brand new gas stove."

Lady Victoria's fine features took on that look of well-bred disapproval: not so much anger as disappointment. "When you divert the conversation so melodramatically, dear, you leave me no graceful way to present the truth. But very well. Dr. Bones, are you a superstitious man?"

"Not particularly."

"Marvelous," Lady Juliet said before her mother could reply. "A gas leak killed the previous resident in her bed, and now half the village thinks the house is haunted. There. Didn't I deliver the news gracefully, Mother? Two sentences, and not a word over three syllables."

Lady Victoria ignored that. "The ruptured gas line has long since been repaired," she told Ben. "The stove replaced merely to set folks' minds at ease. As for this rubbish about ghosts, well. That rumor will fade once you take up residence."

"I'm sure it will." Ben wasn't concerned with disturbances from beyond the grave. But a cottage just off the high street? That was more worrisome. He wouldn't miss Foss's bitterness or the pub's noise, but having his meals delivered to his room had permitted the isolation he craved. Today he'd done more—spoken more—than he had in several weeks; already, so much social exertion had strained him to the breaking point. Yet tomorrow, he was meant to start keeping house? Cooking for himself? Perhaps even seeing patients, if they were desperate enough to let a fellow invalid advise them?

"Forgive me, but my legs hurt a great deal," he lied. Actually, it was his head that throbbed, from pure aggravation. "Can we get on? Lady Juliet mentioned a maid in need...."

"Yes, of course. Well, Mother, we're off to the staff wing to sort out poor Dinah at last." Once again Lady Juliet took the wheelchair by the handles, prompting Ben to clutch his doctor's bag to his chest, just in case. To his relief, Belsham Manor's staff resided on the ground level, in that long, unsightly arm that had been stitched onto the house's hip about fifty years back. So there would be no grand staircase to endure, just one long carpeted hall.

"I mentioned not wanting to prejudice you," Lady Juliet said they approached what he assumed to be the women's dormitory. "But my housekeeper, Mrs. Locke, may have other ideas, so let me give you the facts as I understand them. Our youngest maid, Dinah, has gotten in a few scrapes over the years. She's only eighteen and comes from—well, not the best people, let's leave it at that. Dinah's bright and a good worker some days, flighty and irresponsible others. Over the summer she turned enigmatic, daydreaming and disappearing. I think she had a secret love, which is against the rules, but we've always turned a blind eye. At any rate, now Dinah's taken to her bed. Mrs. Locke says she's a skiving brat who's abusing our good nature and should be discharged. I say something may truly be wrong with her. I won't send her packing until illness is ruled out."

Belsham Manor's staff dormitory was surprisingly agreeable; in fact, its common room was nicer than the one Ben had shared with other young doctors in medical school. Framed watercolors decorated the walls, and it boasted a small fireplace, bookshelf, and reading nook.

Bowls of white chrysanthemums, as large and showy as those in Lady Victoria's parlor, gave the recreation area a homelike touch. Just as Ben started to say so, a slim woman in a black uniform swept in. Catching sight of Ben and Lady Juliet, she seized the nearest bowl and advanced.

"Jenny cut these flowers and scattered them about without my permission, ma'am. I'll remove them at once." White lace trim did nothing to lessen the severity of her uniform's cut, which emphasized her long neck and narrow shoulders. Her gray hair was swept up flawlessly in two victory rolls, one curled above each temple. Judging by the woman's scant makeup and ringless fingers, her hair was her lone vanity, at least of the physical variety.

"I've told Jenny to cut what she likes. We have more than enough for every part of the house." Lady Juliet let the words hang for a moment. "Please leave them, Mrs. Locke."

Sighing, the housekeeper turned her attention on Ben. "Ah! You must be the doctor. I do hope you can settle a difference of opinion between Lady Juliet and myself. I find when I am second-guessed on a large concern, I gradually lose authority, even on smallest matters." Her eyes cut to the flowers: *Exhibit A*, the look seemed to say. "Belsham Manor is very dear to me. The restoration of order is my utmost priority."

There was nothing Ben could say to that but, "Where is the patient?"

"Follow me." Mrs. Locke led them into another long chamber with only one window and a double row of iron-framed single beds. In the last one, a figure huddled beneath a patched blanket.

"Dinah!" Mrs. Locke called loudly, as if addressing a deaf pensioner. "We've fetched a doctor to winkle out what ails you. I see in the meantime you helped yourself to Martha's bed linens."

A muffled voice issued from beneath the covers. "I don't need a doctor. I'll be back on my feet tomorrow, I swear it. And Martha won't mind that I borrowed her blanket. I'm cold."

"I find it quite warm in here." Flashing Ben a theatrical look—*watch this*—Mrs. Locke strode to the bed, grasped the covers with both hands, and pulled them off Dinah like a magician yanking off a tablecloth. Fully clothed in a maid's uniform, stockings, shoes, and sweater, the girl sat up with a strangled cry. For a few seconds there was a tug-of-war for the blanket, Mrs. Locke pulling hard, Dinah clinging desperately. Then she saw Lady Juliet and let go.

"Ma'am! I'm sorry. I got dressed this morning and tried to get up, but I just couldn't." Whey-faced with ginger hair and a smattering of freckles, Dinah sounded well enough, but her pale eyes darted from side to side, settling on nothing

"Got dressed this morning?" Mrs. Locke tutted. "You were still in your nightclothes when I saw you at ten o'clock. And look—you made it out-of-doors from the state of those lace-ups. Tracked mud on your sheets, too. Dinah, perhaps you don't realize it, but every gainfully employed person can think of more diverting things to do than earn an honest wage. The temptation toward idleness and sloth is universal. Yet most of us subvert such impulses in service of the greater good. You, as I am sure even Lady Juliet sees, are incapable of taming your baser nature. May the good Lord help England if our soldiers prove as undisciplined as our young women."

She turned to Lady Juliet. "Madam." She pronounced the excessively formal term like an insult. "I really must insist Dinah be discharged. She should leave the premises at once. Furthermore, I have no intention of writing her a character."

"Mrs. Locke, please. You're employed by Lady Victoria, not Queen Victoria." Lady Juliet approached the maid's bedside. "Dinah. Whatever we decide, this won't end with you being thrown into some Dickensian gutter, I promise. You've said you're ill. I've brought Dr. Bones. Allow him to—"

"Don't need a doctor," Dinah insisted. Swinging her legs off the bed in an apparent attempt to prove it, she winced, sucking in her breath.

"I'd like to speak with Dinah," Ben told Lady Juliet.

"Please, examine her with my compliments." Mrs. Locke folded her arms across her chest, smiling tightly. "I look forward to your diagnosis."

"I meant I'd like to speak with Dinah alone." Ben spoke as if he wore his white coat, turning anxious relatives away from the operating theater. It was a tone that said *Mere mortals are unwelcome*. Coupled with an unblinking stare, his healer's hauteur vanquished Mrs. Locke's confidence.

"Very well," the housekeeper said. "The verdict will be the same whether I witness it or not. I'll wait for you in the staff parlor."

"We both will. And we'll close the adjoining door for privacy," Lady Juliet told Dinah reassuringly. "Remember, Dr. Bones is here to help you. He's taken an oath, like all physicians, to do you no harm. Whatever the trouble is, tell him the truth."

Once the footsteps of Lady Juliet and Mrs. Locke receded down the corridor, Ben placed his bag on the floor and rolled to the girl's bedside. This close, her face glowed with perspiration. Was she running a fever? Or just overheated after hiding her sweater and muddy shoes beneath that patched blanket?

"So. Dinah. How long have you felt ill?"

"Since last night, sir."

"Any pain?"

"No. Well—yes. A little. In my head, sir."

"Fever or chills?"

"No. I mean, yes. I mean… I'm not sure, sir." As she spoke, she stared at the opposite wall, as if evading Ben's gaze might make him give up and go away.

"I see. Well, it's true what Lady Juliet said, you know. When I became a physician, I took the Hippocratic oath. 'I will prescribe regimens for the good of my patients according to my ability and my judgment and never do harm to anyone.' I have to abide by that oath."

She said nothing.

"Dinah, do you want to stay on at Belsham Manor?"

"Yes sir."

"Have you any family to turn to, should you lose this position?"

"No sir."

"Well, that settles it. I'll be careful not to report anything to Lady Juliet that will result in you being put out. May I…?" He reached out.

She flinched. Then, seemingly overriding her instincts by force of will, Dinah allowed Ben to feel her forehead. The girl was a little warmer than being fully clothed beneath a blanket could account for. Not entirely skiving, at least.

"It seems you have a touch of fever. Now I need to examine you. I'll turn my back so you can disrobe to your undergarments. The exam will be swift and professional, I promise."

"I can't. I… er… my other clothes are in the wash, sir."

"Come now." Aware that females from rural areas could sometimes be excessively modest, Ben maneuvered his chair to the wooden chest by the bed's footboard. "I happen to know a housekeeper as, shall we say, *rigorous* as Mrs. Locke would never gather up every stitch of clothing to wash all at once. Risking an indecent staff isn't in her nature. Surely you have—" He stopped. Except for a bible and the Book of Common Prayer, Dinah's chest was empty. No spare uniform, stockings, nightgowns, undergarments. Not even a handkerchief.

Dinah kept her eyes on the opposite wall. Slowly, twin spots of pink blossomed on her milk-white cheeks.

As Ben considered what tack to try next, a familiar scent teased his nostrils. It reminded him of—what? Home?

No, but someplace like home, someplace he'd almost forgotten during those long, dismal days at the Sheared Sheep. Leaning closer to the open chest, he took a deep breath but got nothing but mothball residue.

"Right. Let me think," he muttered. It was one of his more annoying habits, speaking aloud when a puzzle gnawed at his brain. "Only one door out of the dormitory, and that leads to the sitting room. From there you'd have to pass through the kitchen—always busy—and then the dining room and parlor. Even if you felt strong enough to walk that far, someone would have seen you. So...." He rolled to the nearest window. The black and white tiles beneath it were spotless. "Not this one. Must be the other one."

"Sir, I only got dressed because I want to work, I swear it," Dinah quavered. "Please tell Mrs. Locke I'm feverish. She'll listen to you."

Ben was already at the window opposite Dinah's bed. As he expected, a smear of mud marred one tile. Not the brown mud of Birdswing's rutted roads, which he'd bounced over all the way to Belsham Manor. Rich black soil from a well-composted garden, matching the dirt on the soles of her shoes.

Ben tried to open the window from his wheelchair, but the sash was positioned too high. "Nothing for it." Gripping the sill with both hands, he hauled himself to his feet. After the day's jostling, his left knee surprised him, not with a thunderbolt of pain, but only moderate throbbing. From his right, just a mild ache as he balanced his weight on that foot. Sticking his head out the window, the first thing he saw was a cultivated strip of earth. A thorny rose bush, still covered in late blooms, with a pile of fallen leaves at its base. Though far from a gardener, Ben was observant by nature—a tendency honed to razor-precision by his medical training. It was too early for winter precautions. Besides, none of the other rose bushes along the wall had fresh mounds of leaves beneath their lower branches.

He remained standing for what felt like a very long time, weighing the possibilities in his mind. Then he eased back into his wheelchair, closed the window, and returned to Dinah's bedside. The pink spots had faded, leaving her face white again—too white. Mrs. Locke and even Lady Juliet had probably put down such pallor to fear, but he should have known better. Just as he should have recognized the faint, coppery scent of blood the moment his nose detected it.

"Dinah, did you cut yourself?" The question was absurd, but he had to start somewhere.

"No sir."

"One corner of your sheet's untucked. Did you vomit? Try to change the sheets yourself rather than ask for help?"

"Y-yes sir."

"Shift to one side—no, don't try to stand, just shift. Let me help you." As the girl slid over reluctantly, biting her lower lip, Ben made as if he intended to tuck the unmade corner beneath the mattress. Instead, he pulled it back, revealing a wide pink stain beneath the sheet. The mattress had been flipped, leaving the bloodiest side face down. But Dinah had bled so much, the odor of blood wafted up from below, and even the mattress's underside had been discolored.

Making a soft sound, Dinah covered her face.

"Please remember. I'm a physician. Nothing under the sun is new to me." That wasn't true, not yet, but Ben spoke to his patients as if it were. They needed to believe at least one person didn't judge them. Besides, although circumstances could be startling, even shocking, human misery was all too similar, no matter the cause. "When did you give birth?"

"T-two days ago."

"Obviously you managed to conceal the pregnancy from your employers. How?"

"Ate as little as possible. Wore a corset. Moaned about getting fat. It wasn't hard." Wiping her eyes, Dinah gave a determined sniff, as if silently vowing not to weep. "No one here cares about me, or even sees me. Not really."

"If that were true, Mrs. Locke would have been permitted to discharge you, and I'd be having my tea at the Sheared Sheep. Dinah." Despite his urgency, he worked hard to radiate calm. "What did you do with the baby?"

"When the pains started that morning, I begged off work by trading with another maid. I was meant to be gone for an hour. I was gone all day. That got Mrs. Locke's nose out of joint, and after going through it alone inside Mr. Cranford's old granary, I couldn't come up with a story. All I wanted to do was sleep. But I couldn't, not when I kept thinking—"

"*Dinah.*" He squeezed her hand. "What did you do with the baby? Is it still inside the granary?"

"Lord, no! He'd freeze to death. I wrapped him up in rags pinched from the kitchen and crept down an alley—the one between Miller's Sundries and St. Mark's," she said, voice shaking. "People kept passing by. I hurt, I hurt so much, and I was so thirsty. I couldn't wait no longer, so I left him by the delivery door at Miller's. I *hated* doing it," she cried as if Ben had reproached her. "Every time I closed my eyes, I pictured him blue and still. Dead with a dumb slut for a mother. But in the morning it was all over the village—a foundling baby. A living baby," she sniffed, shaking her head as if searching for words to express her gratitude. "Carried by Mr. Miller's clerk to the church and taken into the vicarage for now."

"So it was bloodstained clothes you buried under that rose bush." Ben's shoulders sagged in relief. "When did you hemorrhage?"

"What?"

"Bleed, when did you start to bleed?"

"It doesn't matter. Are you going to tell Mrs. Locke? She'll put me out, and you swore an oath...."

"Did any of the plac—tissue come along with the blood?"

"I don't know."

"You must know. It's important."

"But will you tell her?" The girl's eyes were wild, the only color in her moonlike face. "If you're going to tell her, it doesn't matter!"

"It does." Ben kept a firm grip on her hand as she tried to pull away. "If you don't receive proper care, your life may be in danger. You could die. I'm not trying to frighten you, Dinah," he added as she began trembling all over. "I'm going to help you. Now tell me everything, and I promise you'll come to no harm."

***

"And so," Ben concluded, employing the tone he used when giving orders to nurses, "Dinah will need to be conveyed to St. Barnabas's hospital for a procedure. It's called a D&C, or dilation and curettage, which means—"

"Dr. Bones, Lady Juliet and I are both married women," Mrs. Locke said severely. The three of them were conferring in the staff sitting room, which had been locked against interruptions. Lady Juliet had taken a chair near the cold fireplace, watching Ben's face as he spoke. Mrs. Locke had remained standing, arms folded across her nonexistent bosom, eyes fixed on a point just above Ben's left ear. "You needn't explain such terms to us as if we were innocent young girls. Indeed, one suspects this house contains no such creatures."

"Yes. Well. At any rate, Dinah will likely be kept overnight for observation, then allowed to return home. I see no reason why she can't resume light duties in a day or so."

"No reason?" Mrs. Locke let out a bark of incredulous laughter. "She will never return to Belsham Manor. Indeed, she'll never show her face in Birdswing again, not after this becomes known."

"Where would you have her go, Mrs. Locke?" Lady Juliet asked. "She has no family to speak of, and no skills beyond what we've taught her. How do you propose she keep from starving?"

"She has one skill, it seems, that we certainly did not teach her. Perhaps she can ply that trade like so many women before her." Mrs. Locke's smile faded as Lady Juliet rose, her broad, sunburned face becoming masklike. "Oh, very well, perhaps that was harsh. But there's no need to turn Dinah's situation, which she brought entirely upon herself, into a paperback melodrama. We're a country at war. She has a strong back, and the government needs women to work the farms and bring in the harvest while the men are away. She can become a Land Girl."

"Brought entirely upon herself?" Lady Juliet's question had a dangerous ring to it. "What of the man? Did he play no role?"

"Whatever role he played, he'll soon be in France, if he isn't already. And his culpability is not our affair," Mrs. Locke said. "Men are men, as I am sure even Dr. Bones would readily agree. The woman who fails to see that is no better than a child playing with matches. But enough of this hand-wringing! We knew Dinah was lazy. We suspected she was a liar. Now we see she is immoral, and ladies of our good character cannot allow her to poison this house. I couldn't possibly stand by and permit such a thing."

"I've made up my mind." Lady Juliet spoke coolly, her face still unreadable. "Dinah will remain. You will go. I imagine you'd prefer to leave without delay, so please know I'll be happy to pack up your things and send them on. Along with a week's wages to help you on your way."

"What?" The word came softly enough to be almost inaudible. Mrs. Locke looked so stricken, Ben almost pitied her. "But… you can't mean it. You can't actually choose that wretched little trollop over me."

"Of course I can. I'm the lady of the manor, I can do anything I like." Lady Juliet sounded brisk and cheerful again, as she had with Mr. Foss at the Sheared Sheep. "And it's no good ducking around me to tug on Mother's skirts. We Linton women always stick together, everyone knows that."

"But I've been here ten years. Nearly eleven. Besides—" Mrs. Locke trembled so violently, the perfect gray victory roll above each temple started to quiver. "I'm fifty-one years old. How on earth can I possibly start over?"

"From what I've observed, you've a moderately strong back. Become a Land Girl. Now then, Dr. Bones," Lady Juliet said, stepping behind his wheelchair and gripping the handles. "Dinah needs to go to St. Barnabas. Shall we make the arrangements?"

***

"Thank you," Ben told Lady Juliet, as white-haired, stoop-shouldered Robbie, Belsham Manor's only remaining male employee, headed for the hospital in the manor's bottle-green Bedford truck, Dinah on the seat beside him. Lady Juliet had promised the nervous girl she would meet her at St. Barnabas as soon as she conveyed Ben back to the Sheared Sheep.

"For what? Driving you back myself instead of leaving you to poor old Robbie? He's past seventy, with rheumatism in his arms and shoulders," Lady Juliet said. "He'd never be able to lift you out of that chair."

"I mean, thank you for not discharging Dinah. I promised I wouldn't get her turned out if she told me the truth. It seemed reasonable at the time, but I seem to have underestimated Mrs. Locke's… resolve."

"Her cruel delight in the misfortunes of others, you mean." Lady Juliet gave Ben a sidelong smile. "I really don't know what I'm going to do, what with Dinah staying on and my housekeeper leaving. I suppose Dinah will be better now that she won't be corseted within an inch of her life, not to mention bearing a terrible secret all alone. As maids go, she could hardly be worse. And Mrs. Locke, for all her unpleasantness, was really very efficient. Still, she shouldn't have said that. Not to me."

Ben tried to recall the housekeeper's more inflammatory statements, but couldn't remember any that seemed aimed at her employer. "What do you mean?"

Lady Juliet appeared not to hear. "As a woman who bore several children, Mrs. Locke may know why a D&C is necessary, but I do not. Can I assume because Dinah delivered the baby herself, some part of the process was incomplete?"

"Possibly. If the placenta wasn't fully delivered, it could explain her hemorrhaging and fever. If infection had taken hold inside the uterus and gone untreated, the result might have been fatal."

"So. By getting her to confess, you saved her life?"

"I wouldn't put it so dramatically."

"Perhaps not. But whether you saved her from death or something less dire, you did her a great service, Dr. Bones," Lady Juliet said. "One that could not have been rendered from inside the Sheared Sheep."

She was kind enough to say no more on that score, but Ben took her point. When he'd briefly stood to look out the window, his mended bones had troubled him less than his quadriceps and hamstrings, now unused to such exertion. Pain during recovery was inevitable; as a physician, he knew that. Yet he'd tried to avoid it by staying put in his chair, just as he'd tried to evade a different sort of pain by staying put in his room. It hurt to know Penny had died violently, skull crushed beneath the lorry's wheels. It hurt worse to know he was relieved to be free of her, instantly, easily, without scandal. How could he go on thinking of himself as a good man when his grief was overshadowed by such powerful relief?

"Well, rumor has it I'll be leaving the Sheared Sheep tomorrow," he said, mustering some false heartiness to fill the silence. "Call upon me the next time you've an illness at the manor."

"Or a mystery, it seems." Whatever Mrs. Locke had said to guarantee her dismissal, Lady Juliet seemed to have put it out of her mind. "Very well, Dr. Bones. Let's get you back to Mr. Foss for what's sure to be a tear-soaked farewell."

***

Foss gladly received the news of Ben's departure. He was so happy, he sent a celebratory pint of bitter up to Ben's room along with his supper. The beer tasted watered down, which was typical, but Ben drank it nonetheless, savoring it as the sun went down. Only after he put the glass aside and got his blackout shade in place did he notice a sealed envelope atop his pillow.

Love note from Foss? An itemized bill, more likely, Ben thought, opening it. Inside, a piece of stationary rested, marred by smudged fingerprints. Unfolding it, he found a single sentence, unpunctuated, created by mismatched words and letters clipped from newspaper advertisements.

FORGIVE ME IT WAS NEVER MEANT TO BE YOU JUST HER

Chapter 3: The New Office
11 October, 1939

"Now then, Dr. Bones. No sense getting in a hurry. Getting in a hurry never helped anyone," Mr. Clarence Gaston, Birdswing's air raid precautions warden and acting constable, announced in a pedantic tone Ben had already begun to hate. Slim and spare, with thick spectacles, white hair, a white mustache, and meticulously pressed tan trousers, Gaston occupied the hotel room's sole guest chair. His white helmet with the black letter W hung by its chin strap from a canvas bag containing his gas mask; a silver badge with the crowned letters ARP was pinned to his lapel.

Licking the lead of his pencil, he positioned it above a blank notebook page. "Where was the communication discovered?"

"Just there. On my pillow." Ben had said so twice already. Still, Gaston cocked an eye toward the bed. He studied it for a good ten seconds before making a careful notation in his book.

"Very good. What did the note say?"

"It's, er, on the bedside table right beside you, Mr. Gaston. Beneath the lamp."

"Yes, yes." Gaston's face was bent toward his notebook, pencil re-licked and poised once again. "Read it out to me."

Ben suppressed a sigh. True, the country was at war, but was Mr. Gaston really the best the Council could appoint in terms of an acting constable? Suppose this message wasn't some crackpot's idea of a lark? Suppose it meant just what it implied—that Penny's death had been no accident?

Rolling as close as he could in the small room, particularly given Gaston's outstretched legs, Ben found himself still too far from the note to grasp it. Gritting his teeth, he put his feet on the floor, pushed hard on the wheelchair's armrests, and—one hand still on the chair—stood unassisted for the third time that day. The pain was less distressing than the weakness, the trembling muscles, the realization his legs might give out at any moment.

"Oh, lad, that will never do," Gaston scolded. "Sit down before you rupture something. Here's the letter," he added, passing it over as Ben sat down heavily. "See how easy that was? *Now* you can read it out to me."

Ben studied the sixtyish air warden's face, wondering if all this absurdity wasn't some form of village amusement: the sort of put-on eccentricity to which country folk occasionally subjected Londoners. Gaston's expression—half grave suspicion, half excessive self-regard—gave no clue. Either he was a sincere imbecile, head inflated by the responsibilities of his wartime appointment, or a brilliant prankster.

"Very well." Several times during his nearly sleepless night, Ben had switched on the lamp, unfolded the note, and examined the letters pasted across the page. Though he'd memorized the words, he nevertheless kept reading it anew, as if he might suddenly discern some hidden quality.

"Forgive me," Ben read. Was that irony? A taunt? A genuine plea for absolution? "It was never meant to be you. Just her."

Gaston took an absurd amount of time to transcribe the message. His notebook was plain, the sort sold alongside stationary and envelopes, but its brown cover bore OFFICIAL AIR WARDEN BUSINESS in huge block print.

"Very well, Dr. Bones." Gaston looked up at last. "Now. Who is responsible for placing this curious note in your room?"

"If I knew that," Ben said a shade louder than he intended, "I don't suppose I'd have called you here." Taking a deep breath, he added more calmly, "According to Mr. Foss, the pub was uncommonly full. Someone could have crept up to my room while he was back in the taproom, and he would have been none the wiser."

Gaston, who'd stiffened when Ben raised his voice, frowned. "There's no call for speculation. Speculation," he said severely, enunciating each syllable, "never helped anyone. Though it may be impossible to determine how the note was delivered to your room, I can still compile a list of your enemies and question each in turn."

"Impossible? *Enemies?*" Staring at Gaston's compressed lips and mournful jowls, Ben decided this impenetrable ignorance was no joke. Birdswing's ARP warden and acting constable was in over his head. The man's apparent obliviousness to his own inadequacy reminded Ben of a very senior doctor from medical school: a late Victorian relic who believed smoking opium was healthy, aseptic technique was unnecessary, and all unmarried females suffered in some degree from hysteria. Medical students who wished to progress without poor marks had no choice but to agree with the ridiculous old doctor while ignoring his directions and undoing his handiwork. Dealing with Gaston might require a similar approach.

"I'm not sure how I might have acquired enemies in Birdswing," Ben said. "I've mixed with the public very little since my injury. But since I have no experience in these matters, I'll defer to yours, Mr. Gaston. I suppose it would be impossible tracking down who left this note. Asking Mr. Foss for the names of the patrons he served last night, questioning them all in case one noticed a person slipping upstairs, dusting the envelope for fingerprints after ruling mine out, of course—you're right. All quite impossible."

"Deference to authority is very wise," Gaston said. His eyes had widened slightly as Ben recited the obvious steps any investigator would take; now the wheels creaked behind those eyes, where in a moment or two, the light would dawn.

"Shall I attempt to compile that list of enemies?" Ben asked with a straight face.

"No, no. A fine idea, as amateur notions go, but not helpful." Rising, Gaston tucked his notebook into his breast pocket and smoothed his shirt, adjusting his cuffs minutely. "How could you have acquired such foes from your sickbed? We're friendly folk in Birdswing. Whoever left this note is probably disturbed, lacking full possession of his faculties, and in need of a stern talking to, you'll see. Best course is for me to have a word with Mr. Foss. See if he can recall the patrons served while you were away. As for that…." Gaston plucked the folded note from Ben's hand. "I'll preserve it till I unearth the constabulary's fingerprint kit. Purchased special from London years ago and never unboxed. No time like the present! Thank you for your assistance with these inquiries, Dr. Bones. I'll be in touch."

As Gaston thudded down the stairs, Ben's amusement at the acting constable faded. The note was probably the work of a sick individual. But if it was truly an admission of guilt—an admission of murder—Ben's only hope for answers, for justice, rested on Gaston's narrow shoulders.

There has to be someone else. Someone capable of heading up a true investigation, Ben thought. *I'll ask Lady Juliet.*

***

"Well, you seem in good spirits despite all the excitement," Lady Juliet told Ben by way of greeting. Once more, he'd been forced to rely on Foss to carry him and his wheelchair downstairs, as well as assistance from the maid, Edith. A pretty girl with jet black hair and Clara Bow lips, she'd lugged his suitcase down to the curb with a look of sullen bemusement, as if never asked to perform such a duty in her life. Then, instead of returning to her typical chores—assuming they existed—she'd taken a break. Currently she leaned against the fence between the Sheared Sheep and a large shop called Daley's, puffing a Pall Mall in Ben's general direction.

"Excitement? You mean over Dinah? How is she, by the way?"

"Quite well. The procedure was carried out this morning, and she came through like a trouper." Lady Juliet, again driving herself in the Crossley 20/30, was attired today in marginally more ladylike fashion: white cotton blouse, jodhpurs, riding boots, and overlarge tweed jacket. As before, she wore no lipstick, rouge, or jewelry, her lusterless brown hair contained in the same severe bun. "But the excitement to which I referred was that shocking note on your pillow, asking your forgiveness and claiming Penny alone was the target."

Ben let out an inarticulate sound of disbelief. "How the devil do you know about that?"

"Come, Dr. Bones." She appeared to suppress a grin, but her eyes sparkled. "You're in lonely country now, where a juicy piece of news is as nourishing as red meat. London may permit anonymity, may even encourage it, but 'the birds sing in Birdswing,' as Father Cotterill likes to say. I heard all about it over luncheon. The note's contents are rumored to be, 'Forgive me. It was never meant to be you, only her.'"

"Nearly word perfect. Who told you?"

"Mother. Who had it from our cook. Who had it from the greengrocer, who wouldn't say where she heard it, except the news had already been disseminated up and down the high street." She emitted that incongruously melodic laugh. "I suppose you've been visited by ARP Warden Gaston."

"I have. He appears to be the sole villager who didn't know what the message said. Took a great deal of time copying it down."

"Into his notebook labeled 'official business?'" Lady Juliet smiled. "Vexatious man, he's been filling up notebooks since taking the ARP post. Nothing delights him more than to catch one of us in an infraction that might endanger the village or somehow give aid and comfort to the enemy."

Ben wanted to ask who else handled police work in Birdswing, but having been made aware of how freely news traveled in the village, he could practically feel Edith behind him, straining to catch every word from her supposedly casual position against the fence. "Well, I'm keen to put the note out of my mind and see this place you've secured for me. Fenton House, you call it?"

As before, Ben was obliged to let Lady Juliet assist him into her vehicle, but this time he managed to stand while she loaded his wheelchair, clutching the Crossley's door for support as he tried to bring his left leg up. But no matter how he gritted his teeth, such a feat was still beyond him.

"Can you give me a boost?" he asked Lady Juliet, forcing a smile.

"Well, I… I'm, I'm happy to try." It was the first time she'd stumbled over her words in his presence. "Only, to get you from, well, standing on the ground to sitting down on the passenger seat, I'm not sure how to take hold of you." Her eyes raked him up and down. "Where to, er, place my hands, as it were."

"I see." He looked up and down the rutted tracks that passed for a street, leading into the village proper. Edith, now on her second Pall Mall, wasn't the only native watching this operation with undisguised fascination. Foss lurked in the Sheared Sheep's doorway; across the fence at Daley's, a woman with toffee brown skin and shoulder-length waves had stationed herself on the porch, arms folded across her chest and face blank. A second face, just a small blob, watched from between parted lace curtains in the shop's upper window. Ben sighed.

"Perhaps you should fetch back my chair, let me sit down, and lift me with both arms."

Lady Juliet seemed to think about it, then firmed her mouth. "That won't do. No, if Birdswing is to have any confidence in you, they first need to observe you're growing stronger. Perhaps all that's needed is a friendly—" As she spoke, she attempted what was probably meant to look like casual assistance, one arm about his shoulders. But as Ben tried to work with her, to flex that now-throbbing left knee, his right leg gave out, forcing her to clutch his belt to prevent a fall. At the same time, her other hand, flailing for purchase, grabbed his rear, squeezing hard as she narrowly managed to land him on the passenger seat.

"Oh! That was good, wasn't it?" Ben blurted. *Why in the name of God did I say that?*

Panting with exertion, Lady Juliet glared at him. Wisps of hair escaped her bun, dangling before one eye as color spread across her cheeks.

"I only mean… I didn't ." He stopped. The only other thing he could think to say—"I hardly felt a thing"—seemed more perilous than awkward silence.

Lady Juliet tucked the wisps behind an ear. Taking a deep breath, she adjusted her overlarge jacket, which hung askew. Then she slammed the passenger door shut and marched to the driver's side. Climbing inside, she shut her door with still greater vigor. Her color had progressed from rosy pink to blotchy red, beginning mid-throat and rising straight to her hairline.

"Er. Lady Juliet," Ben began. "I feel… that is, I think…."

"Dr. Bones. You and I shall never speak of what just transpired. Is that clear?"

"Crystal."

Fortunately, the journey from the pub to Fenton House was brief and gave Ben his first look at Birdswing's high street. It was unexpectedly beautiful. The dirt track, marred with the occasional muddy pothole, smoothed out, then became paved by wooden blocks set in tar. It broadened as meaner establishments on the outskirts, like the Sheared Sheep and Daley's, gave way to cottages or bungalows with neatly-kept front gardens. Each patch of green was delineated by low stone walls with wooden gates; every porch was decorated with a window box, potted plant, or scrap of furniture. Penny had regaled her London friends with tales of Birdswing's distressing sameness, with the dreary conformity of village life, but when Ben thought of dreariness, he thought of London. Not the city itself, brimming with layers to discover, but the people, particularly the other young doctors at his former hospital, grim and harried and not-so-secretly terrified of failure. A village where neighbors kept their lawns trimmed and their front steps swept by common consent? Charming.

Unless someone behind one of those red or black-lacquered doors sent me that note. Either as a cruel joke or a genuine admission of murder.

"That's Mr. Jeffers's butcher shop with the ridiculous sign—no words, just a great pink porker. His grandfather had it carved last century, when literacy was rare, and though times have changed, mercifully, he refuses to change with them," Lady Juliet said. She sounded wholly recovered from her earlier mortification, so Ben dared a glance. No, not wholly—those cheeks were still red.

"Beside the butcher shop, there's Laviolette's Fine Dining. Despite the name and the extravagant claim which follows, he is not French, nor has he ever set foot out of Cornwall. Not even for rudimentary cookery classes," Lady Juliet continued, slowing the Crossley as she indicated a tea room with lanterns out front.

"City folk are accustomed to deceptive names and claims. How's the food?"

"I never speak ill of my fellow villager to an outsider. And you, Dr. Bones, are still an outsider, however well-regarded and welcome."

"I only asked for an opinion on the food."

"Yes, and I gave you an answer. Go round!" Lady Juliet called, putting her arm out the window to wave the muddy Citroën past as its driver honked again. As it did so, the lady at the wheel waved back to prevent hard feelings. Lady Juliet's answer was a stiff nod.

"Mrs. Abigail Sutton. Short-sighted and always in a hurry. Since she insists on gadding about, I prefer her in front of me," she told Ben. "And that's not speaking ill of a fellow villager. It's relating a sad truth to a man who's already suffered one grievous injury on our roadways."

"I've resolved not to cross any more thoroughfares while the blackout is on. As for this business of never speaking ill of your fellow villagers: it's admirable, but I'm a physician, used to hearing all sorts of truths." Ben waited a moment to let this statement penetrate. "And when it comes to my late wife, I must admit some curiosity. Not just because of the note. Yesterday, when we met, you seemed—"

"Here we are!" Lady Juliet called cheerfully and a shade too loudly. "Fenton House."

As she fetched his wheelchair from the back of the Crossley, Ben studied the cottage. Gray stone with light blue shutters and a white door, it struck him at once as too feminine. But that was absurd, as like most houses awaiting an owner, it lacked the softening touches a wife would bring: no welcome mat, empty window boxes, and an unswept walk.

Appropriate, as I have no wife, Ben reminded himself. And yet….

The rest of that thought, which seemed to come from somewhere else, made the hackles rise on the back of his neck. *There's a woman here already.*

"Wasn't there some nonsense about the place being haunted?" Ben asked as Lady Juliet lowered him from passenger seat to the wheelchair. He was careful to keep his tone light.

"Oh. Yes. And you must forgive us in advance for what's sure to be a round of superstitious questioning. It's not that Birdswing has more than its fair share of imbeciles and gothic novel devotees. It's just that Lucy's death was such a terrible shock. And by gas. As if we all haven't meditated all too much on *that* fate. In fact…."

Reopening the Crossley's passenger door, Lady Juliet felt around the floorboards until she came up with a medium-sized cardboard box on a long string. Putting it on cross-body, as a Girl Guide might wear a canteen, she patted the government-issue gas mask now resting on her ample hip. "There. Should the Nazis appear overhead to blanket the countryside with mustard gas, or whatever they're threatening us with these days, I'll be ready."

"Lucy?" Ben asked as Lady Juliet propelled him toward the door.

"Lucy McGregor. Lovely thing, just twenty-three. I suppose it was a peaceful death, going to sleep and never waking up. But the neighbor who found her had a nervous collapse. Left the house wide open, so half Birdswing trooped in and out, gawping at poor Lucy stiff in her bed, working themselves into a frenzy over what could have done it. When they heard it was gas, everyone who'd ever scoffed at carrying a gas mask ran right home to get it."

"'Hitler will send no warning, so always carry your gas mask,'" Ben quoted from memory. In the newspapers and on the wireless, there were dozens of such public service slogans, all offering earnest messages of volunteerism or self-reliance. While they were easy to mock, such propaganda did its job, since it sprang to mind so easily.

"I notice you aren't carrying yours."

"Yes, well, I'll remedy that as soon as I unpack." In truth, Ben had little hope an unfitted, mass-produced mask could save him from the sort of attacks that had killed thousands of tommies in the Great War. Still, he was this community's physician, and there was such a thing as setting an example.

"Here we are." Lady Juliet pushed him through the doorway into a poky hall, opening to the right into a little parlor. Down and to the left was the dining room, and beyond that, the smallest kitchen Ben had ever seen. As Lady Victoria had warned him, there wasn't a refrigerator, just the bare necessities: cool larder, sink, draining board, coke-burning boiler, and gas stove. As promised, the latter was new, which Ben found simultaneously reassuring and sad.

After viewing the kitchen, they doubled back to the parlor, its plaster walls painted the same blue as the shutters outside. Ben hadn't expected furniture, but the room was crammed with it: love seat, armchairs, bookshelf, coffee table, lamp, and embroidered fireplace screen. Though well-used and clearly from various eras, the pieces harmonized surprisingly well.

"I'm sure you'd prefer your own things, but until you have them sent down from London, the Council voted to provide everything you need."

"Thank you." The swell of emotion took Ben by surprise. It was only odds and ends; if Penny had seen the furniture, she would have blanched, then found a way to take the villagers' kindness as an insult. The last time she'd received a letter from someone in southwest England—two months ago, Ben estimated, though he wasn't certain—she'd seemed on edge for days. When he'd asked, Penny had insisted it was nothing but an invitation to a church fête and jumble.

"So I can get to know Birdswing again? No sooner than I must," she'd huffed. "And mention of the jumble was salt in my wound. Bad enough to live there.

But to be reminded that practically the only entertainment will be church socials is just too cruel."

"This," Lady Juliet said, opening the door, "used to be Lucy McGregor's sewing room. No doubt you'll someday wish to use it as a study, as it's too small for anything else, but for now, you have a place to sleep without risking your neck on the stairs."

There was an iron-framed single bed, table, lamp, and alarm clock, all of it squeezed against the wall. There wasn't room enough for a wardrobe, or even for Ben to fully maneuver his wheelchair inside, but having a temporary bedroom downstairs was worth the inconvenience. Besides, it would motivate him to work all the harder, walking with crutches. For the second time, Ben was astonished and pleased by how far the Council had gone to make him comfortable. At this point he had only one burning question, but kept it to himself, certain the answer was about to be revealed to him.

"Now old Dr. Egon—he of the bad eyes, bad hearing, and overtaxed liver—lived next to the butcher shop in a squalid little hole that should have been condemned. When he died, Mr. Jeffers bought the space, knocked down the wall, and expanded. Then war was declared, rumors of government meat rationing started, and—well, you'll never find anyone who hates Nazis more than Mr. Jeffers. He insists the Fuhrer timed matters to bankrupt him personally." Chuckling, Lady Juliet turned Ben's chair around, pushing him toward another closed door on the parlor's opposite end. "Since taking over the previous doctor's office was impossible, the Council decided to convert the library into your consulting room. We'd no notion of what to purchase, so we simply brought over Dr. Egon's things for you to sort out." With that, Lady Juliet opened the door with a flourish; apparently, this was the moment she'd been waiting for.

Ben was rendered speechless—thankfully. After all the village's many kindnesses, it would have been monstrous to spoil the great revelation with an honest response.

If Dr. Egon was in his seventies, he was born around 1865, Ben thought, fixing what he hoped was a smile on his face. *He must have inherited all this after he qualified—probably bought it lock, stock, and barrel from some Victorian quack—and practiced all his life without changing a thing.*

A polished black desk dominated the room, equipped with an articulated human skull, three milky apothecary jars filled with unknown granules, and an ancient leather-bound copy of *Gray's Anatomy*. Against the wall, a tall glass cabinet held dozens of bottles, red and blue and green, most with peeling labels and corks instead of screw tops. Its bottom shelf held a stained, ominous-looking travel case that Ben suspected was a field amputation kit. Beside it, an open, velvet-lined box contained four brass syringes. Outside of his medical training, when his wilder classmates had occasionally nicked antique equipment from a professor and threatened one another with it—every last item looked like an instrument of torture—Ben had never seen syringes that weren't made of glass and steel.

Sniffing, Ben asked, "What's that smell?"

"I'm sure I don't know. We cleaned the room very thoroughly. Perhaps a bit of camphor?" Lady Juliet asked. "Mrs. Cobblepot was in charge of airing out the rooms, and camphor is her secret weapon."

"No, not chemical." Ben sniffed again, concentrated, and suddenly thought of the library at university. Specifically, his own favorite study corner, not far from illustrated volumes dating back to the Crimean War. "Like very old books."

Lady Juliet breathed deep, nostrils flaring. "No. I can't claim to smell it. But this was poor Lucy's library. Perhaps the books left a bit of themselves behind." Pointing at a turn-of-the-century electrotherapy machine, she confessed, "I have no idea what that is," as if any modern person could be expected to recognize a Tesla coil on sight. "What does it do?"

"Relieves the gullible of their money, I'm afraid." Ben kept his false smile in place. "I've no doubt Dr. Egon did his best, and I'm deeply grateful to inherit his, er, arsenal of healing weapons. But times have changed, so please don't be put out if I make one or two small changes."

In a cabinet with deep cubbies and a dozen drawers, Ben found a mishmash of items. Some, like the porcelain enema basin, glass eye wash cup, and collection of scalpels, were usable. Most, like the pill-making press, monaural stethoscope—little more than an ear trumpet to press against the chest—and phrenology bust, were useless. Fortunately, he'd traveled to Birdswing with the basics: stethoscope, sphygmomanometer for measuring blood pressure, thermometer, reflex hammer, otoscope for ears, ophthalmoscope for eyes, and his minor surgery tools, including hemostats and forceps. This "office" lacked an examining table, a screen for the patient to undress behind, a scale, an eye chart, and even a diagram of the human body, but it did boast an imposing black desk. Ben resolved to keep it, even if he would have preferred something less intimidating. Perhaps doing so would save the villagers' feelings when he discarded almost everything else.

"That door," Ben said, pointing. "Does it open onto the garden?"

"It does. And you'll find we've cleared away the grass and put down some stones, making a secondary path from the front gate to your office door. It shan't take long to train patients to call at the side for medical consultations." Brimming with obvious pride, Lady Juliet added, "We even wired up a buzzer with a flat tone quite unlike the front door chime. That way, you'll know from anywhere in the house what sort of caller awaits." Her happiness in what had clearly been her idea transformed her face. Smiling that way, her wide, beautifully formed mouth balanced those broad cheeks, making her almost pretty.

"I find myself parroting the same words over and over. Thank you." Ben took her hand. It was as large as his but still feminine, fine-boned despite its proven strength. "Thank you so very much, Juliet."

Her smile faded. She started to pull her hand out of his grasp, stopped for a moment, then gently slid away. Clearing her throat, she blinked twice, folded her arms across her chest, and put on a smile as patently false as the one he'd employed minutes before.

"My mother is head of the Council, and I sit on it as well. We have a vested interest in making you comfortable, Dr. Bones. And we Lintons know our duty."

Mystified by her sudden stiffness, Ben could only nod. Who would have thought impulsively omitting "Lady" from her name would produce such an unseasonable chill? As he struggled to think of something to say, noticing and trying not to notice the redness creeping up her throat, that flat buzzer sounded.

"Your first patient," Lady Juliet declared, looking as relieved as Ben felt. "Rather than linger on and be in the way, I'll be off. But I'll pop in again later, never fear."

Ben hoped so. Not only did he want to smooth over whatever offense he'd managed to give, but—he was ashamed to admit—he would need a great deal more help just to get through the night in his new home. Naturally, there was a toilet downstairs, but no tub. Even if the kitchen was fully equipped with groceries, which didn't seem to be the case, he was hopeless at cookery. And to so much as get down his front steps, he'd need crutches or a cane, which at this stage meant courting a broken neck. In truth, he wasn't terribly chuffed about seeing his first official patient in this strange new office, a mostly useless place that smelled of moth balls and missing books, but his medical training had armed him with a doctor's secret weapon: faking the confidence he didn't feel.

"Until you return, Lady Juliet. And thank you again," he said, but she was already walking away.

Chapter 4: Mrs. Cobblepot
11 October, 1939

Never again, Lady Juliet Linton Bolivar thought, and meant it. Absolutely.

Well. Almost entirely.

And if not entirely, as near as made no difference.

I made a bloody fool of myself over one man. Mother would die of mortification if I did it again.

She often framed her worries that way, heaping anxieties at Lady Victoria's door instead of her own. Her mother's chronic poor health, which had begun after the death of Juliet's father, was both a genuine concern and a convenient excuse. Juliet herself cared not a fig for what anyone thought of her, so the internal monologue went, but Mother's tender feelings had to be spared.

And usually Juliet was on guard against such perils, but this one had slipped up on her. There were few females in her life she'd disliked—no, it would be fairer to say, hated—as fiercely as Penny Eubanks, or Mrs. Penelope Bones. It followed, therefore, that a woman with so many vile qualities would marry a suitably loathsome man, the sort of person Juliet could endure for only brief intervals. Of course, the man would possess a few requisite charms; Juliet had expected Penny's husband to be wealthy, sophisticated, and handsome. Dr. Bones had confounded those expectations in every way.

Wealthy? Not at all. As a professional man, he stood to earn a fine living, perhaps even grow rich later in life if he invested wisely. But the Bones family had no connections to real money or power, as Juliet, patroness of the Birdswing lending library, had stooped to confirm one day when overcome by curiosity. So Penny hadn't married him for money or even the expectation of an inheritance.

As for sophistication—well, in the eyes of some villagers, he would tick that box. Many of Birdswing's residents had left school at fourteen, either to apprentice in a trade or work full time on the family farm. Perhaps a quarter of the villagers were functionally illiterate, and at least half had never traveled farther than Plymouth. So for them, a university-trained physician from London would seem the height of metropolitan glamor. But Juliet had known real sophistication, in the original Greek sense of the term—known it, married it, and come to despise it. She'd assumed Penny's husband would be cut from the same cloth: witty, extravagant with his compliments, glittering like fool's gold. Instead, Ben struck her as intelligent, sincere, and even decent, based on his kindness toward Dinah.

Finally, there was the little matter of looks. Juliet had put off meeting Ben, avoiding the Sheared Sheep for weeks (no great sacrifice) because she didn't care to see the man Penny would have paraded around Birdswing like the ultimate matrimonial trophy: dashing, debonair, black-haired and broad-shouldered, the perfect mix of Cary Grant and Clark Gable. If Juliet wanted her senses overloaded with granite jaws and dimpled chins, she'd go to the cinema and get a happy ending in the bargain, thank you very much. But Ben wasn't what Juliet would call handsome. He was, in a purely masculine sense, beautiful. Reddish-brown hair, wide blue eyes, red lips, and those faintly ginger sideburns. Looking at him too long without legitimate purpose produced distressing physical sensations Juliet had no patience with, at least in theory. Leading her inevitably back to the declaration, never again.

Thank heavens I'm not the sort of silly cow who flusters easily, she thought. *Mrs. Parry is probably spying from across the street, planning to report all to anyone who'll listen. Exuding calm dignity is a must.*

Eyes on Mrs. Parry's lace curtains, Juliet misjudged the second step, turned her ankle, and nearly took a header into the garden. Trousers saved her from flashing her knickers, but catching herself on the stone path dirtied her hands. Brushing them off, she limped to the Crossley, climbed in, slammed the door for vengeance, and roared away. Before falling, it had been in her mind to pay a visit to Mrs. Agatha Cobblepot, whose heretofore unsolvable personal problems might at last have found an answer. Post-fall, Juliet drove away blindly, thoughts reverting to Ben.

Leaving aside the fact she was still technically married to Ethan Bolivar, at least until that slippery devil was forced to sign the papers, and leaving aside the fact Ben was newly widowed and probably wouldn't look at a woman for a year or more, ignoring all other objections, there was one incontrovertible barrier: Juliet stood six foot one in her stocking feet. And Ben, according to her well-honed powers of vertical estimation, was no more than five foot eight.

She disliked being a person for whom so many things boiled down to one simple consideration, height, but there it was. A woman who approached six three in modest heels committed a social faux pas simply by appearing in public, and when such a woman forgot her transgression, ridicule followed. Heartbreak, too. At school, Juliet had discovered most men in the five six to five ten zone not only yearned to be six foot specimens, they pretended they were until confronted by facts. Since they lied to their mates, their dates, and themselves, nothing infuriated them more than the necessity of looking up at a woman when she spoke. In fact, some men refused to do it; Juliet had suffered through many an otherwise pleasant conversation where the man kept his gaze resolutely fixed on her shoulders, as if force of will could accomplish what gravity would not. It was one of the silly things she liked best about men: as a species, they were optimists. And the very short ones, below five foot five, often possessed a damn-their-eyes sort of élan she very much admired. Like her, they'd been forced to accept a physical appearance the world found vexing. But men in Ben's height range were best forgotten. Even when Juliet had dared punch far above her weight in loving Ethan Bolivar, she took comfort in the fact he stood six foot four. If she'd towered over Ethan the way she towered over Ben, so much misery could have been averted.

The high street's stop light loomed. As Juliet downshifted and applied the brake, something made her notice her jodhpurs, really see them for the first time in months. They were paint-splatted on one leg, frayed around the hems, and unflattering, particularly when she shoved the Crossley's keys into her front pocket. Had she even looked into a mirror before she went out that morning? How ludicrous, a woman dressed like a scarecrow fretting she was too tall for—

"Keys," Juliet muttered, realizing there was no familiar lump in that pocket. Absurdly she patted her thigh, as if the Crossley's keys might have melted into it, but the pocket was empty. "Oh, good heavens, I must have left them at the cottage," she announced to the air, frantically running her hands along the dash, the seat, and her pocketless blouse. "I will throw myself off a cliff before I go back there. I will—"

Someone honked. The light had changed, and in Juliet's rearview mirror, Mr. Piedmont offered a timid wave. Given his famous reluctance to disturb anyone, he'd probably been waiting some time.

"Oh, very well!" Juliet bellowed, gunning the engine, and sped along for another five minutes in agony, wondering how she dared return to Ben's cottage so soon. Then it struck her: she was driving. The ignition key resided innocently where it belonged, the other keys dangling just below the steering wheel.

That's it. I've gone mad. Ten years sooner than anyone predicted.

Her distracted driving had taken her far from Mrs. Cobblepot and more than halfway to St. Barnabas's hospital. Sighing, Juliet allowed herself a moment of deep aggravation at her own folly, then pushed it away. The petrol, that first public commodity to be rationed, had already been used, so she might as well go the rest of the way and look in on Dinah. No one else was likely to visit the girl. Perhaps her unconscious mind had directed her toward St. Barnabas for that very reason? As a passionate admirer of Carl Jung, and quite possibly the only person in Birdswing who had read all his published works, Juliet decided that was precisely what happened.

"Until you make the unconscious conscious, it will direct your life and you will call it fate," she quoted aloud, tapping the Crossley's dashboard as if it understood. Madwomen could have conversations with thin air; it was expected, perhaps even compulsory. And with her attention shifted to the psychoanalytic theories of Dr. Jung instead of the personal charms of Dr. Bones, she took the road to St. Barnabas's.

***

Juliet left the hospital around eleven thirty, just as the sisters began serving lunch. Dinah was in good spirits, all things considered, but obviously fretting over the baby she'd abandoned. Twice Juliet skirted the topic, opening the conversational door wide, but Dinah only sighed and bit her lip. She didn't seem mentally or emotionally equipped for motherhood, Juliet thought, but who could dare stand in judgment if Dinah decided to try? But if she wanted to regain custody of her child, if she was willing to start over in some new village where she could call herself a widow and find work to support them both, she'd have to make the first move. Dinah's physician had guessed the connection between his young patient in need of a D&C and the foundling baby under St. Mark's care, but he was a sympathetic sort who would not contact the authorities. That was fortunate, since for now "the authorities" amounted to Clarence Gaston and his delusions of competence. It was also fortunate that lawmen in England didn't carry firearms like their American counterparts, or Acting Constable Gaston would no doubt shoot himself in the foot.

Perhaps even pistol-whip a litterer, Juliet thought as she parked by the curb outside the Gaston bungalow. *No wonder Mrs. Cobblepot is beside herself. Living with a brother like that would push anyone over the edge.*

"Hallo," she called, rapping smartly at the front door. ARP Warden Gaston's bell had been on the fritz for weeks. Apparently repairing things around his own house took a distant second to involving himself in his neighbors' lives.

She waited. No answer came, nor were there any sounds within. Juliet tried the doorknob, which turned freely, and gently pushed it open. The front parlor was empty, yet hints of feminine madness were everywhere for those wise enough to read the signs. The hearth rug had been boiled till it faded and put through the mangle so severely, it looked like a dog had chewed it. The curtains had been starched until they hung like planks, motionless in the breeze. If so much as a mote of dust had survived the morning's clean sweep, Juliet couldn't see it. She could, however, see threadbare fabric on the sofa, where overzealous spot-cleaning had nearly disintegrated the chintz. The same fate which had made Clarence Gaston a widower with an empty house had left his sister, a recent widow, penniless. She had no one else to turn to, and he had driven off every housekeeper in southwest England. If she wasn't rescued soon, Juliet feared one of Gaston's neckties would be put through the mangle as violently as that rug—while still snugly knotted around his throat. And then poor Mrs. Cobblepot would hang for what most of Birdswing would consider a justifiable homicide.

Juliet decided to check the back garden. Just as she started toward the fence, a whistle shrilled. Next came a door banging, then an indistinct cry between a gasp and a moan, that Juliet recognized as Mrs. Cobblepot in distress.

"What's all this?" Juliet demanded, marching up to the gate and pushing it open. In Birdswing gates were rarely locked, though neighbors were usually polite enough to behave as if they were. "Good heavens! Mr. Gaston, what on earth are you doing back here? Mrs. Cobblepot, stay where you are, let me help you!"

The garden, once a pleasant venue to read a book or enjoy a spot of tea, looked as if a bomb had gone off. Two shrubs and a little tree had been dug up and cast in a heap, along with unearthed stones and patches of turf. The culprit stood red-faced with a shovel in one hand and a whistle in the other. Stripped down to his undershirt, which was damp with sweat, he wore a pair of hideous plaid shorts, black socks, his usual brogues, and a curiously triumphant expression. By contrast, Mrs. Cobblepot was on her knees in the dirt, having run out the back door and onto freshly broken ground. For a heavyset, sixtyish widow, rising after hitting both kneecaps could be no easy task, so Juliet hurried to assist her, scowling at Gaston all the while.

"That wasn't a rhetorical question, Clarence," Juliet said, getting an arm around Mrs. Cobblepot. The poor woman clung to Juliet like a life preserver. Her stockings were ripped, her spectacles askew, and she was shaking all over. "Why are you blowing that whistle? And why have you torn your garden to pieces?"

"This will be the site of our Anderson shelter," Gaston announced, indicating the crude six foot by six foot rectangle he stood inside. "The place that will keep us safe and snug in the event of bombing by the enemy."

Whenever Juliet heard Gaston say "enemy," she visualized the word with a capital E and had to bite back a laugh. It wasn't that she lacked a healthy fear of the Germans or the devastation air raids would surely bring. It was just difficult to keep such concerns at the top of her mind when confronted with blue-green plaid and knobby knees.

"There will be unannounced shelter drills day and night. Agatha here just botched her first," Gaston said severely. "Now she's dead, blown to bits, because she didn't heed the sign—three short whistle blasts—and failed to get inside the shelter before the Hun rained fire on Cornwall."

"Oh, Clarence, please don't say such things." Giving Juliet a grateful nod, Mrs. Cobblepot released her, wiping her hands on her apron. "Sorry if I got a bit of egg on you, dear. I was making a pudding when the whistle sounded. Came running as fast as I could, but I had to cover the bowl so the flies wouldn't get it. Clarence gets cross if he doesn't get pudding after supper." Straightening her glasses and smoothing her gray pin curls, she added, "Besides, I did well in the morning pantry inspection, brother. You said so yourself."

"That compliment is rescinded. While I was digging, I came across *this* scattered beneath the hedge." Reaching into a pocket, he drew out a handful of crumbs. "What's this, then?"

"Oh." Mrs. Cobblepot's mouth twisted. "Just a bit of stale bread I put out for the sparrows. Surely that won't count against my pantry inspection?"

"Wasting food is an offense. Not only immoral but deserving of a citation. Stale bread crumbs are a meat extender. There may come a day when you hunger for meatloaf and remember my words." He tucked the crumbs back into his pocket, patting it.

"I'm sorry, Clarence," Mrs. Cobblepot said meekly. Juliet could stomach no more.

"I have come," she announced loud enough to frighten an illicitly-fattened bird out of a tree, "to inform ARP Warden Gaston our community is endangered. I'm at my wit's end and afraid for us all."

"God save us," Mrs. Cobblepot gasped.

"Go on." Gaston's eyes shone.

"I've just come from Dr. Bones at Fenton House. He's in deep distress. I fear he cannot go on, and the Army will soon ship him off to a sanatorium for treatment. *Indefinite* treatment." Juliet sighed deeply.

"Distress? He was well enough yesterday." Gaston frowned. "Asking silly questions and making foolish suggestions."

"Mr. Gaston." She gave him her saddest smile. "Do you imagine a man who's lost his wife—who's lost his love, his very reason for living—would unburden himself to an air warden? I got the truth out of him when I showed him his new home. I was pushing his wheelchair into the kitchen. He looked quite helpless, what with two shattered legs, and confessed he'd never boiled an egg." Inspiration struck. "He took one look at the cooker and burst into tears."

"Oh, that poor boy." Mrs. Cobblepot wrung her hands even as Gaston made a disgusted noise. "It's not good for a man to be without a woman taking care of him. Widowers are far worse off than widows."

"Yes, indeed," Juliet said, heartily wishing Ethan Bolivar dead. "Widows are made to endure. Men are so delicate. A man without a wife is like—like a pot without a flower."

"You're both daft," Gaston said. "I'm widowed ten years and still strong as an ox!"

Mrs. Cobblepot ignored that. "Lady Juliet, I can't bear to think of losing Dr. Bones. Bad enough he was hurt and his wife killed. But to lose him altogether, when we *need* a doctor…. It's been terrible since Dr. Egon died. Traveling all the way to Plymouth for the least little thing, and what if a farmer cuts off a leg or pokes out an eye?"

"What, indeed?" Juliet pressed her lips together. For someone so plain in appearance, Mrs. Cobblepot clearly had a flair for the dramatic. "But lose him we must, I think. He has no wife now, no mother…."

"He has that nurse," Gaston said. "What's-her-name, the sour one who must have been weaned on a lemon. And if the kitchen frightens him so badly, he can take his meals at Laviolette's. Or kip at Morton's café like old doc Egon."

"As long as Dr. Egon had a tot of scotch in his morning coffee, he was perfectly happy. But Dr. Bones is poised on the cusp of a nervous breakdown. I must turn to you to break the sad news to our village." Though Juliet addressed her words to Gaston, she stared hard at his sister. When the bolt finally hit home, the plump little woman steadied her horn-rimmed specs with both hands, as if prepared to make an announcement daring enough to knock them off.

"I can take charge of him! I can cook for him, keep his house, mend his clothes. He needn't pay me more than a few shillings. I'd be ever so pleased to help him adjust."

"Splendid. I'll tell him you—"

"Hang on." Gaston sounded appalled. "You're going to leave me—your own brother—for some townie quack you've never met?" Casting down the shovel, he left his imaginary bomb shelter, closing the distance between himself and Mrs. Cobblepot. "Agatha, be reasonable. I have grave responsibilities. I'm acting constable as well as ARP warden, charged with keeping us safe from the enemy. If spies parachute in, I can't be off darning my socks or doing my own fry-ups!"

Juliet swallowed the temptation to recommend Laviolette's or Morton's. Overplaying her hand now could make the whole scheme collapse.

"Oh, Clarence, love, I've reinforced all the heels and toes. You could march to Berlin and kick Hitler in the face without tearing those socks." Mrs. Cobblepot gazed at her brother sympathetically but unbending iron was in her voice. "Can't you see I'm needed for the war effort? The Army seconded a physician to us to care for our community. Now I'm being seconded to care for him. Billeted in Fenton House like one of the troops. How can you forbid it when it's part of the war effort?"

"I can't march to Berlin. There's a bloody ocean in between," Gaston muttered.

"You wouldn't let that stop you." Mrs. Cobblepot touched his cheek lightly, smiling as their eyes met. "And you'll accomplish so much more without me here to slow you down. Why, you'll have the shelter walls up in no time." She nodded toward a stack of corrugated steel panels. "And once official rationing starts, your portion will stretch so much farther without me to waste it."

He looked at the ground. "Don't care for Morton's pies. Or Laviolette's puddings."

Mrs. Cobblepot, who'd been awarded many cups for baking over the years, shot Juliet a worried glance. *Sacrifice*, Juliet mouthed back her.

"I know, Clarence. It will be a sacrifice for you."

Gaston's head came up. In seconds, the man fully reinflated, chest rising as his shoulders lifted. "We must all make sacrifices. I said it in 1915, and I say it again now. None of us are immune, not till this war is won."

"That's the spirit!" Mrs. Cobblepot sounded as giddy as a schoolgirl. "Give me just a moment to gather an overnight bag, Lady Juliet, and I'll be ready to go."

"Go? Now? But what about my supper?" Gaston asked.

"That poor man needs me! Two broken legs and no wife. You can bring the rest of my things to Fenton House tomorrow, Clarence," Mrs. Cobblepot called over her shoulder, ducking into the house for her bag with the sprightliness of a much younger woman as she claimed, "It's a sacrifice for me, too, brother!" But for all her competencies, Mrs. Cobblepot was no liar, even when her happiness and freedom was on the line. Only the very thick or terminally self-absorbed could fail to hear to the relief in her voice.

Juliet hazarded a glance at Gaston. Sure enough, he'd picked up his shovel again, satisfied by his sister's declaration of duty.

Penny, if you're looking down on us—or more likely, up at us—I do hope you don't expect justice. Not if Clarence Gaston is responsible for working out who killed you, and why. Once upon a time, such an unkind thought would have given Juliet a rush of satisfaction, a tiny taste of being the "bad" girl: the role young Penny had known so well and earnest, bookish types like Juliet could only aspire to. And even now, years later, to pretend she felt even a sliver of sympathy for the dead would be the height of hypocrisy. But there was Ben to consider. For his sake, Juliet wanted Gaston to succeed, to astonish them all in ways he knew too little of police work to even dream of.

Not that I'm much better. Miss Marple and Lord Peter Wimsey have been my tutors, and I probably learned more of wit from them than detective work.

Still, she had her brains, her curiosity, and once the snow fell and the gardens went dormant, time on her hands to boot. She wouldn't need to solve the case, if there was indeed a case at all, just fill in the obvious gaps and drop the results in Gaston's lap. Of course, some people, including her own dear mother, might leap to the conclusion that Juliet had undertaken amateur sleuthing as a way to get close to Ben.

But that's ridiculous. I've made up my mind. Never again, she told herself. And she clung tight to that thought even as the excited Mrs. Cobblepot reappeared with bag in hand, even as it was time to drive back to Fenton House and see him again.

Chapter 5: Old Enemies
12 October, 1939

Ben's first day of medical practice was gentle. His caller at the side door turned out to be the vicar's wife with a covered dish—pear crumble—and an invitation to church that Sunday. She'd accepted his vague assurance to visit St. Mark's "soon," complimented his new office, and offered condolences on the loss of his wife. Like Juliet, the woman seemed reluctant to speak of Penny or reminisce about their school days. Clearly, the rector's wife had never counted Penny as a friend.

Perhaps I actually should be compiling an enemies list, he'd thought. *Not for me, but for Penny.*

The special patient-door buzzer didn't sound again, leaving Ben free to examine his new home's lower level more thoroughly. In addition to the donated furniture, rugs, framed art and wireless, someone had provided a battered old steamer trunk filled with distractions. Inside its newspaper-lined, camphor-smelling depths, he found a jump rope, two decks of cards, eight metal darts, a paperback copy of *Treasure Island*, some watercolors, a bag of marbles, a cricket bat, a baby doll whose porcelain head was only loosely connected, and a wooden board carved with letters and numbers. Ben, who'd grown up playing anagrams with plastic letter tiles, puzzled over it for a moment, taking it for some sort of word game. Then it all came together: A-Z, 0-9, a rayed sun on the upper left, a crescent moon on the upper right, HELLO at the top and GOOD-BYE at the bottom. His grandmother had owned one of these "talking boards," as she called it, though most people referred to them now as

Ouija boards. There was no planchette for alleged spirits to move and spell out messages, however, which made Ben unaccountably grateful. He was a man of science, not superstition, and certainly not old Victorian parlor tricks. But as a little boy, he'd feared the talking board, the collection of letters that could bridge the gap between life and death. His grandmother had forbidden him to so much as touch the planchette. So its absence was comforting, though he could hardly admit it, even to himself.

By four o'clock he was hungry. The pantry contained a few staples like flour, baking soda, and Lyons Golden Syrup; the icebox held margarine and one brown egg. He had no idea how to transform those raw elements into what he really wanted—a filet mignon and mashed potatoes—so he uncovered the dish of pear crumble and went to work. He'd demolished half of it, washing it down with a mug of tap water, when Lady Juliet and Mrs. Cobblepot arrived. What they discovered—dessert eaten straight out of the pan with the first utensil he could find, a gravy spoon—apparently confirmed their opinion he was a man incapable of surviving alone.

"A housekeeper?" he echoed as the determined pair swept into the kitchen, Lady Juliet armed with something wrapped in butcher's paper. Two impulses warred inside. One resented the interference of officious, condescending females bursting into his new home, clucking over a perfectly serviceable meal as if it were anyone's affair what he chose to eat. The other wanted to cheer in relief. Rescue had arrived and brought along a nice leg of lamb. He could keep the food and shoo them out, but he couldn't properly season and cook that joint, not if it meant the firing squad.

"A housekeeper, cook, and light nurse all rolled into one," Lady Juliet confirmed as Mrs. Cobblepot unpacked her grocery basket: onions, potatoes, sausage, oats, dried currants, coffee, and tinned milk. "No doubt you'll be on your feet soon enough, and while I'm sure you can brew your own tea and sew your own buttons, don't forgot you're the only physician for miles. That means Barking and the outskirts of Plymouth, as well as Birdswing. Once word gets out, you won't have a spare moment. In a time of war, it's criminally inefficient to task a doctor with doing the washing up. Besides, this cottage is too large for one person. Best go ahead and take in a useful sort like Mrs. Cobblepot, someone who can contribute, before the Army billets a stranger in your spare bedroom once evacuations resume."

Lady Juliet sounded so matter-of-fact as she said this, so sweetly rational, Ben found all shreds of resistance draining away. At the same time, he regarded her with fresh admiration. How very deft of her to prop up his ego, promote Mrs. Cobblepot's abilities, and make it all sound like patriotism in the process.

"I agree completely. And feel certain Mrs. Cobblepot will soon make herself indispensable." Ben nodded at the matronly woman, sixty if she was a day, her smile as bright and unfiltered as a little girl's. "But I can still depend on you to carry me around from time to time, can't I, Lady Juliet?"

He expected a laugh, but received a glare. "No, indeed, Dr. Bones. Such expectations only breed sloth. Arise and walk as quick as you may, or I'll tear a page from the Sir Shackleton's book and have you transported around the village via dog sled." Shoulders back and head high, Lady Juliet swept out of Fenton House without a goodbye for the second time that day.

"I can never tell if I've offended her or not," Ben told Mrs. Cobblepot.

"Oh, don't fret, love. No one understands Lady Juliet. Dog sleds and South pole explorers! She always says the oddest things." Clucking indulgently, Mrs. Cobblepot drew aside the curtain concealing the larder shelves, pulling her spectacles down her nose to read the tins' labels. "It's why she and your Penny never got on. But I'm sure you know all about that. Penny was the belle of the ball. She expected the other girls to hang on her every word, not try and change the subject to bygone eras and faraway places. I was their elementary school teacher, you know, before I married." Peering into the flour canister, she let out a grateful sigh. "No creepy-crawlies, thank goodness. Mr. Vine's raised the price of flour twice since war was declared."

Intending to rinse his gravy spoon, Ben wheeled to the sink. "I have the impression no one much cared for Penny."

Mrs. Cobblepot gave him a stricken look. "Heavens, listen to me! Lady Juliet's not the only one who has trouble controlling what comes out of her mouth. Only what I say is all too easy to decipher. Never mind that, dear." She plucked the spoon from his hand. "From this moment forward, the kitchen is my domain. And do forgive me if I seemed to speak ill of the dead."

"Yes. Avoiding that is a nice custom, a well-meaning custom," Ben said carefully, hoping his new housekeeper liked to talk as much as he suspected. "But at the moment, I'm more interested in honesty. I realize we've only just met, Mrs. Cobblepot, but would you permit me to share something with you in confidence?"

Her eyes widened. Smoothing her dress with both hands, she said, "Why, yes, Dr. Bones. Yes, of course."

"Penny and I had a brief courtship. Some would say we married in haste. As we became more accustomed to one another…." Lord, he sounded like a patient, launching into a saga starting with his birth in response to the question, "How long have you had that rash?" Was it really so hard to admit the truth?

He started over. "The fact is, we were on the point of separating when the accident occurred. And as I come to know Birdswing and the people who live here, I suspect I hardly knew my wife at all."

Mrs. Cobblepot didn't answer right away. Locating the kettle, she filled it with water and set it to boil. Placing a pair of cups and saucers on the table, she sat down on one side of the table while he maneuvered his chair to the opposite side. When she spoke again, her manner had changed. Gone was the housekeeper, eager to please. This was the woman behind the amiable mask, her tone more serious, her sentences not peppered by self-conscious smiles or laughs.

"Tell me, doctor. Have you known many pretty girls in your life? No doubt London's full of them. Perhaps there Penny was just one in a crowd, but here… here she was a beauty. There's only one of those per village per generation, thank goodness. No small community could ever survive two." Lifting her cup, another donated bit of neighborly goodwill that didn't match its saucer, she ran a finger along the chipped rim. "But back to my question. Have you known many pretty girls?"

"Only by acquaintance, I suppose. I had no sisters, and Penny was the first girl to give me the time of day when I was still a gawkish student. Though I'd like to think I don't categorize anyone, male or female, solely by their looks," he added, hoping it was true.

"Of course not. I don't mean a pretty face guarantees any particular qualities. But we're only human. We always think what we see is what we get. And girls like Penny know that and take advantage. It's almost as if… oh, Dr. Bones, you mustn't think us terribly unchristian, but there's a touch of the old religion in Birdswing. In all of Cornwall, really. My mother believed in fairies, the good and the bad. She would have said a bad fairy slipped into baby Penny's nursery and whispered in her ear."

"Old religion?" Ben repeated, lost.

"The faith of the first people in Britain, before the Anglo-Saxons. The people who raised the standing stones. There was a henge here once, when it was a hamlet called Crow's Wing. Long before Sir Thaddeus Linton turned up in 1840 and renamed it Birdswing."

"And… fairies?" Ben fought to keep a neutral expression. "Whispering what?"

"Why, what bad fairies always tell us. 'You're the only one who matters.'" Mrs. Cobblepot flicked at a crumb on the tabletop. "You must remember, I was Penny's primary school teacher. I watched her spread stories about her little friends, the very girls she played dolls with, telling half-truths and lies. I don't know which child was the first to give her a present—her own favorite toy—to make Penny stop. But I know after that she had power over all of them. And the power grew every year. She always had ha'pennies, mint humbugs, a new ribbon for her hair. Sometimes a parent would make an accusation but naught ever came of it. Penny's father worshipped her, and for him she was sweetness, dimples, and curls. Maybe he should have seen through her." Mrs. Cobblepot shrugged. "Some say the mum and dad are always to blame, and since I was never blessed with children of my own, I have no right to my opinion. But I taught little ones for more than fifteen years, and all I know is, she came to me like that. All time and experience did was strengthen what was already there."

"She didn't look back fondly on Birdswing," Ben said. "She told me the villagers were envious of her father's fortune."

"But Mr. Eubanks hadn't earned it yet." Mrs. Cobblepot looked surprised. "That came later, when Penny was about sixteen. They packed off to London soon after." The kettle began to whistle. Rising, she went to the stove and filled the teapot. "I do hope these tea leaves aren't stale. Let's give it extra time to steep." Placing the pot between them, she resumed her seat. "It's just as well they left when they did, after that awful business with the Archers and the Hibbets."

He waited.

"But you know about all that, don't you?"

Rather than meet her eyes, Ben picked up the teapot and poured. He'd only just met the woman, passed only a little time in her company, and yet he was tempted to spill it out to her, that first betrayal, the thing that had come between him and Penny. He'd never confided in anyone, telling himself it was dishonorable to share his wife's secrets but really just ashamed to admit the truth. The mad impulse to blurt it out, to get it off his chest at last, held sway until he realized there was no cream or sugar on the table.

"Oh, we're missing a few things. No, stay there, Mrs. Cobblepot. This wheelchair works, I assure you." Maneuvering carefully in the tight space, he found teaspoons but nothing else. "Ah, well. I often drank it plain on hospital rounds. And no, if Penny had some trouble before she left Birdswing, she never saw fit to tell me. What happened with the, er, Hibbets, you said?"

"The Archers came first. That story was always muddled, and I know so little, it's naught but gossip. Still, you have a right to know what folks might say about your late wife, so I'll repeat it to you." She blew on her tea before tasting it. "I didn't live in Birdswing when it happened. I lived in Plymouth with my husband Tom. We married late, you know, and had only sixteen years together before he went—boom!—like that. But as I was saying. Bobby Archer and his wife Helen were a young couple, new to the village. Helen had twin boys, toddlers, and it was all she could do to get hot meals on the table and clothes on the line. One of those who gives birth and loses her looks forever, poor thing. Bobby was a handsome man with a roving eye. He used to plop himself down in the Sheared Sheep when his dinner was burnt and complain to anyone who'd listen that his wife was a slattern, starving him to death." She snorted. "Penny was fifteen then. Pretty as a picture she was, and started going round with Bobby. Maybe she was a sympathetic ear. Maybe she was more. What actually went on between her and Bobby is pure gossip. What's fact is, Helen Archer rowed with her about it in the middle of Vine's Emporium. Ambushed Penny by the tinned mackerel and accused her of—of interfering with her husband. Only she was a deal more specific. Not to mention loud. My brother Clarence was there shopping. He said it was the only time he ever saw Penny shaken."

"Was that an end to it?"

"Not quite. Bobby Archer left Birdswing a few days later. Helen stayed and brought up the boys alone. She still can't hear Penny's name without getting angry."

Ben took a moment to digest that. Perhaps the notion of compiling a list of Penny's old enemies wasn't as absurd as it had first seemed. "And the other business?"

"That wasn't just gossip." Looking unhappy, Mrs. Cobblepot took a sip of tea as if to fortify herself. "I knew Ursula Hibbet from birth. She was a sweet thing, and one of Penny's oldest friends, though she took her lumps along with the rest. One Saturday night she and Penny went to a Plymouth dance hall. They came back in the wee hours along Stafford Road."

"A road I'll not soon forget," Ben said. If he thought about it, he could still feel the impact, not pain or fear so much as a rush of impossibility, of unreality as potent as suddenly taking flight. So he did his best not to think about it.

"Well, the car went off the road. It was Penny's father's car, an Austin Twenty she used to careen around in, sailing through crosswalks and giving fright to the old and young alike. They were drinking, of course, but still might have made it home, if not for the milk float idling outside Daley's co-op. John Leigham was unloading crates when they struck him. Old doc Egon said he died instantly. It took time for Mr. Daley—this was before he married that poor foreign girl—to sort through the crash, but he found Penny in the passenger seat with a great bruise on her chest and Ursula Hibbet dead behind the wheel." Another sip of tea. "Both girls had been drunk; it didn't take Sherlock Holmes to work that out. But John's wife and Ursula's father were both convinced Penny was the one driving, and should have been held to some kind of account. The constable questioned her. A detective from Scotland Yard even came to talk to her after Ursula's father went to London about it. But no one could prove Penny switched places with Ursula, and the matter was dropped."

Ben sighed. The note said, *Forgive me, it was never meant to be you, just her.* Was it a coincidence Penny had died on Stafford Road, struck down in the dark just like that milkman?

"Do Ursula's parents still live here?"

"No. Mr. Hibbet died of a heart attack three weeks after the case was officially shut. Mrs. Hibbet went away to live with her sister. Poor woman lost everything, her husband and her only child, in the space of a month."

For a long time, neither spoke. Ben, casting about for something to say that had nothing to do with Penny, finally said, "I believe I saw Mrs. Daley when I left the Sheared Sheep. And perhaps her child at the window?"

"If you saw a colored lady and a mixed child, then yes, you did. She's from some island in the Caribbean. The little mixed girl is Jane. Mrs. Daley runs the co-op in Hugh's absence, but I don't suppose she has many customers."

"What's she like? Mrs. Daley?" Ben asked. He'd known of Caribbean immigrants in London but even in the city they often kept to themselves, buying and selling from one another, renting to one another as much as possible, seeing doctors originally from Jamaica who mostly practiced in secret. How strange must it be for this woman, marrying into English village life and probably viewed as a bit of a curiosity on her husband's arm, only to be left alone to carry on in wartime?

"I don't know. I've never had the courage to speak to her. And I shop at Vine's, because… well. I can't say. Habit, I suppose." Mrs. Cobblepot grimaced. "Oh, forgive me, doctor, but let's put all this behind us for now. If I'm going to pass along gossip, I prefer it to be the happy sort. No, don't!" she cried, as he lifted his teacup to drain it.

"What?"

"I told you, there's a touch of the old religion in these parts. I've been known to leave out a dish of cream for the fairies on St. John's Eve—Midsummer's Eve, as my mother called it. And I read tea leaves. Swirl your cup three times and pass it to me so I can see."

He did as she asked, wondering how a woman who seemed so grounded in everyday life could practice such superstitious nonsense. As he watched, she took the cup in both hands, closed her eyes, and tipped it to the four cardinal directions. "Spirits of the North… spirits of the East… spirits of the South… spirits of the West…." Opening her eyes, she carefully poured the remaining fluid into his saucer, then overturned the cup onto hers. The pattern of soggy brown leaves looked meaningless to Ben.

"Oh, yes," Mrs. Cobblepot murmured. Staring him right in the eye, she said in a commanding voice, "Your every move in this village will be noted and commented upon. Your doorbell will ring all hours of the day and night. Your peace will be intruded upon by a very tall woman with iron resolve, who shall bring round equipment from her own gymnasium, the better to strengthen you…."

He chuckled. She did, too, eyes sparkling as he took her hand. "I'm glad you've come to stay, Mrs. Cobblepot."

"So am I, Dr. Bones. So am I."

***

The next two weeks were busy, pleasantly so, as all of Mrs. Cobblepot's not-so-psychic predictions came true. According to the orders the Army had issued him, Birdswing village was home to over one thousand souls, and its neighbor, the hamlet called Barking, had just under a thousand. Of course, with most men aged eighteen to forty conscripted into the service, that population was down by almost half, but it was still a goodly number for one physician to serve. Once Ben was back on his feet, he would be expected to help at St. Barnabas Hospital as well, particularly in the event of air strikes. The villagers knew this, knew Ben might even be required to travel back and forth to Plymouth if the southwest was heavily hit. Still, the steady influx of new patients not only kept Ben busy but Mrs. Cobblepot, too. After "requisitioning" a dented filing cabinet from her brother, Acting Constable Gaston, she now spent each evening sorting Ben's notes and transferring them into neatly labeled files.

"You shouldn't have to fret over that. You work hard enough as it is," Ben said one night as he rested against the parallel bars set up in his front parlor. As the tea leaves foretold, Lady Juliet had sent them over, announcing that a woman as busy as she had no use for old gymnastic equipment gathering dust in Belsham Manor. Ben's right leg had responded beautifully to his self-directed therapy, but his left leg was a different story. So it wasn't the housekeeper's organizational skills that put him on the verge of suggesting she retire with a novel and a cup of tea, and let him worry about chart making. It was the vicious throb in his left leg, radiating from his poorly mended femur to his knee, that made him eager for an excuse to stop. He wasn't certain he'd ever enjoy another day altogether free from pain.

If so, what of it? Men will be back soon enough without arms or legs, or never return at all, buried in foreign soil. At least I've graduated from wheelchair to crutches and can stand five minutes without falling. Some would give their eyeteeth for that.

"I enjoy it." As she looked up, Mrs. Cobblepot's horn-rimmed glasses flashed in the lamplight. To ensure they obeyed blackout restrictions, she not only covered Fenton House's windows with cardboard, she did all her evening chores—washing up, mending clothes, chart work—by the light of a single lamp. The result was heavy gloom from supper to dawn but prevented her brother from pounding on the cottage door shouting, "Douse that light! Douse it in the name of the king!" Mrs. Cobblepot professed love for her zealot-brother, but had also mentioned in her matter-of-fact way that if he accused her of signaling enemy aircraft once more, he'd be the one pulling himself along on the parallel bars, learning to walk again.

"It's you who needs a rest," she added, placing a completed chart on the day's pile. "Next Monday will bring another flood. Two or three may even be sick, if you can find them amid all the friendly mums and marriageable young women."

Ben mopped his brow with a flannel. "I suppose it would be churlish of me to complain."

"Nonsense. You're newly widowed. It's a scandal the way these mothers hurl their daughters at you. You'd think the menfolk were never coming back." She picked up the next page, a brief note—"healthy, well-nourished, mild headaches, recommend fresh air and adequate sleep"—on yet another ostensibly ill young woman who'd turned up in his office perfumed, beribboned, and kitted out in her best frock and patent leather heels. "Mind you, many of them won't be coming back. And Lord knows how long the war will go on. Men in reserved occupations are more romantic than dukes and cinema stars."

Fitting his crutches under each arm, Ben let that remark pass. Romance was the last thing on his mind, as each day was struggle enough. Not just with his rehabilitation but with running a medical practice with Victorian paraphernalia, not to mention a local chemist who seemed to have crawled straight out of the Dark Ages.

Mr. Dwerryhouse, a little man with a hooked nose and a left shoulder several inches higher than his right, distrusted Ben's prescriptions for sulfa drugs. And though he'd stocked the newfangled medicines Ben requested, he advised his customers not to take them. At his shop, cod liver oil was the supreme cure-all, followed closely by a health tonic made with arsenic and mercury for stubborn cases. Apparently he'd enjoyed a close working relationship with old Dr. Egon and felt obliged out of loyalty to thwart the man's replacement at every turn.

Heaven only knew when the modern medical equipment Ben had sent away for would arrive. The Army got first pick of everything, naturally, and many scientific companies had converted their factories to manufacture nothing but military supplies. Viewed from that height, the needs of a country physician were too small to be seen.

At least no more mysterious notes had arrived, although Ben sometimes wished they would if it would light a fire beneath Mr. Gaston's rear. The man toiled from daybreak to well past dusk, laboring on his backyard bomb shelter, painting curbs white so they would be more visible during the blackout, and conducting surprise inspections of rubbish bins to determine if food was being wasted. According to rumor—and it was true what

Lady Juliet had said, the birds did sing in Birdswing—Mr. Gaston had also advised Mr. Vine and Mrs. Daley to begin voluntarily rationing food in advance of government decree, offering to stand guard himself as the new rules were applied "to forestall a riot." For a man of his years, Mr. Gaston seemed to be in all places at once, his fingers in every pie but one—the question of whether Penny Bones's death had been an accident or murder.

I'll ask Lady Juliet how to proceed. Ring her up at the manor first thing tomorrow, Ben thought, suddenly too tired to follow through with his plan of sitting down beside Mrs. Cobblepot and helping her finish the day's charts. So he said good night, squinted against the semi-darkness, and went half-blind to his temporary bedroom, crutches thumping all the way.

As always since moving into the cottage, sleep came swiftly and deeply. When Ben sat up in bed, jerking awake to the sound of more thumps, he had the absurd notion his crutches were roaming Fenton House by themselves. He started to laugh, but the sound froze in his throat, swelling like water into ice that seemed to cut off his air.

Why was the bedroom so cold?

Passing a hand over his face, he waited, listening. Just as he started to settle back under the covers, there came another *thump*, then a smaller noise like a rattle.

Someone is in this house.

He knew it, knew it absolutely, and wished he owned a hunting rifle or cricket bat to drive them away. In a village like Birdswing, the housebreaker might be a tramp. But might also be a fringe dweller, a smallholder desperate enough to break into the crippled doctor's home.

There's a cricket bat in that old chest. Or my crutch might do. Ben swung his legs over the side of the bed with a suppressed groan. He was decent, at least, wearing the striped cotton pajamas he'd purchased after Mrs. Cobblepot moved in, lest a midnight air raid reveal he preferred to sleep nude.

Decent? Fitting the crutches beneath each arm, he exited the converted sewing room. *I'm turning into a true villager if I'm worried about decency while surprising a housebreaker* . . . .

It was pitch black inside the parlor. As Ben ran his fingers along the cold plaster wall, searching for the light switch, he heard another sound, dry and slithery, like rustling robes. It sent a jolt of fear up his spine and directly into his heart, which leapt into overdrive.

"Who's that?" he shouted into the dark.

Silence.

Heart thudding hard against his ribs, he ran his shaking hand over the wall again. It touched something clammy.

The switch!

Even as he flipped it and the low-wattage lamp came to life, casting yellow incandescent light in a muted circle, he felt—imagined?—something brush against him as it passed by. It was like passing a hand through water and feeling spiders instead; life where it shouldn't be, eyes where they *couldn't* be, a vitality both familiar, alien, and utterly out of context.

As his eyes adjusted to the lamplight, he noticed the battered old steamer trunk. It was pulled forward a few feet, and open. The cricket bat he'd thought to arm himself with lay on the carpet, no doubt the cause of at least one thump. The "talking board" he'd examined, so similar to the one his grandmother had once forbidden him to touch, was also out. So was the doll, in two pieces.

"Dr. Bones! You almost frightened me to death!" Mrs. Cobblepot appeared in the opposite doorway in kerchief and wrapper, face oddly defenseless without her horn-rimmed glasses. "Did you get up for a glass of water and trip in the dark?"

"No. I heard something. A housebreaker," he said, still staring at the Ouija board. The doll's body had fallen in a heap. Its round, wide-eyed, solemn face stared at him from atop the word HELLO.

"Housebreaker?" Seizing the cricket bat from the floor, she announced in tones that must have terrified many a naughty student, "Anyone who trespasses here will get a right walloping!"

Chuckling weakly, Ben realized the worst of his fear had passed. It was hard to maintain superstitious terror with an armed old woman bellowing threats into the night. "I'm not sure anyone was ever here. Fringe benefit of the blackout—no need to go round checking windows for one that was jimmied open. This place is shut up tight as a drum."

"Well, someone must have been here. They've rifled poor Lucy's things."

Gooseflesh rose on Ben's arms. "That stuff belongs to her?"

"Belonged, yes. We let the house remain furnished for too long after she died," Mrs. Cobblepot said, replacing the cricket bat inside the battered trunk. "People were so afraid of the gas, you know, after all that on the wireless about possible gas attacks from Germany. We didn't make a clean sweep until Lady Victoria and Lady Juliet decided Fenton House would be yours. Almost everything went at auction, but most of us who knew her took a keepsake or two. Miss Jenkins—she teaches primary school now—took this trunk, but brought it back a few days later. Said it gave her bad dreams." Putting the broken doll and Ouija board inside as well, she closed the trunk and pushed it back into its usual spot. "Just wait until the next evacuation sends a wave of city children our way and her little class is overflowing. She'll have no time for dreaming then!" Peering at the mantle clock, she added, "We still have a good few hours before dawn. Would you like me to warm some milk for you?"

"No, thank you." He always frowned when the housekeeper coddled him like that, but in his secret heart, he rather liked it. "Only—if no one broke in, what happened? Who rifled Lucy's things?"

"Well, I don't sleepwalk, so it must have been you, Dr. Bones."

"No. I heard the thumping… at first I thought my crutches were walking around by themselves… something about being decent…." He stopped, realizing how silly it sounded, as garbled as the average dream.

"And woke up in here," Mrs. Cobblepot concluded for him. "When I called your name, you looked stupefied. Hair mussed, mouth open. Asleep on your feet."

Ben, who'd never walked in his sleep, took up the notion eagerly. "You're right, of course. If I still used the wheelchair, I suppose it would have been sleep-rolling. I'm sorry to have disturbed you. Goodnight, Mrs. Cobblepot."

Once in bed again, it took a long time to drift off. Upstairs, a proper bed awaited, as soon as he was strong enough; this mattress was thin, the sheets scratchy, the pillow as flat and uncomfortable as a punctured tire. Lucy

McGregor had used this room for sewing; he would make it his chart room, and possibly store emergency medical supplies here as well, assuming the Army allowed any to be shipped his way. Curling up as much as his stiff left leg allowed, Ben started a mental inventory. Gauze bandage rolls. Iodine. Cotton wool. Smelling salts....

He tried to keep his thoughts marching stolidly down the list, but the last thing he saw before he fell asleep was that pale solemn doll's face, lying beside the word HELLO.

Chapter 6: Venom
28 October, 1939

"Yes, indeed," Lady Juliet said before Ben could finish asking her to lunch. The telephone lines between Birdswing's high street and Belsham Manor often yielded a static-filled connection, but her strong voice came over like she was in the next room. "We're preparing to winter the roses here, and I've never been more thoroughly frustrated in the whole of my life. If I ever profess so much as a passing fondness for children again, have me dragged into the village square and flogged."

"Children?" he repeated, thinking he'd misheard.

"I fear so. Mother continues her crusade to be of use to the community, and therefore, I continue to suffer. She's invited Miss Jenkins and what can only be described as a passel of little ones to spend Saturday in the gardens, learning about horticulture by *helping* me," Lady Juliet scoffed. "Next year I shall grow carnivorous plants large enough to make a dent in any would-be assistants. So, yes. Lunch. But I fear you must come to me, as even reluctant hostesses are permitted no egress. Are you driving yet?"

"No." Clearly she hadn't heard about his attempt a few days before. The vehicle had three pedals—clutch, accelerator, and brake. And while he could manage the clutch with his left leg, trouble braking had caused a near-collision with the speeding Mrs. Sutton and her mud-spattered Citroën.

"Very well, I'll send the car around. I fear Cook will be serving boiled mutton with potato pastries and prune sponge. Are you averse?"

"Not at all. I should tell you this is more than a social call. I intend on begging a bit of advice."

"Naturally. And you needn't plead for it to start, though you may plead for it to stop." She rang off.

Chuckling, Ben put the receiver back in its cradle. Perhaps Lady Juliet's tendency to skip goodbyes was only a habit, not a form of censure.

He arrived at Belsham Manor just before noon. It was a lovely day, mild enough to be late summer, with a gentle breeze that sent puffy clouds scudding across a bright blue sky. Oaks in their reddish-orange autumn finery still looked robust, but the yews were half bare already, drifts of golden leaves around them. The manor itself was less jarring on second viewing, though with Halloween approaching, Ben had no trouble superimposing a little agreeable spookiness atop the asymmetric heap. That reminded him of Lady Juliet's comment—"Until I was eight, I assumed we were secretly vampires"—and he smiled. What would she make of his apparent sleepwalking the previous night?

"Over here, Dr. Bones!" Lady Juliet boomed as he disembarked from the car. After thanking the driver, Belsham Manor's ancient retainer, Robbie—once in normal tones, then twice in a shout, since Robbie was deaf as a post—Ben thumped along on his crutches over dying grass and gravel paths toward the sound of her voice. Children were everywhere, a few older ones pulling weeds or raking leaves, the rest dashing here and there, giggling, shouting, calling back and forth. Alone by a wrought iron obelisk covered with white climbing roses sat Mrs. Daley's daughter, Jane. She couldn't have been more than four years old, with skinny limbs, *café au lait* skin, and a storm cloud of frizzy brown hair. Her eyes followed him as he went, perhaps because of the crutches, but when he tossed out, "Hallo," she looked away.

Ben found Lady Juliet seated in a summerhouse alongside Lady Victoria and a petite young woman with shoulder-length ginger hair. Seeing him approach, the redhead smiled, and Ben smiled back, some automatic masculine instinct warning him not to grin too widely. In the last two weeks, the hopeful mothers of Birdswing and Barking had paraded some pretty girls across his path, but now he'd come face to face with the prettiest.

"Dr. Bones!" Lady Victoria looked splendid as ever in a pale blue tea-length frock, hat, and gloves. Rising, she came forth to greet him, beaming as he easily traversed the summerhouse's three shallow steps. "What progress you've made. I know you've been practically under house arrest in your new office, held captive by all the aches and pains of Birdswing. So perhaps you haven't yet been introduced to our primary school teacher, Miss Rose Jenkins." Turning to the redhead, who was dressed in a practical chambray skirt and blouse with a yellow kerchief round her neck, she said, "Miss Jenkins, I'd like you to meet Dr. Benjamin Bones."

"Hello, doctor." Rising gracefully, Miss Jenkins accepted his hand, meeting his gaze with sea-green eyes. "I've been meaning to bring over a pie to welcome you to Birdswing, but there was practically a line to the street."

"All of them female," came a comment from Lady Juliet's vicinity, but when Ben managed to look away from Miss Jenkins, Lady Juliet seemed not to have spoken. Hands folded in her lap, she watched the children.

"Yes, well, it will keep me out of the bread line." Usually Ben could think of something to say, could make polite conversation like grown men had done since the dawn of civilization, but at the moment his mind was blank. Instead of commenting on the fine weather, the children's efforts to help, or gardening in general, he heard himself say, "With those eyes and that hair, I can't help but wonder, are you Irish?"

"God save the King," Lady Juliet burst out, surging to her feet like a force of nature. "No, Mother, I'm not swearing, I just suffered a sort of patriotic spasm. To answer your question, Dr. Bones, Miss Jenkins is as English as you or I, a wonderful teacher, and *very* pleased to meet you, if I do say so myself." With scarcely a pause for breath, she continued, "Now. Lunch was promised and I'm famished. Mother, Miss Jenkins, would you mind terribly if Dr. Bones and I drove into Birdswing for lunch? He's come seeking my advice, and I intend to give it at length, which is sure to bore you to tears. No doubt you two have something wonderfully feminine to discuss in the meantime."

Folding her arms across her chest, Miss Jenkins looked away. "I'll be glad to stay with Lady Victoria and the children," she said in a determinedly cheerful tone.

Lady Victoria gave her daughter a cool-eyed smile, conveying refined disapproval without saying a word. As rebukes went, it was so discreet, Lady Juliet could have pretended not to receive it. Except she appeared incapable of letting her mother have the last word, even if that word was silent.

"It was a compliment," she cried. "A mere acknowledgement of how beautifully your gentle, harmonious natures fit together. Allow me an hour or so off the lead, and I'll return fed, rejuvenated, and altogether presentable." She looked down at her overlarge tartan shirt, corduroy trousers, and big black boots. "Well, perhaps not presentable."

"Go with our compliments," Lady Victoria said, radiating genuine warmth in Ben's direction. "Miss Jenkins and I will dine on mutton and summer wine, and miss you not at all."

"You seem a trifle out of sorts," Ben said when they were past earshot.

"'Are you Irish?'" Lady Juliet retorted. Instantly, she sucked in her breath, as if trying to draw the words back in. "Oh, never mind me, I *am* out of sorts. I'm accustomed to being aggravated all over Birdswing and in every room of the manor, but being aggravated in my garden is a new experience. Well. That is to say, the plants aggravate me sometimes. And the insects. And the soil." She laughed. "Upon reflection, I'm an entirely unsatisfied creature, and nothing but an enormous piece of pie can set me to rights."

She set a rapid pace through the red-painted oaks toward Belsham Manor's mews, a place where sometime in the last twenty years, carriages had given way to automobiles. Ben found that on crutches, he could nearly keep up with Lady Juliet's great stride. And now that he wasn't traveling by wheelchair, he didn't have to crane his neck as far looking up. "So we're leaving to escape the prune sponge, not the children?"

She tossed him a surprised glance. "I like the children. They're utterly useless, and I won't let them *touch* a rose bush, but they're no bother in small doses. It's Mother. Please understand, I love her dearly, and I really must admire any woman who can waft amongst the soil and manure without ever staining a glove." She stripped off her own gloves, cowhide and well-used, hooking them in her belt. "But by inviting the children, she invited Miss Jenkins, and I cannot abide Miss Jenkins."

"She seems pleasant enough."

"Oh, for heaven's sake, she's a pretty face and nothing more. She spent ten minutes discussing her ensemble with Mother. How she bought the chambray from Vine's and sewed her blouse from a pattern in *Women's Weekly* so it would match the skirt. Just as I was about to go in search of hemlock, she switched topics. To her scarf. Canary yellow, because her soldier boyfriend adores her in yellow."

"Boyfriend?"

Lady Juliet emitted a pained sound. "Boyfriend. Did you think she wouldn't have one? Ask her about him. He's a favorite topic of hers, or so I imagine."

"Imagine? You don't know?"

"I spend as little time around her as possible."

Ben's crutches were crunching against gravel now, the stone and timber mews only a hundred yards away. White-haired, white-mustached Robbie puttered along obliviously just outside the cavernous entrance. "Sounds like you've condemned her more for her looks than anything she's done," he said mildly.

Lady Juliet drew up short, rounding on him so fast, they almost collided. "That's quite an accusation! A reckless, unwarranted, *egregious* accusation!"

He grinned. "That's the thing about people with an overgrown vocabulary. They can turn a simple observation into a perfidious recrimination quicker than you can say *antidisestablishmentarianism*."

Her broad face froze as if caught between a retort and a chuckle. Finally she softened, settling for the latter. "Usually you employ smaller words."

"Yes, well, never use a bone saw where a scalpel will do. Now drive me somewhere, and let me buy you lunch."

"Nonsense, I'll pay my own way and yours too. It's the least I can do." She led him into the cool, shadowy mews where the Crossley waited. "Have you learned anything more about that odd little note?"

"No, and that's what I'd like to talk to you about. If Gaston's conducting an investigation, it's so top secret, he should spy for Britain. But Mrs. Cobblepot told me a thing or two. About Penny's trouble with Mrs. Archer and the Hibbets. I don't mean to make another accusation," he added lightly, "or say I've come to the conclusion the note was genuine and Penny's death was no accident. Still." He stood back as Lady Juliet opened the passenger door for him. "To say she made enemies is no lie. And if he won't look into it, perhaps I should."

"I agree. And that makes our choice of where to dine simple," she said as he used his left leg's growing strength to pull himself into the cab. "I only hope Archer's still has pie on the menu."

***

Archer's restaurant was located far off the high street, in a converted semi-detached house with a patched roof and weed-choked front garden. Its four-paned windows had been painted black, and hastily, too, judging by the dried black splotches marring the sills. A hand-written notice affixed to the front door read:

NEW HOURS 8 TO 3. SUPPER SERVICE CANCELED INDEFINITELY DUE TO GOVERNMENT HARRASSMENT.

"Our intrepid air warden threatened to fine her because a patron left the door open a crack after sundown," Lady Juliet told Ben in a low voice. "He's threatened to fine every person in this village, including me, but Helen Archer takes things personally. To hear her tell it, she needs the income from her evening diners—she's the only villager I know of who claimed she was too poor to buy cardboard and curtains, and went straight to black paint. *And* she's petitioning the Ministry of Defense for reimbursement, or so she says. Still, the first time Mr. Gaston cautioned her, she was deeply offended. Called off supper and tacked up that sign."

Ben thought the writing on that sign, overlarge and a bit wobbly, boded ill. He asked, "How's the food?"

"Excellent. Or else we'd be in Morton's café discussing the Hibbet side of the equation." Lady Juliet opened the door, setting off a jangly bell over their heads. As they entered, Ben felt oppressed by the paneled wood walls and matted burgundy carpet. A single electric fan in the far corner could not move the air fast enough to dispel the sense of suffocation, and a few electric wall sconces did not make up for the gloom perpetrated by those blacked-out windows. The predominant kitchen odor, some kind of roast meat, smelled good. But not good enough to change Ben's impression of Mrs. Archer's restaurant as a nursing home for grudges.

There was a long Formica-topped counter with mismatched stools, some round tables and a handful of booths. All the booths were taken, mostly by older women lingering over cups of tea.

"This place used to cater to laborers the way Morton's caters to old men, and Laviolette's to those lacking sense of taste or smell," Lady Juliet whispered to Ben. "Now with most of the men leaving, I suppose Mrs. Archer truly does face hard times. Perhaps I should stop mocking the paint. Though if she hadn't been in such a rage over the blackout rules, she would have made a better job of it."

"Lady Juliet. And that must be Penny's husband," a flat female voice said. It did not sound pleased.

"Mrs. Archer! What a pleasure, we were just about to claim our seats," Lady Juliet said, taking a stool beside the dessert case. Ben spied caraway seed cake, custard tarts, and apple pie, and then the proprietress stepped around the counter.

Helen Archer was under forty, he would later learn, but looked fifty. Her gray hair, parted in the middle, had been combed neatly on the left side, yet remained wild and tangled on the right. The left side of her face was unremarkable—cold blue gaze, flared nostril, sullen lips. On the right side, her upper lid drooped over a white shrunken eye. The nostril and tip of the nose were scarred, and her mouth turned down, twisted by pain.

"My scalp hurts. Even my hair hurts. I wear a cap when I cook, which is God's own torment, but the rest of the day I let it breathe. The shingles," she said, still in that flat tone. "Being a doctor, you'll know about that."

All too well, Ben thought. Some of his older professors at medical school had still thought of this condition, caused by a virus called herpes zoster, as a form of erysipelas, or "holy fire," the burning red skin disease that killed St. John of the Cross. Its origins were still somewhat unclear, but the ability of those weeping red sores to flare up without warning, often around the sufferer's trunk, was well known even to the ancients. In fact, the common name, shingles, came from a Greek word meaning "girdle." Why the virus attacked one branch of the nervous system over another was still a mystery. But when it flared in the trigeminal nerve, the result could be a scarred nose, a blind eye, or scalp pain that lingered for years. Ben saw no active lesions, which meant Mrs. Archer's disease, though quiet now, had left her with all three.

"I'm afraid I do. And I'm sorry for your trouble. Shingles is beastly. I'm Ben. Ben Bones." He offered his hand.

Mrs. Archer studied it for what felt like such a long time, he feared he'd have to withdraw it. Then she sighed, clasped his hand, and gave it a perfunctory shake. "I'm sorry for your loss. That's not me being insincere, mind you, only decent. What will you have to eat?"

"Is that beef I smell?"

"Minced beef and dumplings. For two?"

"For two," Lady Juliet agreed.

As Mrs. Archer disappeared through the kitchen's swinging door, Ben took the stool beside Lady Juliet. "Now that we're here, I haven't the faintest idea how to proceed," he said close to her ear. There it was again, that scent he liked, less heady than a perfume but more pronounced than soap or *eau de* stick insect.

"I believe the standard course is to demand she account for her whereabouts on the night of the murder," Lady Juliet whispered back. "Alternately, you tell her you know all, even though you know nothing, and intimidate her into confessing."

"Trick her into boasting about it while you get Gaston to eavesdrop around a corner?" Ben chuckled. "The cinema makes detective work look so easy."

"Did you know Mrs. Archer had shingles before she told you?"

"Of course."

"How?"

"Observation."

Lady Juliet's interest seemed genuine, which was rare in non-medical folk. Most of them ascribed godlike powers to doctors, who were in turn emboldened to ascribe still greater godlike powers to themselves. "But surely many conditions look similar."

"They do. That's where questioning—taking the history—and sometimes laying hands on the patient comes in. Plus the differential diagnosis."

He could practically see the gears turning behind those brown eyes, working out the meaning of the phrase. "Sort of like gardening, eh? Say the whole plant is wilted. Are the leaves a normal color? If yes, check for holes in the stems. If no holes… well, you get the picture. Once you've eliminated all the things it isn't, you arrive at what it is. That must be how a criminal investigation goes, Dr. Bones. Observation, questioning, laying hands on the evidence."

"So you think I should ask her about Penny?"

Mrs. Archer returned with two steaming plates of minced beef and dumplings. Without asking, she put out two cups and saucers, poured tea, left the pot between them, and disappeared into the kitchen again.

"Oh, do ask her." Pausing to taste a dumpling, Lady Juliet made a little sound of approval. "This is better than half of what we eat at the manor. Mrs. Archer could put Morton's out of business if she wasn't so prickly all the time. And don't look sidelong at me. Yes, I'm prickly, too, but I don't rely on the public to pay my salary. And rest assured, she'll want to discuss her husband's indiscretions. She's been quite free on that topic since the day he walked out. Myself, I prefer a narrow list of confidantes. The birds here sing readily enough without me buying them sheet music."

After that, they ate in companionable silence. When Mrs. Archer returned to take away their empty plates, Lady Juliet ordered a slice of apple pie and asked if she might carry it into the back garden. "I adore your hornbeam tree's yellow leaves. I'll sit on the grass and gaze up at them as I eat."

Shrugging, Mrs. Archer looked at Ben. "Same for you?"

"Yes. And I wonder—might we have a private word?"

"Why? You have a tonic for shingles?" Mrs. Archer's sagging right eyelid lifted slightly as her left eye went wide. "Oh. *Right.* I'll talk to you, doc, but I didn't write you any note saying sorry."

"You've heard about that?"

"Everyone from here to Barking's heard about it. Maybe from here to Land's End. Either Penny was done in by a killer with a conscience, or someone in our midst has a vile sense of humor. You'd think," she added, ordinarily flat voice gaining sudden expressive bite, "the law in this village would be rooting out that sort of thing, not harassing a poor woman trying to run a business."

She led him through that swinging door into the kitchen, a reassuringly clean place being made cleaner by two identical boys of about nine. Each had broad shoulders, firm features, and a shock of black hair. Both looked equally sullen, too, one mutinously pushing a mop, the other scouring a prep table with treasonous eyes.

"Caleb and Micah. My sons," Mrs. Archer told Ben. "On punishment in the kitchen. Lying, this time. Telling our fool of an air warden they saw a plane with German markings flying over Pate Field. Put half the village in an uproar."

"The stupid half," one of the twins muttered.

"It's not for you lot to criticize your betters." Mrs. Archer glared at them.

"You call Mr. Gaston doolally all the time," the other twin said.

"Yes, and when you're a grown man and a taxpayer, you can, too. Now off with you! Get upstairs to your books and see that your homework's done. I'll see Miss Jenkins at church tomorrow, and she'll tell me straight away if it's not handed in."

As the boys put away their cleaning gear and hung up their oilcloth aprons, Mrs. Archer led Ben to a table in the far corner. There she put out two cups, and as he sat down to pie and more tea, she produced a box of cigarettes. Taking the seat across from him, she said, "I never smoke around my cooking, not even when it's safe in the oven. But in the afternoon, give me a ciggie over pudding any day." Shaking one out, she lit up and pushed the box at him. "You?"

He gave her what he hoped wasn't a weak-willed smile. "I try to avoid them. And tobacco's sure to be rationed soon, so now's the perfect time to go off it."

Mrs. Archer took a deep drag. "Some days tobacco's the only relief I get. What you got against it?"

He shrugged. Heaven knew dozens of physicians endorsed tobacco. A few, including a German doctor, had suggested cigarettes were linked to cancer, but the medical establishment took little notice, especially since that unpopular notion was championed in Deutschland. Still, it seemed reasonable to Ben that the deliberate daily inhalation of fumes courted throat and lung irritation, if not worse maladies. So after his injuries, he'd stopped buying cigarettes, and most days he didn't miss them much. Yet now, after a bite of pie and a sip of tea, he couldn't resist Mrs. Archer's offer. Lighting one up, he inhaled with as much pleasure as when he'd picked up the habit, in a place where smoking was ubiquitous: medical school.

"Now. I got to ask." Mrs. Archer's tone was flat as ever, giving no hint of what would come next. "Are you broke up over losing Penny? Or thanking God she's gone?"

Startled, Ben coughed, drank some tea, coughed again, and wondered for the second time in three minutes what his face looked like. Not just now, but in general. Did he seem too cheerful? Had he looked like a happy bachelor, ordering up lunch with Lady Juliet, when a proper widower should have been marinating in his own gloom?

"You don't have to say it out loud. I just wanted to know for sure." A faint smile curved the left side of her mouth. "People don't look at me much since the shingles, but I look at them. Closer than I ever did when I had two good eyes. You seem decent enough to me, Dr. Bones. Toff manners, King's English, ever so polite with no double-talk, no mockery. Good appetite, too. You aren't grieving. You were never her sort. I don't think she even bit you. And if she did, you cut the wound and drew out the venom before it was too late."

Ben thought about that. And since Mrs. Archer was so frank about her powers of observation, he returned the favor, taking in all she'd said and everything about her, from the wild half of her hair to her frayed shirt collar to that plain gold band, glinting on the third finger of her left hand. "But it was too late for you?"

"Yes. Bobby was the only one for me. So good-looking he put those handsome sons of mine in the shade. I worshipped him, and what's worse, I trusted him.

But he was weak." Another drag on the cigarette, followed by a slow grudging exhalation. "Penny didn't even want him, not really. It was a game to her, like everything else. A bit of fun, turning a weak man's head. Making him believe he was good enough for her sort, that she saw past his wife and babies and dirty hands. She poisoned him, turned him against the life he was made for, left him fit for nothing but the drink. Poisoned me, too. But she didn't eat me. Only wrapped me up tight and left me hanging in the web. Forever, I suppose."

"It sounds like you hated Penny enough to kill her."

"No. I hated her enough to wish her dead, and that's not the same thing. No crime, either, thank God, or I'd swing ten times over." Mrs. Archer's chuckle was as flat as day-old champagne. "And I wouldn't stand alone on the gallows. Your friend Lady Juliet couldn't bear Penny." She twisted the ring on her finger. The band was snug, bought for her hand before its joints reddened and swelled, and now moved only with difficulty. "Lady Juliet's friend in Plymouth, Mrs. Freeman, grew up in Birdswing, and she loathed Penny, too. But when they get together to moan, they never include me. Likely I don't use posh enough words when I complain."

Ben's instincts told him Mrs. Archer was telling the truth, that her calm, matter-of-fact delivery was no pose. But were the instincts that told him when a patient was being honest sufficient to sort the innocent from the guilty in a murder case?

"Why did this Mrs. Freeman loathe Penny?"

"Penny's dad cheated Mrs. Freeman's husband, or so the story goes. I never got it from the horse's mouth. Some bad business in the last year or two."

Ben made a mental note to ask Lady Juliet about those moan sessions, assuming Mrs. Archer was correct. Just because she spoke the truth as she saw it didn't mean those statements were accurate. "Where's your husband now?"

"In Plymouth." Mrs. Archer stubbed out her dog end. "Lives with his aunt and stays down the pub more than he works. Never sends a farthing home to the boys, so I won't let him put one boot over my threshold. At least we aren't divorced." She sighed. "I thought of him, truth be told, when you and Penny were struck down. Wondered if he'd started romancing the bottle on the job as well as off. Wouldn't that be something, if he'd managed to kill his one great love because of his other great love?"

"Wait. Are you saying Bobby drives a lorry?"

"Yes, of course he does. If I were trying to investigate a murder—and heaven knows I'd have no choice in this village, what with that fool of an acting constable—I would have started with who owns a lorry, or drives one. That makes the most sense, doesn't it?"

Warmth crept up his throat, threatening to rise in his cheeks. Naturally, she was right. In London, the scope of such an inquiry would be impossible for a citizen acting alone, but Birdswing was perhaps small enough to manage. Why hadn't he thought to begin with the murder weapon?

"You *are* going to smoke the rest of it, aren't you?" she asked, indicating his cigarette, which was transforming itself into a long cylinder of ash on the edge of his saucer.

"No. I really must quit." Ben passed it to her. "Mrs. Archer, I'm terribly grateful to you for sharing so many personal details. But I must ask you a still more difficult question. Do you think… do you imagine it's possible—"

"No." She put him out of his agony with that one word, then puffed contentedly for a time before speaking again. "I told you. Bobby thinks Penny was his own true love. He'd never have killed her, except with whiskey breath and soppy promises. His aunt sent me word after he heard Penny was dead. Said he tore his clothes and pulled his hair and bawled like a baby. I never laughed so hard in my life."

He turned that over in his mind, wishing he had seen something, that he had some useful memory of that moment beyond the earthshattering *smack* of impact.

"But you don't have to take my word for it," Mrs. Archer continued in her dull, uninflected way. "Bobby drove Singer's lorries, the ones that carry furniture and carpets. Why don't you call Mr. Singer and ask him if one of those lorries got a dented bonnet two months ago?"

***

"I told you she'd be happy to relate her tale of woe," Lady Juliet said as she drove them back to Belsham Manor. "And the notion of asking about a damaged lorry is sound. I would have thought of it myself, I'm quite certain, if I weren't trying to get my preparations for winter concluded. It's the sort of gardening I don't fancy at all. Raking, and loading the wheelbarrow, and dumping, and doing it all over again until you want to strike a match and have done with it."

"Isn't that why your mum called in Miss Jenkins and the children? For help with all those menial tasks?" Ben allowed his first needle to sink in, then jabbed her with another. "Yet you said something about not letting them come near your roses, didn't you?"

Lady Juliet upshifted rather abruptly as they left the village, turning right onto Old Crow Road. As a result, the Crossley leapt forward so sharply it jarred him from tailbone to back teeth. "Don't vex the driver."

"Point taken."

"However," Lady Juliet went on, lifting her chin as she kept her hands at ten and two and her eyes on the road, "while you had your tête-à-tête with Mrs. Archer, I enjoyed a period of reflection beneath the hornbeam tree. Your suggestion that I may have misjudged Miss Jenkins is noted. When we return, I shall extend the hand of friendship. And, if she deems it appropriate, allow her class a more active role."

"That tree worked a miracle."

"I rather think it was the pie."

Once again they slipped into easy silence as they traveled. To his surprise, Ben found himself enjoying the ride, letting questions of Bobby Archer, the man's affair with Penny, and a dented lorry temporarily fade. He often did the same with troubling patients, and these brief mental breaks seemed to help him redouble his concentration later. Though it still seemed somewhat unreal to him, Britain was a country at war. This land around him, these gentle hills and green-brown fields, was no longer safe; no part of the England he'd taken for granted would necessarily remain in a year, a month, or even a day. Lord Gort and over one hundred thousand men Ben's age were already in France, with more preparing to go. He'd been chosen to remain at home—not his old home, London, but his new home, Birdswing. Surely that conferred upon him a responsibility to enjoy autumn's splendor in the English countryside as much as he could.

The first sign something was wrong came as the Crossley's tires struck gravel, signifying the start of the long, winding drive that ended in a loop in front of Belsham Manor. Robbie trundled toward them in the manor's old Bedford truck, hunched over the steering wheel with his gaze pointed down, as usual. Lady Juliet had to blow the horn to make him look up and perceive they were on a low speed collision course. When he did, he veered left, half onto the grass, and honked back at her, gesticulating behind him. It was the first time Ben had seen the old man appear agitated. It was the first time he'd seen the old man appear *anything*, come to think of it.

"Good heavens. Is he having a fit?" Lady Juliet accelerated, taking the next rise fast enough to kick up dust. Near the stone fountain were Lady Victoria, Miss Jenkins, and her entire class. A few of the children were wandering here and there, but most had formed a loose cluster around their teacher, who knelt before something. The moment Lady Victoria caught sight of the Crossley, she began calling, "Dr. Bones! Dr. Bones!"

As Ben approached on his crutches, wishing he'd thought to bring his doctor's bag, Lady Victoria shooed the children aside. "We're of no use here. Miss Jenkins and Dr. Bones will take care of Jane. Let's all go inside and see if Cook has any treacle tarts left over, shall we?"

As the class followed Lady Victoria up the stairs and through the manor's double doors, Ben found Jane Daley sitting on the fountain lip. Her eyes were red, but she wasn't crying. Her breath came in the quick, shallow hitches of a child in pain. Releasing Jane's hand, Miss Jenkins rose to her feet so Ben could get closer. The girl looked up at him and moaned.

"She's shy of strangers," Miss Jenkins said. "Jane, dear, Dr. Bones is here to help you. Tell him where it hurts."

The girl jumped off the fountain, or tried to. Her knees struck the gravel, eliciting a high thin cry almost like a whistle. Ben looked at Lady Juliet. "Help me down beside her."

It hurt, of course, getting down on both knees, but it had to be done. Jane's thin chest heaved up and down inside her dress; her eyes were wild, darting like a cornered animal's. Above him, Miss Jenkins was trying to give a history, but Ben tuned it out.

"I'm not going to hurt you. I'm going to fix this," he told Jane. "Have you thrown up?"

Jane shook her head, frizz bouncing.

"Been to the lavatory a lot?"

Another head shake.

"Does something hurt?"

"We think perhaps she ate something spoilt and her stomach—"

Ben silenced Miss Jenkins with a stern look. Bad enough to put ideas in the minds of adult patients. Prompting a little one at the wrong moment could confound everything, because young children, trained to please adults, would nearly always declare the statement true.

"Jane." For the same reason, his physician-tone was useless—no point intimidating the chronically intimidated—so he spoke normally, person to person, looking her in the eye. "What were you doing before you started feeling bad?"

"Climbing… a, a… tree."

"Why did you stop?"

The girl's eyes flicked to Miss Jenkins. Clearly she'd been told to come down.

"What did you do next?"

"Put…." More quick, shallow breaths as Ben felt her forehead, which was damp with perspiration and a little warm. "Put my shoes on."

"Then what?" He shifted to her upper arm, pressing two fingers against her brachial artery. Her pulse raced.

"It… it hurt."

"What hurt?"

"My foot."

The girl whimpered when Lady Juliet lifted her back onto the fountain lip, and Ben tried not to whimper as she hauled him to his feet. Leaning hard on his crutches, he said, "Get Jane's shoes and stockings off." A thought had come to him, a notion put there by Mrs. Archer, of all people. It seemed today was his day for guidance from an unexpected source.

The right foot proved unblemished, but a bit of blood marked the white stocking on the left. Beneath it, in the center of Jane's heel, was a small wound surrounded by a circle of redness.

"Is that a snakebite?" Miss Jenkins cried.

"Spider bite, more likely," Lady Juliet said. "Look, here's the little bugger, flattened inside her shoe. A false widow, I'll bet, though it's too squashed to tell. Autumn brings them out."

"False widow? Like a black widow?" Miss Jenkins shrilled. "But those are deadly!"

Jane tried to gasp, but all that came out was another thin whistle. Her airway was closing.

"Pick her up!" Ben ordered Lady Juliet. "Take her to the car, now!"

"Hospital?" Lady Juliet already had Jane in her arms.

"Is the chemist's closer?"

"Yes."

"The chemist's, then, fast as you dare!"

And if that snake oil salesman didn't stock every drug I asked for, Jane Daley's as good as dead.

Chapter 7: "I Saw Him"
28 October, 1939

Although the tires of Lady Juliet's Crossley struck every pothole between Old Crow Road and the sharp left turn onto Stafford, Ben hardly registered his own pain. Holding Jane tight in his lap, he stroked her hair and murmured to her, thanking God each time the jolting car forced a high-pitched moan from her lips. But as the Sheared Sheep and Daley's Co-Op came into view, Jane sagged in Ben's arms, silent but for a soft, tortured whistle of breath. Her airway was nearly closed.

"Should we stop for her mum?" Lady Juliet asked, or tried to ask.

Ben cut across her. "I said the chemist!"

The Crossley lurched forward as Lady Juliet floored the accelerator. A dozen things came to Ben all at once—what if a farmer chose this moment to drive his sheep from east pasture to west? What if timid Mr. Piedmont was on the road, creeping with glacial slowness from home to grocer and back again? What if Mr. Dwerryhouse had nothing but castor oil and excuses when they—

"Clear the road!" Lady Juliet cried, honking several times for good measure. The boys in the street, who appeared to be setting up some type of roller skate relay, leapt out of the way, knocking over a row of rubbish bins in the process. Shouts, a thrown rock, and some surprisingly adult words followed, but then the boys disappeared in the Crossley's cloud of dust. Up ahead was Birdswing proper—neat houses, paved high street, and just visible, Dwerryhouse's CHEMIST sign in black Gothic letters. Ben shook Jane gently, but her eyes were half-closed, and she made no sound. The child's skin was clammy, pulse thready.

"I can't leave her," Ben said as Lady Juliet skirted a car moving at normal speed, striking the curb and shaking the Crossley in the process. Something *popped*—a tire?—but it didn't matter, nothing mattered, except that he issue orders and be obeyed. "Park as close as you can. Run inside—no, don't look at me like that, you can run and I can't!" Pretending not to recognize the terror in Lady Juliet's face, he issued his instructions, forcing her to repeat them twice as the car thumped and bumped to a halt outside the chemist shop. A tire was indeed blown, and as Lady Juliet threw open her door and leapt out, Ben saw she'd struck a fence when she jumped the curb. The white wooden gate hung from the Crossley's side panel, still trailing a few torn clematis vines. As Lady Juliet sprinted into Dwerryhouse's shop, ARP Warden Gaston emerged from Morton's scowling ferociously, his OFFICIAL AIR WARDEN BUSINESS notebook in hand.

"Hang on," Ben told Jane, praying in that wordless way that sometimes came to him: desperate, fervent, hopeful beyond reason. He'd never prayed for a miracle for himself, not in his entire life, but he'd often asked on behalf of his patients. "Don't be afraid, sweetheart. You'll be all right, you'll be all right." Her lips were turning blue.

"What's the meaning of—" Sticking his head into the cab on the driver's side, Gaston trailed off when he saw Jane in Ben's arms. "Something t'matter with the wee one?"

"Anaphylaxis," Ben shouted, hearing Dwerryhouse's objections as the stooped, crooked-shouldered little man emerged with a cardboard box in one hand and a bottle in the other. Gaston hastily moved aside as Dwerryhouse passed over the box. Tearing it open, Ben fitted the 25 gauge, stainless steel needle into the glass hypodermic.

"Lady Juliet told me spider bite." Dwerryhouse's high thin voice sounded more suspicious than usual. "What use is adrenalin chloride for—"

Snatching the bottle away, Ben checked the concentration, did the math for a pediatric dose in his head—*please God, please God, a misplaced decimal point could kill her*—and flicked the hypodermic twice. A bit of adrenalin chloride, also known as epinephrine, squirted out, taking the air bubble with it. He plunged the needle into Jane's thigh. "Gaston, do you have a car?"

"Of course."

"We'll need it to get her to St. Barnabas. Even if this works…." Ben stopped, staring at Jane. The blueness was spreading through her face. Her pulse still beat in her brachial artery; he could feel it against his fingertips, and that meant the adrenalin was coursing through her, undoing her allergic response to the false widow's bite. Jane's airway, temporarily sealed by swollen tissues, should be opening enough to permit at least shallow breaths. But the child still wasn't breathing.

Only desperation could have triggered what came next. He'd done such a thing twice in the maternity ward, once to a happy ending, once to no avail. Sometimes during labor, the baby received too little oxygen, emerging blue-faced and terrifyingly silent. Most textbooks recommended nothing but vigorous backside slaps. Yet seasoned doctors and nurses knew that sometimes, sealing one's mouth around the infant's nose and mouth and breathing into its lungs could elicit the babe's own respiration. Jane was much too old for that;

Ben had never heard of anyone trying such a thing. He didn't know why he covered her mouth with his and forced his air into her lungs, because he wasn't thinking, not truly. He was still praying that stubborn, fervent prayer, permitting his physical instincts to take over.

"Doctor!" Mr. Dwerryhouse sounded shocked.

"What on earth—" Gaston began, breaking off with an *oof*. Something or someone had silenced him, but Ben's concentration was fixed on Jane. He filled her lungs twice, drew back, did it again. The fourth time, her legs jerked, and she pulled away, coughing.

"God almighty," he breathed as the girl's cheeks regained their natural color, lips turning pink again. "Thank you."

"What did you do?" Dwerryhouse's usually mistrustful tone carried a hint of wonder.

"Something an old midwife taught me." Ben rocked Jane in his arms as her weak coughs continued. She was damp with perspiration and trembling all over—shock was setting in—but St. Barnabas Hospital would treat her for that. And monitor her throughout the night, as her body disposed of the false widow toxin that usually left only a minor flesh wound yet had caused such a catastrophic reaction in one susceptible little girl.

"You hurt me," ARP Warden Gaston accused Lady Juliet. Rubbing his side, he gave her a dark look.

"Write me a citation for disrespect. I'll happily pay it. *After* you drive Dr. Bones and Jane to St. Barnabas. And I *am* sorry for elbowing you," she said, not sounding sorry at all. Eyes meeting Ben's, she smiled. "I've never heard of such a thing, but it worked. You saved Jane's life."

"We saved her life." Everyone was watching him, seemingly expecting him to say more, but he had no desire to hear his own voice. The only thing he wanted to listen to was that thin, pained, steady intake of breath, the sweetest sound in the world.

***

Breakfast the next morning was a special occasion, thanks to Mrs. Cobblepot and the gratitude of Birdswing's high street. Every resident who'd been home when Lady Juliet's Crossley jumped the curb, sideswiped a fence, torn off a gate, and brutalized a clematis had come out to watch the commotion in front of Dwerryhouse's. Ben hadn't noticed; he'd spent the afternoon at St. Barnabas's, getting to know two physicians who were expected, along with him, to oversee triage and direct dozens of nurses should their little corner of England suffer bombing raids. Both doctors were too old for military service, suspicious of adrenalin chloride for anything but asthma treatment, and astonished to hear that maternity ward "rescue breathing" had worked for Jane Daley. The child was well on her way to recovery by then, mother at her bedside, and Ben saw no reason to linger. By the time he made it home, catching a ride back to Fenton House with a gaggle of friendly nursing students bound for Plymouth, he'd missed dinner. But Mrs. Cobblepot had been busy in his absence.

It wasn't that rationing had taken its toll on their daily meals yet—there was only the two of them, after all, and Mr. Vine's efforts to fairly distribute his reduced stock was still informal, though ration books were reportedly on the way. Mrs. Cobblepot insisted to Ben she was always allowed to buy just enough, and with careful management and creative use of leftovers, he rarely noticed what was missing: fish, which was "dear beyond reason" according to his housekeeper, corned beef, bananas, and oranges. The sugary puddings he liked had been replaced with more savory desserts: butter, margarine, and lard seemed easy to come by, while each sugar purchase was noted in Mr. Vine's ledger. Rumors of shiny limousines pulling up to village grocers, and fur-clad city women rushing in to buy up all the sugar and tinned goods, had been taken as fact in Birdswing. Vine's Emporium had even placed a sign in the front window: LOCAL TRADE AND FAIR SHARES STRICTLY ENFORCED. Mrs. Cobblepot could only buy enough bacon to serve twice a week, Wednesday and Sunday. So when Ben entered the kitchen that Sunday morning, the sizzling pop of bacon didn't surprise him. It was the rest of the spread that made his mouth fall open.

There was fresh bread from Abbott's bakery. Éclairs from Laviolette's. Sausage from Morton's. And gathered from donations up and down the high street, from the pantries of his neighbors: beans, stewed tomatoes, ham, black pudding, blackcurrant jam, and two sorts of fish, poached and fried.

"You'll never guess who donated the fish," Mrs. Cobblepot said, beaming. "He's so pale, you wouldn't think he spent time in the sun at all, much less hours on the riverbank."

Sinking into a chair, Ben propped his crutches against the wall. "I have no idea."

"Mr. Dwerryhouse. I can't say he had much confidence in you at first sight. Now he's telling all his customers to stop round and let the *London-trained* doctor have a crack at what ails them." She set a plate in front of him, heaped with a little of everything, with one notable exception. "I don't recommend those éclairs. You know where they came from. There's a dog that makes the rounds once in a while, sniffing at kitchen doors. I may feed them to her, so long as my brother doesn't see."

"Why not give them to him? He helped, after all. Lent us his car," Ben said with only the tiniest twinge of guilt. The pastries appeared edible. Slightly flatter and drier than customary, but edible.

Mrs. Cobblepot laughed. "Clarence is foolish, but not quite a fool. Even he avoids Laviolette's."

For a time, Ben gave himself up to simply eating, savoring each individual taste. After yesterday's wild ride and so much time on his feet—even with the support of crutches—he'd expected extra soreness this morning, perhaps even a lazy Sunday with the wireless and a novel. But after a good night's sleep and breakfast fit for a king, he felt surprisingly restless. Not to mention, curious.

"I take it back. Let's pack some meat, bread, and jam into a basket and pay a call on your brother," Ben told Mrs. Cobblepot. "I want to know what he's learned about Penny's de—murder."

***

They took Ben's car. Like many villagers who'd come to driving later in life, Mrs. Cobblepot was slow, careful, and faintly suspicious of the automobile, keeping an iron grip on the steering wheel at all times.

"I grew up driving a horse and buggy, which suited me fine," she told Ben during the short ride to ARP Warden Gaston's house. "I suppose if the war goes on too long, horses will outnumber cars on the street, what with the petrol rationing."

"Let's hope we get a ceasefire well before it comes to that." Ben's fingers drummed the dashboard, itching for a cigarette. Despite his desire to give up tobacco for good and all, in his mind, traveling by car was indelibly associated with smoking. Had he left a pack in the glove box? Hoping he hadn't but unable to resist checking, Ben opened it for the first time since leaving London. A slender green volume dropped into his lap.

"What's that?" Mrs. Cobblepot's eyes flicked away from the road for only a millisecond, although Sunday traffic in Birdswing consisted mostly of restless chickens or rogue geese.

"Shakespeare's sonnets." Ben studied the worn book. Should he send it to Mr. Eubanks or George as a remembrance? "Penny had taken to carrying it with her everywhere."

"A great fan of the Bard?"

"An affectation, I thought. A way to look cleverer than her friends. More literary." He sighed. "I used to go out of my way to think the worst of her."

Mrs. Cobblepot waited a long time before venturing, "Perhaps she deserved it."

"Probably." He placed the book beside him on the car seat, suddenly unwilling to open it, see her familiar handwriting on the flyleaf—those huge, sloping letters—and risk feeling whatever lurked inside him, safely thrust down, down, as far as he could push it. "But whatever she did, whatever she was, I'm the man who married her."

"You didn't know."

"No. But still. I married her, and there was no gun to my head. What does that say about me?"

This time Mrs. Cobblepot did risk taking her gaze off the road long enough to meet his eyes. *She knows*, Ben realized.

"Yes. Penny was with child. But I'd—that is to say, we'd already—the ring was on her finger, the hall engaged. I assumed… of course I assumed the baby was mine. She told me during our honeymoon, and I was overjoyed." Forcing what he hoped sounded like a laugh, he looked out the window as the high street slid past, all those raked front gardens and scrubbed front steps. "But soon after, I realized she was too far gone—much too far gone. First I confronted her. Then I tried to respond like a doctor. Calmly. Just asking her to help me understand. Both times she laughed in my face."

They had reached Gaston's bungalow. Letting the engine idle, Mrs. Cobblepot turned to Ben, her expression as matter-of-fact as if they were discussing kitchen rations or a laundry problem. Why had he imagined any of this would shock her? Pregnancy was the inescapable center of almost every woman's life.

"Did she tell you who the father was?"

"No. Refused to discuss it. Said—" He stopped. *Said just because I'd been a sad little virgin didn't mean she was. Said I should have wondered what she saw in me, what I could possibly offer, and been grateful. Said even if I knew his name, it would prove nothing, because he was a man to be reckoned with, not a milquetoast.* "Said a lot of rubbish."

"Did she… lose the baby?" Mrs. Cobblepot asked, with that faint emphasis on "lose" that signaled her willingness to hear the whole truth, even if it led into territory where most physicians feared to tread.

"It was fetal demise. I—I behaved rather badly during the last trimester," Ben said, picking up the sonnets and running his fingers along the gold-lettered spine. "I walked away when she tried to tell me about swollen ankles, or cravings, or the baby kicking. Left her alone as much as I could, put her under the care of a Harley Street man her father chose. When the doctor tried to contact me, about two weeks before the baby was due, I ignored it. Thought perhaps she'd gone into labor early, in which case I intended to 'accidentally' miss the whole thing. But finally he got me. It was a condolence call—the baby no longer had a heartbeat."

"All four of mine were stillborn," Mrs. Cobblepot said. "The last time, the midwife broke the news at seven months. Those were the longest eight weeks of my life, hiding inside my own home, terrified some acquaintance would congratulate me, and I'd fall to pieces. It was the worst labor, too. Not the hardest by any means, but the worst. Delivering a child I knew was already lost."

"After that, I tried to be a better husband. To put it behind us." Ben opened the book, saw that bold, unapologetic hand, and closed it again. "I think Penny tried, too, as much as she was able. But it was too little too late, from both of us. And I'm sorry," he added, touching his housekeeper's arm. "For your losses, I mean."

"Oh, love, it was so long ago." A determined brightness settled over Mrs. Cobblepot's features, and the matter was closed. "Since Clarence hasn't come out to check our identity cards and ask our business, I'll bet he's around back. Let's see."

ARP Warden and Acting Constable Gaston was indeed in his back garden. It smelled of freshly turned soil, sheep manure, and something else, soon revealed to be pig slop. Or possibly the pig itself, a hairy pink and black thing, half-mature and already larger than an Alsatian. It had rolled in its slop, as well as the manure-enriched soil, which confused the matter.

"You're right on time!" Gaston cried, looking delighted to see them. "The pig pen's up, the crops are going strong, and I've just put a floor in the crown jewel. What'd'ya think?"

"Well, it's… it's…." Mrs. Cobblepot groped audibly while Ben, uncertain what he was looking at, kept his mouth shut. Was it a sod-camouflaged tool shed? An outhouse with a patch of veg on top? Whatever it was, a brown rabbit sat on the peaked roof, chewing a leek.

"I've never heard of mixing gardening with bomb shelters," Mrs. Cobblepot said at last.

Ben advanced on the corrugated metal structure, coated on the sides and top with packed earth. So much of Gaston's former lawn had been given over to cultivation, he had to place his crutches carefully, lest he trod on rows of parsnip and onion. "Is the soil meant as a bulwark?"

"Indeed it is! An Anderson shelter," Gaston said proudly. "So simple any man can build it, and so sturdy, the Germans can't hope to bomb us out."

Ben studied the construct. The door was open, the interior shadowy, but he thought he made out long shelves attached to the walls. Bunks? Given that the shelter was only two meters long and perhaps a meter and a half wide, even one man might feel cramped inside. Were entire *families* meant to squat in these dirt-floored hovels while falling bombs whistled overhead?

"Is that cabbage you've put down?" Mrs. Cobblepot adjusted her glasses. "I don't fancy winter crops. I've never had a bit of luck. And Mr. Morton predicts a hard, cold winter. You know he's hit it on the nose nine years running."

"Maybe winter will be hard on the rest of the country, but this is Cornwall. Autumn comes a month late, spring comes a month early. It'll grow," Gaston declared. Pointing at the shelter's sprouting roof, he added, "My leeks have already earned the stamp of approval."

"I wouldn't have pegged you for the sort to keep a bunny for a pet," Ben said.

The ARP warden gave him a pitying look. "Oh, you soft city boys will be the first to die if the enemy descends upon these shores. That's no pet, Dr. Bones. That's next month's Sunday dinner. And I'm one-fourth owner of Sally the pig. Me and the lads dreamed up the scheme at the Sheared Sheep, a sort of pork co-op. Plus I get the hogshead on account of being the one who keeps her. Sally'll do nicely for Christmas lunch, you'll see."

From the village square, bells pealed signifying the end of the service at St. Mark's. Mrs. Cobblepot took that as her cue to present her brother with the covered basket. As he poked through it making happy noises, Ben said, "I know you're very busy, Mr. Gaston. But I wonder if you've made any progress with those inquiries into my wife's death?"

His head came up, eyes wide and mouth open. That confirmed Ben's suspicions in one stroke.

"Or perhaps you've had no time," he said, doing his best to hide his irritation. "So I have a few suggestions. Perhaps someone might question Bobby Archer? He seems to have carried a torch for Penny. I understand he drives a lorry, too. Then there's the death of Ursula Hibbet. I realize it was years ago, but might there be someone in Birdswing who held a grudge?"

Gaston's face settled back into its usual mix of disdain and suspicion. "Now don't go all Miss Marple, Dr. Bones. No good ever came of folks going Miss Marple, no matter how clever they are about wee girls and spider bites. I am proceeding with the investigation along the proper channels."

"Oh, good." Mrs. Cobblepot clasped her hands and beamed. "Tell us everything you've learned."

"It's classified. Could have national security implications. I'll not be discussing it with civilians, much less in the middle of the street."

"National security implications? Nonsense." Taking off her glasses, his sister polished them with the slow censure of a disappointed educator. She might have retired from teaching some years ago, but clearly she remembered all the tricks. "And we aren't in the street, Clarence love, we're in your garden. Surely Dr. Bones has a right to hear your findings."

"Not until they're *all found*! I must say, Agatha, there's been a change in you since you went to work at Fenton House. And not for the good, I fear. *Not for the good.*" Transparently desperate, Gaston dug into the basket, coming up with a bit of fried fish and waving it under her nose. "Vine's hasn't stocked whitefish for a week. No one will buy it at those prices. How did you get this? Is this black market fish? Is there a black market operating in Birdswing?"

"Yes!" Mrs. Cobblepot cried. Snatching the basket, she tossed it into the pig pen, eliciting a grunt of approval. "And I'm the kingpin! Corned beef is 6p an ounce, and bananas are a guinea each!"

"I'll take one!" a female voice called over the fence. "Silly me, listening to a sermon while you three are having a fine old time."

Relieved at the interruption, Ben turned to see the primary school teacher, Miss Jenkins. She looked lovely in a navy dress, black heels, and fitted jacket. Her red hair was up, a pillbox hat pinned atop it at the perfect angle. He found himself smiling. "Just admiring the air warden's new bomb shelter. Come have a look."

Ben took it upon himself to give Miss Jenkins the tour, from Anderson shelter to cabbage patch to pig pen.

That gave the siblings time to locate their dignity, shake it out, and drape it about their shoulders once more.

"You're moving well on those crutches," Miss Jenkins told Ben.

"These?" Leaning on one, he lifted the other casually, as if he might pitch it away. "They're just for show. I'm practically fit again."

"I think you're a liar." Quite petite despite high heels, she had to lift her face to speak to him. Unused to that, Ben found it made her even prettier.

"Shall I prove it? Walk you home?"

"Can you?"

He pressed a hand to his heart as if struck. "Now I'll have to carry you. Mrs. Cobblepot! Can I rely on you to drive the car home while I prove myself?"

"Of course." The housekeeper regarded Ben and Miss Jenkins with sparkling eyes, then turned to her brother, mouth quirking as if suppressing a smile. "Come into the kitchen, Clarence, and I'll make us some tea."

"I don't live very far," Miss Jenkins said. "Just up Mallow Street beyond that line of oaks. I'm sure you've seen them. The biggest is over a hundred years old." She matched her pace to his. "And you really are getting along splendidly on those crutches. Quite an improvement from being carried about by Lady Juliet."

In his bachelor days, such a comment would have made Ben blush scarlet, anxious to assert his masculinity and utterly stymied as to how. It had taken marriage to beautiful Penny for him to relax, forget his flaws both real and imagined, and start talking to women like human beings, not potential mates. Penny's careless, often cruel wit had beaten the boyish self-consciousness out of him, a gift for which he'd forever be grateful. "Yes, well, I suppose most country doctors spend years trying to ingratiate themselves with the local gentry. I made my debut delicately cradled in the arms of a bona fide lady. How many men can say the same?"

Miss Jenkins laughed, giving him a flash of those green eyes and curling black lashes. "You're terribly lucky Lady Juliet approves of you. She despises me, though I've no idea why. Although after yesterday, I suppose I deserve her derision. No matter how many syllables she uses to express it."

"Yesterday?" Captivated by the pleasure of walking with Miss Jenkins, Ben could hardly think back to breakfast, much less the previous twenty-four hours. "What do you mean?"

"Poor Jane. I was useless. Saying all the wrong things at the worst moments." Her cheeks grew pink. "You looked ready to give me a slap, and I don't blame you one bit."

In truth, her contribution had been unhelpful at best. But *that* wasn't the right thing to say. "You're too hard on yourself. You're Jane's teacher. It's natural you felt frantic."

"Oh, yes, feeling frantic is one thing. Displaying that emotion before Jane and the other children—" Miss Jenkins waved a hand as if to sweep the memory away. "It's the first time a student in my care has been seriously injured. And I fear it won't be the last. Next time, it might be a bomb. Or a gas attack."

"Or a bloody nose. Or a broken ankle." Stopping to lean on one crutch, Ben touched her lightly on the shoulder. "Next time, you'll do better."

She dropped her gaze and ducked her head, even lovelier with that bloom in her cheeks. "It's wonderful having you in Birdswing. For the children, I mean. Though I'm sure you miss London."

"Less and less." Ben started forward on his crutches, even slower this time, intent on prolonging what remained of their walk. "Did you say an oak near your house is past a hundred? I'd like to see that."

A whistle sounded shrilly from somewhere in the vicinity of Gaston's bungalow. Miss Jenkins drew closer to Ben. "What's that?"

"I rather suspect it's an air raid drill."

"But the last time the village gathered in the town hall, the man from the army said the signal would be hand bells. Wait. Maybe those are for the all clear? I don't know, but I'm quite sure he mentioned rattlers, like at football games." She mimed the action of the red and white striped devices. When whipped in a circle, the inner mechanism created a sharp repeating pop loud enough to cheer a goal, dispute a bad call, or wake a sleeping neighborhood.

"Yes, well, this is a special drill, aimed at punishing Birdswing's black market kingpin."

She peered at him suspiciously, like he might be taking the mickey. "You've spent too much time with Lady Juliet. Soon no one will be able to understand you."

"Then perhaps I'll seek more balance by spending time with you, Miss Jenkins."

"Rose." That smile again, as bright and inviting as the first time he'd seen it. "Call me Rose."

***

It was no use calling Bobby Archer's occasional employer, Winston Singer of Singer's Fine Furnishings and Turkish Rugs, to ask if Archer had driven a lorry the night Penny died. Like virtually every business great and small, the office would be closed on Sunday. So when

Ben returned to Fenton House after passing that very pleasant half hour with Miss Jenkins—Rose—he used up his restless energy on the parallel bars. He alternated walking back and forth with long periods of standing unsupported, continuing until the ache in his legs opened a second franchise just behind his eyeballs. By supper time, he was too pained and worn out to eat—and not all that hungry anyway, after his orgiastic breakfast. So he went to bed, pleased to know he wouldn't be sleeping in Lucy McGregor's old sewing room much longer. Tomorrow, with Mrs. Cobblepot standing by in the event of a disaster, he'd test his stair climbing skills and possibly view Fenton House's upper floor for the first time.

He dreamed he bounded up those stairs as he once would have, effortlessly, two at a time. It was summer, not late autumn, and there was no blackout. The curtains were parted and the windows were open, a night breeze sliding over the sills like moonflower vines up a trellis. In the master bedroom, a blue lamp burned, its indigo-glazed shade enhanced by the blue fringed shawl draped atop it. The bedstead and chest of drawers were shabby. Wallpaper patterned in stripes and clusters of violets… a porcelain wash basin, its cracked pitcher filled with cut daisies… and a young woman sitting cross-legged on the still-made bed, a slender green volume open in her lap.

"Your wife made some notes in the margins. I think it's a sort of diary."

The woman's voice, lower and huskier than most females, suited her. Ben had no idea what she was wearing. It wasn't a frock or nightgown or housedress. It was as blue as the lamp, high-necked and long-sleeved, with silver piping along the bottom of each bell sleeve. Her dark brown hair fell in wild curls over her shoulders;

her brown eyes were wide, hypnotic. She wasn't a traditional English rose, but she was striking, all the more so because she was so very singular.

"You're reading Penny's book?" It was a silly thing to say, but in dreams he frequently spoke like an idiot.

"One of us had to. Some of the notations are just numbers. Did she owe someone money?"

"I've no idea. I paid the household bills; her father provided her spending allowance. But what's that you're wearing?"

She smiled. "A robe. A special one. Open your eyes, doctor. I'm not the only woman in Cornwall known to don one like it." Tossing the book aside, she stretched luxuriously, like a cat awakening from deep sleep. "Sorry I was clumsy before. With the talking board, I mean. This is all new to me."

"I don't understand." Something was wrong; something was nagging at the back of his mind, like a semi-dormant toothache threatening to erupt with fresh pain. The delectable summer breeze had become cold, stale air; the windows, once opened to the night, were shut tight in observance of the blackout. The blue lamp looked spectral now, as if it burned half in his world, half in another.

"Listen to me." The woman's voice faded in and out. "I have something. It belonged to the man who killed your wife."

It occurred to Ben that he must be dreaming, a thought that always preceded waking up. "How do you know?"

"I saw him."

Her lips moved soundlessly, as if saying a name, and he woke up. Not in his bed, but in an icy pitch dark room.

Smooth floorboards were beneath his hands. A lumpy rug was under his knees. For what felt like eons he remained there, heart racing, throat tight, waiting for this madness to pass, to dissolve, proving the blue lamp and the husky-voiced woman only a dream within a dream.

A few feet away, something creaked, like a foot against a loose board.

"Hello?" His voice sounded thin, strange.

Silence.

Slowly, unable to see even his hands in front of his face, Ben crawled forward, groping. His breath came so raggedly, blood rushing so loud in his ears, he didn't even cry out when something small and heavy clattered to the floor. Reckless with fear, he reached out and touched something small, rectangular, and cold. It felt like his own Ronson cigarette lighter, except for an etched pattern on the case.

I was sleepwalking. Except I can't walk yet, not well, so I crawled. All the way up the stairs to the master bedroom.

What he wouldn't have given in that moment for the ability to leap up, to chase away the darkness with the flick of an electric switch.

And while I was here, I spoke to Lucy McGregor.

Chapter 8: Ranunculus
29 October, 1939

"*Bam!*" Lady Juliet Linton clapped her hands together, earning intakes of breath all around. "I struck the gate and just kept going. No idea I was dragging it along. Finally we came upon the chemist's shop—tire blown, gate beating against the passenger door, and poor little Jane *silent as the grave.*"

Her hostess, Mrs. Margaret Freeman, rolled her eyes at the cliché, but the other guests—Alice, Katrina, Eunice, and Betty—looked appropriately alarmed. Two of them lived in Margaret's neighborhood and had never met Ben, Jane, or Mr. Dwerryhouse. The other two, residents of Birdswing, had traveled to Margaret's Plymouth home for the monthly meeting of the Monday Moaners. The alliteration, as well as the lighthearted name, was deliberate. Otherwise, the group could veer out of amusing cynicism and into out-and-out self-pity with relative ease. They were ill-matched in many ways, like a flower bed sown by the wind, with only matrimonial troubles to unify them. Alice, a Cape daisy, lived alone because her husband had walked out on her. Katrina, a pretty little foxglove, was a virtual pariah; her husband had chosen to serve his prison sentence for tax evasion rather than shoot himself, as gentlemen could once be relied upon to do. Eunice, a common cowslip, detested her spouse, who'd placed two of her children in one of those mental deficiency hospitals that everyone knew about but nobody spoke of. And Betty, a wild daffodil, had left the Anglican Church for her husband's faith, reformed Judaism, incurring her family's ire. Now he was in France preparing to fight for his country, leaving her six months pregnant and mostly alone, except for her fellow Moaners.

Margaret, the Moaners' co-founder, could be compared to a bee orchid: beautiful and irresistible. She was the only member with no complaints about her spouse. Yet her entry ticket, as the group called it, nevertheless related to Gerald Freeman; she was his second wife. And since the first Mrs. Freeman, although twenty years Margaret's senior, was still very much alive, Margaret was received in Plymouth society about as well as Katrina, minus the pitying looks.

Juliet, the Moaners' other co-founder, couldn't equate herself with a flower. If she were any plant, it was English ivy: climbing tall, spreading wide, virtually impervious to harm, and strong enough to burrow through walls and crack foundations. Like most gardeners, Juliet hated the stuff, yet related to it all the same. Her entry ticket into the club was Ethan Bolivar. Usually when it was her turn to speak over tea and cake, she regaled the ladies with her husband's latest outrage. If he'd vanished into the mists again, she fell back on Ethan's golden oldies. But today excreting her usual bile held no appeal; nothing could be more boring. It was the story of the false widow bite and that terrifying, exhilarating ride back to Birdswing that she burned to tell.

"I was so frightened for Jane, I'd forgotten everything else, including the fact Dr. Bones was on crutches," Juliet continued, enjoying her rapt audience's attention. "But then he fixed his eyes upon me—blue eyes, bright blue, if I didn't tell you—and spoke so calmly, and with such perfect authority, I positively *shone* with reflected confidence. I swept into that shop like

Boudicca and *demanded* adrenaline chloride to save a dying child!"

Eunice applauded. Betty, Alice, and Katrina leaned forward, cake slices forgotten. Margaret covered a yawn.

"Oh, don't mind me, dear," she said when Juliet threw her a look. "My health's dodgy again, and I'm starved for sleep. It's no reflection on your story. Though if you mention the color of that man's eyes again, I may lob a sugar cube at you."

"Lob away. I'll collect it as part of my ration." Juliet kept her tone cheerful, but inside she was disappointed by such frank disinterest. Surely her friend and fellow gardener—garden mentor, as a matter of fact—didn't begrudge her one happy adventure after years of mutual commiseration?

We haven't met since her last outbreak, and that was two or three months ago. She's probably a morass of unaired grievances. I sound like Pollyanna to her, that's all.

When Juliet finished her story, everyone clapped, even Margaret, albeit with a knowing half-smile. The skin disorder she suffered—a series of rashes and sores that erupted without warning and hurt to look at—never affected her above the neck, which was fortunate. Margaret Freeman had the strength to endure rescinded invitations, powder room confrontations, and a daily gauntlet of *tuts* and whispers. But she didn't have the strength to face the world with a disfigured, well—face.

It would be the same for me if I lost my health, Juliet thought. *I couldn't bear to be bedridden, dependent on others to be fed, bathed, entertained. I'd go to pieces. Margaret could let herself be tended. She does, in fact, whenever Gerald feels like spoiling her rotten. She could survive becoming ornamental. But becoming ugly? Never.*

Juliet listened to Margaret's tale—how her latest outbreak had rendered her "bad as a leper" in the eyes of her own staff—with nods and smiles, but her attention kept slipping away. Contemplating the loss of her health reminded her of Ben. He was doing better, on that everyone agreed, but suppose he never regained full use of his legs? Would the prospect of lifelong reliance on crutches or a cane harm his spirits? Men were so sensitive to the appellation of cripple; quick to brand one another with it while terrified of becoming "half a man." Well, even if the war ended triumphantly in a cascade of fireworks and Union Jacks, a great many Englishmen would return with injured or missing limbs. And if Ben Bones gave off so much as a whiff of self-pity, she'd root it out like English ivy or Japanese knotweed. What difference did it make if he needed a cane? He was clever, compassionate, handsome, decisive, well-spoken, well-built, handsome, deft with his hands, not really short so much as *compact*, handsome—

"Juliet!" Margaret was laughing at her. "What on earth are you daydreaming about, smiling and rolling your eyes like a great sheep? Tell me it's not Dr. Broken Bones!"

Alice, Betty, and Katrina tittered. They were Margaret's friends first and foremost, a situation Juliet was well-acquainted with. As a child, adults had liked her—teachers, vicars, parents. But her schoolmates had never bonded with her, or followed her, or chosen her friendship over some other girl's when the chips were down. Juliet had never been anyone's first choice, except Ethan Bolivar's, and he'd fallen for her money.

Eunice, another loner with a habit of saying the wrong thing at the wrong time, frowned at their hostess.

"'Broken Bones?' That's unkind. Didn't his wife die in the accident?"

"She did! And what a wife she was." Margaret smiled at Eunice and Betty, both Plymouth natives. "Penny Eubanks grew up with us in Birdswing, isn't that right, Juliet? Shall I tell them what she was like, or shall you?"

"Nothing but good of the dead, mind you," Eunice said primly. She was a stickler for that.

"Oh, quite right." Margaret pushed a lock of dyed red hair, rich and deep as crushed velvet, behind one ear. As a girl, she'd lacked Penny Eubanks's natural loveliness, yet made up for it now in a number of ways: a strict diet to keep her figure trim, expertly applied cosmetics, stylish clothes, and red-lacquered fingernails to match that long, luxuriant hair. She was living proof that a woman of average looks could sculpt herself into something close to beauty, given sufficient budget and attention to detail. "Let's talk about her husband, then. Isn't dissecting husbands what the Moaners do best?"

"Vivisecting," Juliet said warily.

"You remember I was in the throes of illness when Dr. Bones arrived in Cornwall," Margaret continued, pouring herself a second cup of tea, "so I've not witnessed this medical paragon in action. And yes, the story of how he saved Mrs. Daley's child is wonderful. It even reached us here in Plymouth, where one or two things of greater importance than a spider bite occur on a daily basis. As a port city, we have our eyes on the skies, braced for German bombers."

Juliet bristled. "As do we."

"Yes, but we may actually come under attack by the enemy. What's Birdswing afraid of, the Archer twins?" Margaret dropped one sugar cube in her cup, then another, *plop*, *plop*, and grinned. "I heard about that false alarm of theirs. No doubt General Gaston wet himself. At any rate, my point is this: to marry a woman like Penny, Dr. Bones must be a man of weak character or surpassing superficiality. Oh, I suppose he might have been a fortune hunter, like dear Ethan. But only if he were dirt poor, since Penny's father's wealth was a flash in the pan. He should have sold that company years ago. He'll be penniless soon, if he isn't already."

"I hadn't heard that," Juliet said.

"Another bit of news more suited to Plymouth or London, where financial realities matter. But back to Dr. Bones. If he *is* a fortune hunter, I suggest you fling a pretty girl in his path, posthaste," Margaret told Juliet between sips of tea. "Otherwise he may cotton on to what you're worth and make you a Moaner twice over."

"What rot." Juliet was too infuriated to turn red; that would happen later, after the shock wore off. "Dr. Bones is still in mourning, as is only fit and proper. In the meantime, our Miss Jenkins has let it be known she's utterly besotted with the man," she lied. "She'll stand up with him before next Christmas, mark my words, and I'll be the first to throw rice. Besides." Juliet pushed her slice of frosted lemon cake away. "I'm still a married woman. Dr. Bones isn't the sort of man who'd interpose himself between man and wife, any more than I'm the sort of woman who'd sully myself so unforgivably."

She'd gone too far. That was nothing new; Juliet often did when truly angry. And although Margaret gave no sign of offense, the party died a swift death thereafter. Alice, Katrina, and Betty fell silent, except for a few bland pleasantries directed toward their hostess; Eunice focused on her tea, in her own world, as usual. When the goodbyes began, Juliet pretended not to notice how the others shunned her. Instead, she drew Eunice into the foyer for a private conversation. There was a delicate subject she'd been working up to broaching, and the best antidote to fear was action.

"Eunice, let me start by saying, I consider you a friend. We've shared many confidences over the years."

The other woman's eyes snaked from side to side. "Have I done something wrong?"

"Not at all. I don't mean to seem so cloak and dagger. It's only… well… I'm at a bit of a loss. I have a question for you, and it may sound like base curiosity, but I assure you, it isn't. Might I proceed?"

Eunice looked surprised. The pain of losing her children to an institution society insisted upon, yet despised—of being expected to pretend they didn't exist—had aged her beyond her twenty-nine years. A dozen slashed lines, like hash marks on a tally sheet, marred her lips; taut cords stood out in her neck. Afraid to conceive and bear other babies that might also be different, and thus taken away, she often kept her lips pressed together, as if anticipating another blow. Now, despite obvious suspicion, she nodded for Juliet to continue.

"Have you considered adopting a baby?"

"Of course. But Leonard says no. It won't work, going on a long holiday and coming back with a child. People will guess the truth and talk."

"Is that so terrible?"

"Not to me. But Leonard says, think of the child. They'll say he was someone's bastard, dumped in an orphanage and living off charity. He'll be teased every day of his life." Taking a deep breath, Eunice repeated the phrase Juliet knew she hated most, words she always attributed to her husband. "'Only normal boys and girls are happy.'"

"Oh, no doubt." Juliet sighed. "But what of my parents? They were handsome, wealthy, and titled. Their little girl was fated to be the most beloved child in Birdswing, wasn't she? Except she had a plain face, a sharp tongue, and towered over all the boys. It's true, I wasn't a normal child, and sometimes I was desperately unhappy. What about you?"

"What do you mean?"

"Were you a normal child?"

Eunice frowned, suspicious all over again. "Yes."

"Were you always happy?"

"Course not. Never very good at making friends. And the boys called me 'Chicken Legs.'"

"So Leonard wants a child destined for utter joy, a child no one can taunt. But we all get taunted," Juliet said. "If you adopt a child, he or she will get put through the wringer for that. Yet if you could have one naturally, he or she would, too—for being too fat or thin or a hundred other things. At least an adopted child can say he or she was chosen. The rest of us simply turn up one day and our poor parents can't give us back."

Eunice's eyes widened at that unfortunate choice of words. Inwardly, Juliet cursed herself, wondering if she'd made an irretrievable blunder. But then Eunice shrugged.

"It's a good argument. But Leonard won't listen. Won't visit an orphanage. I remember how he was with our babies, before—before he knew. He fell in love on sight. I think he's afraid if he sees a baby in need of a home, he'll weaken, so he makes sure never to see one."

Juliet, who'd heard this observation many times when it was Eunice's turn to moan, nodded eagerly. "But suppose I could, to use Margaret's phrase, fling a pretty baby in his path? All you need to do is drag Leonard up to Birdswing to visit Mother and me. I'll take care of the rest."

"I didn't think your village had an orphanage."

"We don't, that's the beauty of it. We have one healthy little foundling boy. The vicar doesn't want him sent away, not while the war keeps everything in flux. And the Council hasn't seen fit to rule otherwise, so the boy remains in St. Mark's care. They're even calling him Mark, for want of a better name. He needs fostering at the very least."

"But I live in Plymouth. And you said the vicar won't—"

"Won't send a baby to an orphanage, maybe to die there," Juliet cut across her firmly. "But giving Baby Mark a permanent home and responsible parents is a very different thing. And you and Leonard can take him to the country yourself, if the bombers come."

Eunice clasped her hands together, smiling so tremulously Juliet's eyes stung. It hurt to see that much hope. But just as quickly, Eunice's visible elation flagged. "Leonard won't allow it. I know he won't allow it."

Juliet had one last arrow in her quiver, but for a moment, she wavered. It was true, while presenting a tale of woe, the Moaners got personal. But otherwise, they maintained decorum, and Juliet was about to touch on very indecorous territory indeed. But as she'd so recently declared, she was a married woman. That gave her certain conversational rights, so long as men were out of earshot. "Eunice, how long since you slept with Leonard?"

The other woman groaned. "I don't know. A year. More."

"Has the olive branch been extended?"

"About a thousand times. I need earplugs to shut out the begging."

"Give in," Juliet urged. "Yield a little ground. Then bring him for an afternoon at Belsham Manor, and I'll introduce him to Baby Mark."

Soon, Alice, Katrina, and Betty crowded into the foyer with their coats on, making further private conversation impossible. Promising to ring Eunice the next day, Juliet groped for her handbag and realized she'd left it in the parlor.

"Looking for this monstrosity?" Margaret appeared, holding it up by its long leather strap. "Attach a canteen, and it could pass for a saddlebag."

"Yes, well, I never did possess any sense of style. The few times in my life I've looked presentable, I had you to thank." Juliet intended to sound cutting, but the words came out humbly. "Forgive me for what I said, Margaret. I've never judged you or Gerald, you must know that. I was just cross."

"I don't blame you. The fault is entirely mine." Graceful in forgiveness as she was in all things, Margaret hugged Juliet, the crown of her fragrant red hair tickling Juliet's nostrils. "Let me see the other Moaners out the door, and we'll talk."

When Margaret returned from the task, she removed her light sweater and hung it up, revealing shapely, blemish-free arms. Juliet was impressed; it often took months for Margaret to fully recover. "You look wonderful. But I thought you said...."

"Dodgy health, yes. Well, people tend to assume I mean my skin, but lately, the trouble's more of an emotional variety. A difficulty with Gerald weighs on my mind." She seated herself.

Juliet was surprised. As children, Margaret had been one of Penny's friends, not Juliet's, and as teenagers, the trio had avoided one another as much as a small village allowed. But after renewing their acquaintance at a meeting of the Plymouth Gardener's Association, Juliet and Margaret had spent plenty of time together, including afternoons in Margaret's hothouse and a great deal of digging, potting, and pruning at Belsham Manor. Yet during all that time, Juliet had never heard the other woman complain about her husband or signal even the briefest bout of trouble in paradise.

"Oh, don't look so terrified," Margaret said. "Gerald hasn't replaced me with a younger mistress. Despite what I can only assume are fervent prayers from Plymouth society." Opening a gold cigarette case, she withdrew a Pall Mall, mounting it in a long black holder. "It's business. And water under the bridge, most likely, though I worry about him. And I wouldn't want to lose all this." Lighting up, she blew smoke at the crystal chandelier. Throwing back her shoulders and lifting her chin, she reclined on the sofa's velvet cushions, managing to look sophisticated, magnetic, and vulgar, all at the same time.

Did I really call her a bee orchid? Nonsense. She's a ranunculus, a prize one, just like the cultivars that won her a silver cup, Juliet thought, seeing the winning flower in her mind: blood-red and showy, with layer upon layer of concentric petals drawing the eye down, down, down. If a blooming rose was like a bride, then an opened ranunculus was like a whore—the elegant sort, all silk stockings and French perfume—that blameless women sometimes envied. But perhaps mention of whores was uncalled for. Margaret had met Gerald at a charity fête, not a jazz club, and no one, not even the first Mrs. Freeman, denied the pair had ultimately married for love, not money. Still, Margaret had fashioned herself into more than a field-flower to be visited briefly. She'd become like one of her own hothouse specimens, destined to be possessed.

"I suppose importing any manner of goods will be challenging with an anticipated U-boat blockade, even—what's that Gerald ships again?"

"Phosphate. And nitrogen."

"Yes, of course." With only the vaguest idea how Gerald made his fortune, Juliet had assumed his business might profit from shortages. Or given the "Dig for Victory" campaign, had the British government stepped in, freezing prices on the chemicals necessary to keep land arable and food crops thriving?

"Yes, well, like good patriots, we'll weather the storm," a man said in a hearty baritone. Gerald Freeman stood in the doorway, dressed as always in a couture suit so understated many would mistake it for off-the-peg. His diamond tiepin glinted; his black homburg hat was in his hand. "And we must be good patriots, or the mob will come with pitchforks and torches, isn't that right?"

"Oh, dear, don't start with another lecture on conformity." Bringing the elegant black cigarette holder to her lips, Margaret took another lungful of smoke the way an oxygen tent patient gulped air. "I've been ghastly to poor Juliet and only just said sorry. The last thing we need is to start arguing about politics."

"I suppose not. Though I must say, Juliet, you've always struck me as a thoughtful woman. And Linton is a fine old Anglo-Saxon name." Smiling at her, Gerald strolled into the living room. Still handsome at sixty, the silver at his temples and in his mustache made him all the more distinguished. "What do you make of this phony war? So many men in France just sitting on their backsides, staring at one another across the border while we face all these rules and regulations. It's intrusive, positively ridiculous. The propaganda on the wireless, the shameless scare tactics—"

"Gerald." Margaret's tone was light as a feather. "As much as we adore you, neither of us care a fig for the excesses of Mr. Chamberlain, the Parliament, or His Royal Highness the King."

He laughed. "Can't blame a man for trying. Perhaps I'll invite Smith into my study for an early-evening cigar. Hear the views of a true Englishman on this country's present course."

"True Englishman?" Juliet repeated when he'd gone. "Have I missed a joke?"

"No, just another of Gerald's ideals," Margaret said indulgently. "He was born with a silver spoon in his mouth, so naturally he romanticizes the working class, particularly those whose families have lived in England since time out of mind. 'The unsung heroes of this sceptered isle.'" She shrugged. "It's an excuse for him to smoke and drink with his driver. Whereas you and I require no excuse. Care for a sherry?"

"Yes, please." Juliet was driving, but a thimbleful of sherry wasn't enough to go to her head. Besides, she'd been so occupied in making up with Margaret, she'd hardly paused to internally celebrate finding Baby Mark a potential home. Surely that called for a toast.

"I still feel I owe you an explanation for my cattiness beyond being in a snit over Gerald's business." Margaret returned from the sideboard with two dainty glasses. Handing one over, she draped herself across the sofa again. Juliet, who still had a schoolgirls' habit of sitting up ramrod-straight, size eleven shoes firmly planted and knees pressed together, envied the other woman's ease.

"Well, we *are* the Moaners, not the Enthusiasts. I went on for much too long about Jane Daley when I was supposed to complain about Ethan."

"But of course you were happy to play a major role in the child's rescue. I didn't mean to pooh-pooh that. It's splendid." Margaret lit another Pall Mall. "It was all that fawning over Penny's widower that made my heart bleed for you."

Juliet lowered her glass. She set it on the table, picked it up again, and mechanically forced herself to take a sip. Her cheeks were warming. "What do you mean?"

"Oh. Sweetheart." Margaret's look of concern was almost unbearable. "I was in Birdswing last week. Delivered some cut flowers to St. Mark's for a wedding. The vicar told me Dr. Bones had settled at Fenton House, so I stopped by and introduced myself. Why not? If I'm suffering another outbreak the next time I'm there, he's sure to be sent for. Anyway, my point is—I've seen him."

Juliet took another sip. Thankfully, the closest mirror hung on the wall behind her, because if she caught sight of herself reddening, she'd blush all the harder.

Margaret didn't continue for what felt like forever. When she spoke again, it was in a brisk, practical tone. "I wish we'd been friends when Ethan turned up. I can only imagine how heady it must have been, singled out by a man so dashing, so sought after. I understand why you fell for him. He made you feel like Cinderella. But now you know he married you for money. And if you'd had an older sister or a friend, a good, loyal friend, you might have heard the truth before it was too late."

Juliet's glass was empty. Her sherry had disappeared. "I can't even pin down Ethan long enough to divorce him. Do you really imagine you must warn me not to marry Dr. Bones?"

"Good Lord, no." A surprised chuckle escaped Margaret. Looking abashed, she covered her mouth. "I'm warning you not to humiliate yourself again. Ju, darling." Margaret reached across the coffee table to take her hand. "However much you're infatuated with this man, let it go, I beg you. There's a saying: water seeks its own level…."

"Oh, for the love of God," Juliet exploded, on her feet so quickly, she sent her empty glass flying. "Out with it. I'm not pretty enough or stylish enough or graceful enough for him! Not to mention the fact I loom over him like a giraffe on stilts! I don't need an older sister or loyal friend to tell me that. The world tells me every single day, in a hundred unsubtle ways!" For a horrible second, Juliet thought she might cry. But it was true, all true, and she prided herself on being someone who could choke down the truth. Choke it down, digest it, and turn up for another helping the next day. "Well! How's *that* for a champion moan?" She grinned at Margaret. "I've been working up to it all week."

The other woman put down her cigarette and applauded. "Brilliant. For a moment I thought I'd ruined our friendship. And I couldn't bear that, I really couldn't."

"Don't be silly. And don't go erupting into boils and welts again," Juliet said. "I mean to have you up to the manor by Advent at the latest, so you can't be bedridden."

"I'll pass the command along to my skin. Not to mention my nervous system. We're throwing a cocktail party tomorrow. Last minute, all Gerald's friends, naturally, since I've so few. The theme is 'Devil Take the Blackout,' and it may go past sunset, if you can believe our daring. Would you like to come?"

"I'm not sure. I'm not much for parties. And I'd have to overnight in Plymouth…."

"You'd be welcome to stay here. Just think about it. I'd love another hen among the crowing cocks." Margaret grinned. They indulged in a bit more banter, mostly to reassure one another there were no hard feelings, and then Juliet embarked on the two-hour drive back to Birdswing.

She was just being kind. Concerned for my well-being, Juliet told herself as the orange sun sank halfway between tree-dotted hills. Stafford Road, a long gray ribbon, stretched into the distance, but with luck she'd arrive at the manor thirty minutes ahead of full dark. The Crossley's engine was tuned, the tires well-patched, the silence perfectly suited to contemplation. A wise woman would look back on her marriage to Ethan Bolivar, review her missteps, appreciate the lessons, and vow to do better.

Juliet intended to do that, she really did. But before she knew what was happening, she fell into a misty recollection of The Jane Daley Affair, as she secretly called it. It bore only scant resemblance to reality, especially at the end, when Ben insisted that she, Juliet, accompany him to St. Barnabas Hospital. There they knelt at Jane's bedside in wordless vigil, except for meaningful glances and a slow, warm kiss. The fantasy proved so engrossing, it kept her occupied right up until her arrival at Belsham Manor.

As she tucked the Crossley's keys into her front pocket, it occurred to Juliet that perhaps it was time to leave the Moaners, or convince the group to adopt a new mission statement. It wasn't that she didn't enjoy their monthly gatherings. But outside of divorcing Ethan, which would necessitate a certain amount of discussion with barristers and the King's Proctor, her future ex-husband no longer seemed worth the breath it took to complain about him.

Chapter Nine: A Lighter and a Lorry
30 October, 1939

Ben was waiting by the front gate when Lady Juliet drove up. It was his first day relying on a cane instead of crutches, so he'd made the short walk from porch to fence a little early to prove to Mrs. Cobblepot he could. But in truth, he was restless after his encounter with Lucy's ghost: jittery and eager to discuss it, yet afraid he might be considered foolish or mad, even by his housekeeper. Cornwall had always been a county apart, famous for haunted mineshafts, mysterious pre-Christian monuments, and the otherworldly beauty of Bodmin Moor. It was one thing for Ben to embrace the ghost stories, the tales of fairy folk, the suggestion of magic. It was quite another for him to admit he'd seen an apparition, even in a dream, or that he'd shut down his office for the day because of it.

"Good morning, Dr. Bones," Lady Juliet called from behind the wheel of the Crossley as he loaded his cane and black doctor's bag in the back. After nearly losing Jane Daley, Ben had decided that the bag, like his gas mask, would accompany him everywhere. And in addition to his usual arsenal, he'd added two ampules of adrenalin chloride, just in case.

"Questioning the second person of interest," she continued as he climbed into the passenger seat. "I'm positively shivering with anticipation."

"Second person?" Ben was distracted by her atypical choice of clothing. "What's that you're wearing?"

She scowled. "Garments, Dr. Bones. Garments were devised by the human race as protection against the elements, including the scorching sun and the relentless rain. You may not have noticed, but as a precaution against discomfort and public censure, I ensconce myself in them daily."

"That's a skirt," Ben continued, undeterred. "Good grief, I can almost see your ankles." He squinted. "No, that's just boot leather. I had no idea skirts were made from Black Watch tartan."

"Skirts are made of fabric. It so happens I once had a deal of tartan left over from a project that is absolutely none of your affair, and I sewed this one to prove to Mother I'm capable of such a feat," Lady Juliet said, tone growing sterner as her broad cheeks reddened. "I chose to wear it today because it so happens that while in Plymouth, I may drop in on an afternoon party. And I may even permit you to accompany me, doctor, if your impertinent observations don't render you *persona non grata*."

Ben doubted a city party was prepared for the sight of Lady Juliet's overlong, unevenly-fringed skirt, but he wasn't about to say so. Besides, this would be his first time in Plymouth, and perhaps styles were different there. "How is Bobby Archer the second person of interest?"

"Helen Archer was the first. She detested Penny enough to wish her dead, which renders her a suspect in my book," Lady Juliet said, pulling away from the curb. "Perhaps she encouraged us to focus on the lorry to throw us off her scent."

"I suppose," Ben said, doubting it. It wasn't until they were truly on their way, traveling down Stafford Road with nothing but brown fields around them and cloudless sky above, that he gathered the nerve to say what he'd been working up to.

"The first time I saw Belsham Manor, you said it was so Gothic that as a child, you assumed the Lintons were secretly vampires. Well, Fenton House may capture your imagination. It's haunted."

"Doctor! Are you having me on?"

"Not at all." He chuckled. "I think of myself as a modern man, a man of science. So I know it's out of character."

"Ordinarily, I adore ghost stories. I *am* Cornish. But Lucy…." Lady Juliet sounded acutely uncomfortable. "I knew Lucy. We weren't particularly close, but I liked her and wish I'd known her better. To imagine her spirit trapped in the place where she died, dead to this world yet barred from the next? No. I don't call that amusing."

"I wasn't joking. I'm quite serious. I've been walking in my sleep, which is quite a feat if you think about it. Last night while sleepwalking, I climbed the stairs to the master bedroom, dreaming of Lucy all the while. She wore robes, blue robes, and sat beside a blue lamp. That meant something, I'm sure, but I don't know what." He paused, struggling to remember. "She spoke to me, I know she did, but I can't recall what she said—I had it for a moment, but then I woke up in that cold room and something fell from the ceiling, or thin air. It landed beside me, I jumped, and whatever she said went right out of my head."

"What fell? The ceiling fixture?"

"No. This." Removing a chrome Ronson cigarette lighter from his inner jacket pocket, he held it up for Lady Juliet to see. "I don't suppose you recognize it?"

She glanced over, checked the road, and glanced again, longer the second time. "No. I like the design. Is that a raven?"

"A magpie, I think. The raised metal in the middle is meant to be its white breast." He hesitated, then added,

"I believe Lucy saw the man who ran me down and killed Penny. I think she brought me this to help me find him."

***

After a long drive, and an equally long discussion of the supernatural, arriving in the port city of Plymouth came as a relief to Ben. Here the natural beauty of Devon seemed to disappear, at least after his weeks in Cornwall, giving way to progress pursued with a fervency perhaps not even London could match. The streets were wide, and many looked new. The storefronts lined up smartly like soldiers, each with a picture window and striped awning; cars and trams clogged Union Street while above, billboards sold everything from porridge to Cartier diamonds. Ben was tempted to seek out a few points of interest, like the Royal Citadel, but he resisted. He and Lady Juliet were bound for the warehouse headquarters, Singer's Fine Rugs and Furnishings, to speak to the man who occasionally employed Bobby Archer.

Winston Singer invited them into his office, which surprised Ben; he'd imagined amateur detectives would be viewed with suspicion, even hostility, but Mr. Singer seemed sympathetic to Ben's request and willing to help. His answers, however, led nowhere. No, Bobby Archer wasn't known to drink on the job. No, he'd never crashed or even dinged a lorry. Yes, other drivers in the southeast were employed by Mr. Singer, and yes, a handful had been involved in accidents with civilians since the blackout. But none in Birdswing. Mr. Singer had his secretary pull the company's accident reports and spread them out for Ben and Lady Juliet to peruse. Sure enough, insurance adjustors verified that all the incidents had occurred in Devon, not Cornwall.

As they left the warehouse, a church tower pealed eleven o'clock, and Lady Juliet turned to Ben. "My friend Margaret's party doesn't start until half past twelve, and she's warned me repeatedly about turning up on time. It seems that with regard to frivolous social intercourse, punctuality is a sin on par with debating religion or refusing to bathe. So between now and one o'clock, would you care to make a circuit of every garage in Plymouth, hoping to chance upon a mechanic who repaired a lorry with a dented bonnet?"

Ben made a pained noise.

"I quite agree. So I took the liberty of unearthing the address of Mrs. Norma Archer. Bobby lives with her on the east side. Mind you, at this time of day, most men would be at work. But since we'll arrive at Mrs. Archer's well before the pubs open…." Before she finished, he was already nodding.

Norma Archer lived in a third floor bedsit on Rosebury Road. The building's red brick front was pleasant enough, but stairs were uncarpeted and smelled faintly of urine. Her door, 304, had peeling paint, a brass 3, a brass 4, and a dark spot where the 0 once hung.

"No, thank you!" a woman called in response to Ben's knock.

"Mrs. Archer?" He felt absurd, introducing himself through the unopened door. "My name is Ben Bones. We haven't been introduced, but I'd like to speak to you, just briefly, about—"

"No, thank you! We don't need any!" the woman called, louder.

"Mrs. Archer, this is Lady Juliet Linton. I've traveled all the way from Birdswing to speak to your nephew, and I insist you open this door."

A muttered conference inside the bedsit followed. One voice was clearly male, though the words were too low to make out. Then a key scraped in the lock, and Bobby Archer opened the door. He looked very much as his estranged wife described, handsome despite his stubbly cheeks, stained shirt, and uncombed black hair. The heroic chin, sensuous lips, fine eyes, and noble brow made him look like a Hollywood actor miscast as a bum. Then he spoke.

"I don't owe you nothing." He pronounced that last "nuffink." "Never seen you in me life."

"This isn't about money. As I said, I'm Ben Bones. Penny's husband."

Bobby's eyes widened as he took Ben in a second time. "What you come here for?"

"Just to talk. May we come in?"

"There's no—" Even as Bobby started to shut the door in their faces, Lady Juliet lifted her skirt hem a fraction, planting one large booted foot over the threshold. That, coupled with her glare, seemed to change Bobby's mind.

"There's nothing to talk about," Bobby sighed, stepping aside to let them in. "I'll give you ten minutes, then I got someplace to be."

The bedsit, meant to accommodate at most two people, seemed filled with the detritus of a dozen. The walls were invisible, covered with postcards, torn pages from magazines, photographs, framed bits of embroidery and oil paintings, the sort that crop up in church jumbles and never get sold. Most of the floor was also obscured, sometimes by tall stacks of possessions—books, hat boxes, cigar boxes, tins—and sometimes by untidy piles that looked like junk to Ben: yellowed newspapers, torn wrapping paper, unopened letters. In the center of this chaos sat a wingback chair draped in mismatched knitted blankets, and in the chair sat an old woman, knitting. Ben saw at once why she might have been reluctant to get up and answer his knock: besides all the disarray, there was only a narrow path from her chair to the door.

"I'd ask you to sit, but that's Bobby's." She nodded at a nearby sofa. Apart from the knitted blankets of many colors that covered it, the sofa was the only spot not being used for storage, as near as Ben could tell. Bobby Archer fell upon it, not sitting but stretching out lengthwise.

"Me bed! Auntie can't pile her rubbish here, or it goes in the bin. That's the rule," Bobby announced.

"Not rubbish," Mrs. Archer said mildly. Her hands worked with slow precision as she studied Ben and Lady Juliet. "You're not as handsome as our Bobby. You rich? I always said Penny would marry up."

"I'm not rich. I'm a doctor," Ben said. "I won't take any more of your valuable time than strictly necessary. Let me start by saying I'm not here to judge anyone or cause distress. But I have questions about the manner of my wife's death and—"

"My time's not valuable," Mrs. Archer said, hands working with a swift precision at odds with her unhurried speech. Her eyes shifted to Juliet. "You live at that manor in Birdswing?"

"I do."

"You said Linton. Thought you were married."

"I was." Lady Juliet's tone was frosty.

"Her husband left the village in the dead o' night, like me." Bobby grinned. "Hell hath no fury. My boys told me he were locked out of Belsham Manor stark naked. Before he could hitch a ride out, he wrote a farmer a promissory note for a pair o' trousers."

"Yes, well, no doubt that gullible soul yet awaits repayment," Lady Juliet said. "Mr. Archer, you mentioned an appointment to keep, and as the pubs will soon open, I'll take you at your word. We have reason to believe your, shall we say, old *friend* Penny Eubanks Bones retained one of your possessions as a keepsake. We'd like to restore it to you, if it is indeed yours."

Impressed with how easily she'd brought them to the point, Ben reached into his pocket to produce the lighter, but Lady Juliet put a hand on his arm. "Not just yet. Mr. Archer, the item is a chrome Ronson with a design on the case. Tell us the design, and we'll know it's yours."

Apparently a bedsit stuffed with odds and ends wasn't enough for Bobby Archer; from the look of low cunning that narrowed his eyes and pursed his lips, he wanted that lighter, too. Perhaps he assumed he could sell it or swap it for a pint.

"The Union Jack!" he burst out, like a child guessing at a riddle.

"No. Think carefully, Mr. Archer," Lady Juliet said. "Have any other lighters with embossed designs gone missing?"

He pondered the question, gears transparently grinding behind those fine eyes, then shrugged and gave up. "No. Carry matches, I do. But I'd like it all the same, if it were Penny's. Your, er, Ladyship."

"Why is that?" Lady Juliet asked.

"Because it were hers," Mrs. Archer said.

Bobby didn't deny it. Instead he looked Ben up and down again, as if whatever he saw, he found wanting. "I rang her up sometimes. Even wrote her a letter," he added, chest swelling. "She wrote me back. It was special between us."

"Forgive me, Mr. Archer, if we view that claim with dubious eyes," Lady Juliet said. "We cannot surrender an item that might ultimately convict Penny's killer, as her death appears to be murder."

Ben wasn't sure that making such announcement was wise, much less warranted, but the suggestion of murder, delivered in ringing tones that would have done the Royal Shakespeare Company proud, electrified Mrs. Archer and her nephew. His face registered naked shock. She dropped her knitting on her lap.

"You think our Bobby done it? You accusing our Bobby?"

"Not at all," Ben said hastily. "We apologize for taking up your—"

"Are you ratting him out?" Lady Juliet snapped back. "Did your nephew's unrequited amour for Penny lead him to—"

"We're leaving." Taking Lady Juliet by the arm, Ben started toward the door, or tried to. The maneuver wasn't actually possible for a man dependent on a cane, at least not with that particular lady. Fortunately for him, she must have seen sense, because with a huff of frustration, she allowed herself to be led out.

"Penny never loved you, you know," Bobby shouted at their backs.

"I know," Ben said.

"Then why you doing it? Looking for her killer?"

Ben had no answer, so he shut the door.

***

"I really think you should have allowed me to continue my interrogation," Lady Juliet said as she guided the Crossley through mid-afternoon traffic on the way to Margaret Freeman's house.

"'Are you ratting him out?'" Ben repeated and laughed.

"Yes, well, if you were a student of what's known as hard-boiled detective novels, you'd realize it's advantageous to speak to the criminal class in their own misbegotten tongue. How do you like Mr. Archer for our killer?"

"Not much. He seems fixated on Penny, that's true. And she got a letter just before we left for Birdswing, a letter than seemed to upset her. But she told me it was about local news. And she said she wrote back but only to say when we'd arrive and what sort of car I owned, so we'd be expected."

"So. Penny sent a letter telling someone, possibly Bobby Archer, you'd be traveling along Stafford Road in an Austin Ten-Four sometime around dusk. Important information for anyone bent on deliberately running you down."

"It was pitch dark when I parked on the verge. Well, almost, but not quite. I suppose someone with good eyes or a pair of binoculars could have seen us approach in the twilight." Ben shook his head. "I'm still thinking about what Bobby said."

Lady Juliet shot him a quizzical glance.

"He asked me why I'm doing this. Trying to discover if Penny was murdered, and why. I know she had plenty of enemies, and it seems like she deserved them, frankly. To say I'm burning up with the desire for justice on her behalf…." He stopped.

"If I were you, I'd be positively ablaze with the desire for justice for myself," Lady Juliet said. "You were nearly killed and put through untold agony. The man who did it must be punished, even if the deed, according to that note, was accidental."

"Punishing the man who did it won't change what happened. I'm not even sure it would give me satisfaction at this point," Ben said truthfully. "When I was stuck in the Sheared Sheep—yes. A little righteous vengeance would have suited me fine. Now…." He shrugged. "Life goes on. If I could have one wish granted, it would be for my left knee to bend properly."

"Perhaps it shall, given enough time and exercise." Lady Juliet smiled. "But you *do* want this mystery solved, I feel certain of it. And Lucy does, too, or she wouldn't have revealed herself by providing a clue. Perhaps you just can't resist a puzzle."

Ben considered that. Physicians were sleuths by nature, listening to seemingly mysterious complaints for the clue that would lead to resolution. And maybe there was a kernel of stubbornness in him, a refusal to give up on something once he'd engaged. During his internship, Ben's very first case had been an old man dying of cancer. All efforts at treatment had failed; what remained was palliative care, which presumably not even a wet-behind-the-ears intern could botch. He'd known that, known that untested young doctors were always given terminal cases in the beginning, partly to reduce the chance of fatal errors, partly to teach a lesson: many patients die, and the doctor who cannot accept that reality cannot practice. And still, he'd researched novel approaches to advanced tumors, he'd harassed pharmacists about unproven drugs, he'd spent hours at the old man's bedside trying to will him back to health. In the end, the patient died, of course, and a bemused nurse had asked Ben why he'd fought a battle which personally gained him nothing and did the mostly insensible patient no good, either.

"Because I can't *not* try," was all he'd been able to say. Perhaps the same was true of tracking down Penny's killer. Getting on with his own life was probably the best course, yet when it came down to it, he couldn't help but try.

They reached the Freeman residence at a quarter past one. Margaret and Gerald lived in a detached townhouse with a stone exterior, peaked roof, and French white viburnums around the front gate. The sort of residence Penny had aspired to, outside and in—black and white tiled floors, soaring ceilings, crystal chandeliers, and a baby grand piano. A paid entertainer in evening dress tinkled the ivories, crooning a love song as uniformed maids served drinks. Most of the guests were older men in business attire, though a few wives were present, all of them in silk dresses, fur stoles, and high heels. As Ben and Lady Juliet entered, every female pair of eyes came to rest on that tartan skirt and well-worn boots.

"Ju! And Dr. Bones! How marvelous!" Margaret sailed forth to greet them. Her cream-colored gown, as well as that flame-red hair, made her a standout in a sea of black, gray, and navy. "I'd practically given up hope." More softly, she said to Lady Juliet, "Somewhere in Birdswing, a dog bed cries out for its missing upholstery. Have you been at the needle and thread again?"

Lady Juliet tossed her head. "It was this or trousers, Margaret dear."

"Then I applaud your sense of decorum. Gerald, leave off that for a moment! Come meet Dr. Bones."

Excusing himself from a crowd of men deep in conversation near the hearth, Gerald Freeman genially presented himself for inspection. "I never disobey my wife," he told Ben. "Crossing a redhead is tantamount to a death wish. Once she was so angry, I fled to the docks and smuggled myself across the Channel for a month."

"Ah, but he came back. He's no fool," Margaret said, gazing fondly up at her husband.

"No, indeed. Dr. Bones, have you given any thought to Mussolini? What's your take on *Il Duce*?"

"Oh, dear, you know where that discussion leads. Into your breast pocket and that bottle of nitroglycerin." Margaret patted her husband's arm. "Dr. Bones, the glass of whiskey in my husband's hand is his second. What's your professional opinion on hard liquor for a man with angina pectoris?"

Ben expected Gerald to look defensive, but instead he appeared interested. "Oh. Well. I'd prescribe moderation in all things. Avoid too much exertion, too much alcohol, and overly emotional debates."

"I shall do my best to obey," Gerald said, and Margaret chuckled as her husband rejoined his friends.

"My poor Gerald is such a hypochondriac. He's obsessed with his health and devours every newspaper article on modern medicine. He has only a touch of angina, but let him suffer the least stab of pain, and he pours those tablets down the gullet like candy. Well. Ju, Dr. Bones, it's wonderful to see you both. But I'd better make the circuit again," she said, and glided off to greet another pair of newcomers.

Ben did his best to mingle, but the Freemans' affair was more like a stiff compulsory hospital affair than the sort of cocktail party Penny used to throw. The men talked nothing but politics, mostly with regard to how their bottom lines were affected. Clearly they were Gerald's industrial contacts: shipbuilders, chemical manufacturers, retired or failed politicians. Ben, who preferred to keep things light when conversing with absolute strangers, was reduced to frequent nods and noncommittal smiles. Before long, no one had anything to say to him, and his host was segregated by another low-voiced knot of businessmen, while Lady Juliet had disappeared altogether.

"Excuse me." He caught a maid's attention. "Is there a library?"

"Mr. Freeman has a study. Just there." She pointed down the hall. "Last door on the right."

The study turned out to be an oak-paneled room dominated by a large, leather-topped desk. One wall was filled with books, the other with framed portraits of Gerald. In pride of place was a photograph of him standing beside a straight-backed, somber man with a dark mustache. He looked vaguely familiar, perhaps from London society, or possibly from Parliament's House of Lords.

No wonder I don't fit in with these people. They're probably social climbers. Wonder what she sees in them? His gaze fell on Lady Juliet, curled up on a pouf reading *Jane Eyre.*

"Oh! Have I been gone so very long?" she asked, guiltily closing the book. "I told myself I'd only slip off for a moment, and then, well. Charlotte Brontë. I realize Emily is all the rage, and *Wuthering Heights* is ostensibly oh-so-romantic, but Heathcliff needed psychoanalysis. Give me Mr. Rochester any day."

"He did keep his wife in the attic."

"True. Probably it's Jane I prefer." Standing up, she slipped the book back in its place on the shelf. "This is Gerald's domain, of course. Margaret says it's the place where conversations and Cuban cigars go to die. I get the impression you're not enjoying the party, either."

"Not really. How do you know Mrs. Freeman?"

"We grew up in Birdswing. But we didn't really get on until we met again at the Plymouth Gardener's Association, when she started mentoring me. To be honest, I hoped the party would be more intimate, and the three of us could speak privately. Margaret's quite clever. She could assist us with our sleuthing."

Ben groaned. "Accusing Bobby Archer is one thing. Tell me you haven't involved a woman I barely know."

"You have absolutely no faith in my judgment, do you? I've said nothing yet. And I wasn't planning to launch directly into the story, just open the door for you to do so. Perhaps give you a little push." Lady Juliet smiled. "But alas, this party seems neither the time nor place. And if we stay much longer, we'll be stuck overnight in Plymouth. If we leave now, we should reach Birdswing before dark."

"That sounds wonderful." Ben assumed it might take a few minutes to locate one of the Freemans and thank them for their hospitality, but they found Gerald in the hallway speaking to a rotund white-haired man with a bulbous red nose.

"I had it from Lady Diana," the man with the red nose was saying. "The ship's called Chain Home, old boy. Chain Home."

"That's very—" Gerald broke off when he saw Ben and Lady Juliet approaching. "By Jove, you two have wandered far afield. We were speaking of those blasted U-boats. Devilish hard to meet shipping deadlines in a war. Dr. Bones, I'd like you to meet my good friend, the baronet. He's troubled by a quite peculiar sneeze…."

Forcing a smile, and hoping to get in his goodbyes before much longer, Ben listened politely and prepared to dispense more free medical advice.

Chapter 10: Freddy
31 October, 1939

It was after lunch the next day when Ben decided to tell Mrs. Cobblepot about Lucy. He wanted to try the stairs, and didn't care to be alone in case the attempt went awry. Besides, if he was very honest with himself, just falling asleep in Fenton House was difficult now. A joint expedition to the master bedroom seemed wiser than going up alone.

"I don't know, Dr. Bones." Mrs. Cobblepot insisted on following directly behind him in case he lost his footing. The fact that they might consequently tumble down together didn't seem to concern her. "Is this really the right time?"

"Past time. I was sleepwalking again, night before last. Or sleep-crawling, since I woke up in the master bedroom." Gaining the landing at last, Ben paused, resting his left leg as it trembled. He was young enough to fall a few times without seriously hurting himself; why was he so afraid of overtaxing it until it buckled?

Forcing himself to release his death grip on the bannister, he leaned heavily on the cane. Mrs. Cobblepot waited serenely, breath still even despite her age and extra pounds. A lifetime of woman's work—backbreaking, time-consuming, never-ending—had kept her fit.

The master bedroom was gloomy, cardboard taped to each pane of glass, and thick curtains besides. Most of the details he'd dreamt about were wrong, except for the wallpaper. It was just the same, a pattern of ribbons and violets. The spot where the blue lamp had been in the dream looked painfully empty, like a toothless socket.

"I dreamt it was summer," he explained to Mrs. Cobblepot. "A woman sat on the bed wearing a dressing gown or sort of robe. She was reading something, a bit of paper or a book…."

"Robe? What sort of robe?" The only thing odder than the look on Mrs. Cobblepot's face was the fact she'd interrupted. As a rule, she never cut across anyone, even when brimming with news.

"I don't know. Definitely blue. Silver thread on the sleeves. I woke up here, on my hands and knees." He tapped a spot with his cane. "I felt a presence. Then something fell from the ceiling, or thin air, and clattered down in front of me. I think perhaps it belonged to the man who killed Penny." Reaching into his jacket pocket, he held up the Ronson lighter with the magpie design.

"My goodness! That's Freddy's," Mrs. Cobblepot said. "What on earth was it doing in this house?"

"I don't know. But something, or someone, wanted me to have it. Who's Freddy?"

"Just Freddy Sparks down by Little Creek. He's a sad sack if ever I saw one. Always asking Clarence if he wants help with his ARP duties."

"Someone *requested* to work for your brother?" Ben asked gracelessly. Clearing his throat, he started to rephrase, but Mrs. Cobblepot only laughed.

"Beggars belief, doesn't it? But Clarence told Freddy no."

"Does he steal, or drink too much?"

"No. He's just… lost." She sighed. "He's only twenty-two. I've known him since he was a baby, taught him in primary school. One of those children who never seemed to have his lunch or a pencil or a coat when it's thirty degrees out. Bruised a lot, too. When he was twelve, most of his teeth were knocked out. He said he fell out of a tree. Doc Egon said, more like he got hit in the face with a tree branch. The Council met about it, quietly, and sent Father Cotterill and some other men to talk to Freddy's dad. Again. And things got better for a time.

"Then, when he was seventeen, Freddy was sent to hospital with two ruptured eardrums. His life raced downhill after that. The girl he was courting married someone else. His father died, the family farm was lost, and even the Army refused to take him, what with his missing teeth and bad ears. Anyone could have predicted that, but not Freddy. So now he drifts. Fishes Little Creek, walks Old Crow Road, and sits in the Sheared Sheep most nights. Hangs about the lads, trying to be one of them." She shook her head. "Even Clarence belongs to that crowd, and you know how vexing he can be. But he doesn't have poor Freddy's wounded, hopeful air. Clarence thinks he's the best man in Birdswing. The finest shot, the stoutest drinker, the sharpest mind. He's wrong on all counts, of course"—she laughed again—"but down the pub, vanity is virtue. Freddy Sparks hates himself and thinks if he finds friends, it'll turn around. But he has the whole thing back to front."

"What else can you tell me about him?" Ben frowned. "Surely he's a bit young for Penny to have broken his heart."

"You'd think. And I find it difficult to believe Freddy would kill anyone. Deliberately, that is. But running away from the scene of an accident? Yes.."

"The note asked forgiveness," Ben reminded her. "For hurting me, not Penny. Penny was the target."

Mrs. Cobblepot sighed. "Oh, I hope he didn't do it. But I suppose it's possible. This year will go down as an *annus horribilis* for me. My husband died after New

Year's. I spent months living with Clarence. Lucy died far too young. And war broke out." Despite the gleam of tears in her eyes, she straightened her glasses and smiled. "But I also met you and came to work at Fenton House. So all's well that ends well."

Mention of Lucy returned Ben's attention to the spot where the blue lamp had shone in his dream. "Mrs. Cobblepot, I haven't the foggiest notion how to ask you this, but here goes. Was Lucy a… well…."

"Witch?"

"I was going to say mystic." His left leg quivered from ankle to thigh, forcing him to sit on the bed. "Those robes I told you about. The way you looked when I described silver thread on the sleeves. I seem to remember her saying she wasn't the only woman in Cornwall to wear them." He watched Mrs. Cobblepot's face closely, encouraged by her faintly enigmatic smile. "And you mentioned the old religion."

"Which simply affirms the power of the natural world." Smoothing her apron over her skirts, she sat down beside him. "I've told you, my mother brought me up in the Church. I was baptized at St. Mark's, and married there, and someday I'll lie in that churchyard just like Lucy. But Mother also taught me about herb potions and charms, and methods of divination. I'm one of many in these parts who remember the heathen folklore. Once, 'heathen' only meant 'from the country.'" She paused, transparently deciding how to continue. "Lucy was the youngest of us, and the most gifted. I've never made contact with spirits or had a talent for turning the cards. If I have any magic, it's in the kitchen making good food—healing food." She gave his leg a motherly touch. "But Lucy had a sixth sense. A way of communing with animals. She was a bit of a weather witch, too—when she was angry, it stormed, believe it or not. I don't know why she didn't *know* that gas line was leaking." Mrs. Cobblepot's voice rose suddenly. "I don't know why she had to die when she was still half a girl!"

Ben would have put his arm around her, but couldn't decide if the action would be intrusive or welcome. And Mrs. Cobblepot, for all the suffering 1939 had visited on her, didn't actually burst into tears. Instead she sniffed a few more times, drying her eyes with a corner of her apron and sitting quietly, lips compressed in a determined line.

Just as he resolved to embrace her, awkward though it might be, she said in a perfectly normal voice, "Let's go downstairs. I want to show you something."

She went first, heading to her bedroom after making certain Ben made it down all right. Shaky from the exertion, not to mention the idea someone named Freddy Sparks had killed Penny, Ben dropped into the nearest armchair. Intent on clearing his head, he closed his eyes and didn't open them again until the housekeeper stood before him, a leather-bound scrapbook in hand. She held it out to him without speaking.

The first ten pages or so contained snaps of Mrs. Cobblepot and her husband, genial-looking and bald as an egg. They'd been captured together at picnics, parties, and Christmas lunches. Next came a photo of her and her brother, ARP Warden Gaston, outside his bungalow, him grinning broadly, her eyeing the camera as if staring down the barrel of a gun. Two blank pages followed, then some very different photos, which was perhaps the reason for their segregation. They were amateur nature snaps, not always artful but pleasing: a riverbank, a mighty oak, a grove of yew trees, dozens more. All four seasons were represented: crocuses in melting snow, summer fields, piles of fallen leaves, a frozen stream. Then came a snap of Mrs. Cobblepot among a group of laughing women.

The venue was impossible to recognize. Some of the women were younger than his housekeeper, some the same age or older, but they all wore dark robes with piping along the sleeves, hair falling loose about their shoulders. Absurdly, Ben searched for Lady Juliet, but didn't find her. He did, however, see Rose Jenkins, looking even prettier with her hair down. Beside her was a smiling woman he knew at once. She looked just as she had in his dream, cross-legged on the bed beside that glowing blue lamp.

"Lucy. That's Lucy."

"So it is." Mrs. Cobblepot studied the photo, sighing fondly. Then she closed the scrapbook and stuck it beneath an arm. "Thank you, doctor."

"For what?"

"For giving me peace of mind. I couldn't bear to think of Lucy dead so young. Now I know a part of her survives. The best part, if she's trying to help you."

Ben wasn't sure such an existence, seemingly caught between this world and the next, was anything to celebrate. And assuming Lucy really had indicated Freddy Sparks—that all of this wasn't simply a mutual delusion shared by him and Mrs. Cobblepot, the phenomenon French physicians called *folie à deux*—there was still the question of why spirits meddled in the affairs of the living, except to create suffering. If Mrs. Cobblepot was truly a student of English folklore, she knew it was crammed with vengeful ghosts. Did Lucy's accusation make objective sense? Why would a twenty-two year old ne'er-do-well want Penny dead?

"Freddy spends most nights at the Sheared Sheep, you say?" Ben asked.

Mrs. Cobblepot nodded.

"Then I suppose it's time I went down to the pub."

***

The Sheared Sheep wasn't as cheerless as Ben remembered. The horse brasses gleamed, the brass ale taps were spotless, and the long mahogany bar had been polished to a warm, deep glow. All the stools showed signs of heavy arse traffic, yet were in good repair and comfortable enough. As Ben settled into one, he saw the walls were crowded with hunting and fishing trophies, photos of local men winning ribbons or awards, framed stories from the *Gazette*, two deeply-pitted dart boards, and dozens of advertisements:

ARE YOU TIRED? TRY A GUINNESS
and
REACH FOR A LUCKY
and
PRINCE ALBERT DOES NOT BITE THE TONGUE

Near the top shelf whiskey, a plaque read: *If You Want Praise, Die. If You Want Blame, Marry.* Down by the well, another said, *This Establishment Does Not Serve Women, Bring Your Own* while a third said, *If You Drink To Forget, Pay In Advance.* Altogether, the Sheared Sheep was clean and pleasant. Why had he taken pains to avoid it after moving into Fenton House?

"That's Blind Bill Hancock's seat you're warming," Angus Foss announced without preamble, entering from the stockroom with a bottle of scotch in each hand. "Pick another."

Right. Mystery solved. Ben made a show of inspecting the length of mahogany before him, as if confirming no names were carved upon it.

"Show your face now and again, and you'll ken where the regulars sit well enough," Foss said. "Keep your arse on that stool, and you and Blind Bill will get off on the wrong foot. Bad break for a man who only just found his footing again."

"For which I'm grateful. Being carried around by you was the low point of my life." Ben shifted down the row of stools. "Is this better? Though I probably shouldn't let the wrath of a blind man intimidate me."

"We don't call him Blind Bill because he's blind." Foss, who seemed to have only two settings, injured or contemptuous, had his dial turned to the latter. "We call him Blind Bill because he married the ugliest woman in Birdswing. Another fact you'd be aware of if you stopped by regular, like old Doc Egan. Liked to hobnob with his patients in their natural state, he did."

And observe the habits that will put some of them in an early grave. "Why, Foss. If I didn't know better, I'd say you missed me."

The publican snorted. "I miss Doc Egan. Worst day of my life when he passed. Don't suppose you fancy Old Crow?"

"The road?"

"The scotch."

"Good God, no. Pint of bitter."

"Suit yourself." Foss selected a glass, gave it a cursory polish, and placed it under the tap. "I bought three crates of the stuff for the old doc, and he croaked."

"Perhaps some other villagers will take a shine to it."

"Look around ye." Foss glared at the otherwise empty room. "Only skint young blokes and bleeding drunks bother with rotgut. The skint young blokes have gone off to war, and the bleeding drunk to his eternal rest. Time was I had half a room at four o'clock. Now I'm empty till the lads file in, and even then, only a quarter full." He pushed the pint, medium brown with a skim of white foam, at Ben. "Think I could entice the ladies to pop round if I stocked up on crème de menthe?"

"I doubt it," Ben said, gazing on the row of postcards tacked up behind the wine glasses. The most tasteful showed half-dressed females beckoning, waving, and winking beneath slogans like "Hello, Sailor!" The others were even less likely to make women feel welcome. Sipping his beer, Ben wondered if he should ask about Freddy Sparks. The inquiry might not seem too unusual; surely the village's new physician could ask after a man who'd suffered so many injuries? Then again, Foss was both suspicious and talkative, a bad combination. Ben resolved to drink slowly and hope "the lads," as Foss called them, arrived soon.

He got his wish. The aforementioned Blind Bill came first, plopping onto the stool Ben had vacated and ordering a pint of stout. Red-faced and brawny, dressed like a farmer just in from the fields, the fiftyish man spoke not a word, nor even looked in Ben's direction.

"Cheers," Ben ventured.

Blind Bill took out a briar pipe. Filling the bowl with Prince Albert, he struck a match on his boot heel and lit the tobacco. Then he stared straight ahead, smoking his pipe as Foss consulted his racing form. The pub filled up with the scent of burley, sweet and faintly unpleasant.

After several minutes, another man arrived. This one was past sixty, a shrunken little fellow in round glasses and an oversized suit. He took a seat well away from Ben, greeted Foss in a squeaky voice, accepted his pint, and drank. Soon the pub was silent again, except for the rustle of Foss's paper and the sound of Blind Bill sucking his pipe.

Mr. Dwerryhouse, the stooped, hook-nosed chemist, was the next to enter. At least he nodded companionably in Ben's direction, but that was the limit of his warmth. Ordering a glass of red wine, he carried it to a small round table beneath a wall sconce, took out a book, and started to read.

If this is the night life in Birdswing, I'd rather spend my evenings with Mrs. Cobblepot. At least at home there's the chance of a truly riveting game of Patience or dominoes.

"Hey ho, hey ho, time to call the banns!" a familiar voice boomed as the door opened. "Sergeant Hancock?"

"Present," Blind Bill said without turning around.

"Sergeant Williams?"

"Present, sir," the little man with the spectacles squeaked.

"Captain Dwerryhouse?"

"Here." Lifting his wine glass, the chemist took a dainty sip.

"And who's this? An interloper in our midst? Possibly a spy?"

Ben had never imagined feeling grateful to see ADP Warden Gaston, much less hear his typical nonsense, but today was full of surprises. Better he talk to anyone, anyone at all, than endure this silence one more second. "What's this about calling the banns? Is someone getting married?"

"Birdswing Anti-Nazi Society. B-A-N-S," Gaston said proudly. "'Calling the banns' is just my little joke."

It would have been churlish to agree that as jokes went, it was indeed quite small. Particularly since Blind Bill, Mr. Williams, and Mr. Dwerryhouse had all noted Gaston's recognition of Ben as a human being and seemed influenced by it. Blind Bill went so far as to make eye contact, and Mr. Williams offered a thin smile. It was a start.

"What brings you into our midst at last, Dr. Bones?" Gaston asked. "Come to lecture us on the evils of drink after shunning us for so long?"

Is that the problem?

Lifting his pint glass, Ben downed what remained in a single gulp. "Another!" he called to Foss.

"I'm right here, and not deaf," the publican muttered. Folding his racing form, he tucked it away, took Ben's glass, and refilled it. At the same time, Gaston pulled out the nearest stool. Dropping onto it with a satisfied grunt, he loosened his tie and undid his collar, lessening the pressure on his thick neck, which bore deep grooves after long confinement. The silver ARP badge remained pinned to his coat, however. Did Gaston wear it to bed, on his pajamas?

"Birdswing Anti-Nazi Society," Ben said, licking away a bit of creamy foam from his second bitter. "An informal club, I take it, for those who want to do their bit?"

"Yes indeed, yes indeed." Gaston didn't have to ask; Foss automatically handed him a Guinness. "The young bucks are going to France, and the womenfolk are doing their best, too, learning about rations and prudent cookery and what not. Keeping pretty with the rouge and the victory rolls so we don't lose heart." He gave a low-throated chuckle. "But it will fall to seasoned men to defend this nation if the invader comes. Eyes on the skies, ears to the ground. Patrols on the coast, along the rivers, and the main thoroughfares, too. It won't just be Fritz storming the beaches or Jerry spraying mustard gas. The enemy within can't be underestimated. They may spread propaganda and lies, or scout our countryside for Berlin."

"The enemy within," Ben murmured. It sounded like paranoia, but there *was* such a thing as the British United Fascists, or BUF, as well as other, less ideologically transparent organizations. They doggedly called themselves patriots while singing the Third Reich's praises. Virtually all such groups were unified by anti-Semitism, though some concealed it better than others. They claimed lofty objectives, like lasting peace and social harmony, but proposed achieving it by shunning or destroying supposedly inferior cultures. Some of these homegrown admirers of Herr Hitler were scientists and physicians enamored with eugenics, a philosophy of strengthening the human race by eliminating those "unfit for life." Ben doubted Nazi sympathizers had their eyes on Birdswing, but in London he'd witnessed such men attempt to sway public opinion, sometimes with disturbing results. And the eugenicists he'd met in medical school frightened him in certain ways more than mustard gas ever could.

"Aye, lad, and just because you're young doesn't mean you can't aspire to join us. *If* we decide you can be of use," Gaston said, slapping Ben on the back.

Surreptitiously Ben glanced around the pub, which had gained a few more patrons since the air warden's arrival. He'd neglected to ask Mrs. Cobblepot what Freddy Sparks looked like, but everyone in sight had most of their teeth, and Ben was the only man under forty-five.

"Do you take anyone who volunteers? I heard Freddy Sparks was eager to do his bit."

"Sparks?" With all the subtlety of a bull elephant, Gaston craned his head to check out half the pub. Turning completely around on his stool, he scanned the rest, looking high and low.

Brilliant. A born investigator.

Satisfied that Sparks wasn't hiding under a table, Gaston leaned so close to Ben's face, the individual hairs in his mustache were visible.

"I won't let Sparks join," Gaston whispered, "but I'd rather not make that obvious."

"Because he's hard of hearing?"

"No. It's his carryings-on with Edith. Not acceptable for a man in uniform."

"Uniform?"

Gaston took a pull on his Guinness. "We don't wear them yet, but it's only a matter of time. The government will formally call upon us to serve before much longer, just you wait. Until then, the BANS is an independent group, but that don't make us lax. I won't tolerate men who, er. Fraternize."

"Somebody say my name?" It was Edith, she of the short blue-black hair and sharply defined Clara Bow lips. Though still in her maid's uniform, she'd removed her starched white cap and apron. The unlit cigarette between her fingers floated in Ben's vicinity.

Gaston cleared his throat. "Sorry if you misheard. No one called you. Just men here, speaking of men's concerns."

"Right. Like the sight of men ever scared me off." Edith smiled at Ben, her unlit cigarette still bobbing between them. "You're looking better these days."

"Kind of you to mention." Feeling inside his coat, Ben found his lighter. Opening the metal lid with a *clink*, he thumbed the flint wheel, holding the flame level as Edith lit up. The scent of naphtha and a long tendril of smoke, curling toward him as she took a drag, tempted him to beg a cigarette, but he resisted. When the rationing noose tightened, the one and two-pack-a-day smokers would suffer, while his cravings would be only a memory.

"Thanks, love. I don't suppose either of you boys have seen Freddy around?"

"Not since yesterday." Gaston's manner had cooled since Edith's arrival, but if she noticed, she gave no sign.

"He'll turn up. He always does. Angus!" Edith called across the bar. "Pull me a pint!"

When he placed it in front of her, she picked it up without dropping any coins in return. Apparently publican and maid had an agreement when it came to drinks.

"I'm going up," she told him, pointing to the ceiling. "Have to play my records, now that the wireless is all rubbish, all the time." Like many who'd relied on the BBC's erstwhile regional programming for radio drama and popular music, she appeared to consider its wartime replacement, the Home Programme, distressingly news-centric.

"Did you know it's high treason to listen to the BBC in Germany?" Gaston asked Ben. "A crime punishable by death. The truth frightens the Hun."

"Bugger the Hun. I'd rather hear Shep Fields and His Rippling Rhythm Orchestra." Edith winked at Ben.

"Come up if you can manage those stairs, and I'll play it for you." Humming "South of the Border," she strolled off, cigarette in one hand, pint in the other, hips swaying in between.

"Indecent," the ARP warden muttered. "Your poor wife's scarcely cold, yet here she is, making suggestions. No shame, that one."

"Do a lot of men go up to, er, listen to Edith's records?"

Gaston *harrumphed.* "I do my best not to notice."

"Someone left that note on my bed," Ben reminded him. "And just now, when Edith took the stairs, no one paid any attention. It could have easily been her. Or a man known for visiting her up there, like Freddy Sparks."

Gaston's heavy brows lifted. "Never thought of that."

I'll bet. You've been too busy with your garden and your Anderson shelter to question a soul, haven't you? Despite his irritation, Ben refrained from saying as much. He'd long realized he alone was responsible for discovering who killed Penny; no sense manufacturing fresh resentment now. Still, the urge to needle Gaston a little was overwhelming.

"Did you ever dig up that fingerprinting kit?"

"Aye. Ferret out some new evidence that wants dusting, and I'm your man," Gaston said proudly. "I've put the ordnance depot in good order, too."

"Ordnance?" Ben almost choked on a swallow of bitter. "What sort of ordnance are you in possession of?"

"Oh, just the usual for a country village. Rope and sandbags in event of flooding. Hooks and nets to drag Little Creek in event of a disappearance. Shotguns and birdshot in event of the crows becoming a nuisance. A half-dozen Winchester long guns. And a matched pair of Webley revolvers."

"In event of…?"

"Martial law, should the invader arrive on our shore." Judging by Gaston's tone, that grim scenario was one of his fondest hopes. "And ammunition, of course: cartridges and shotgun shells. It's all stored safe in the back of the constabulary," he said, referring to the office located on the high street. "I keep it under lock and key with the nitro."

"Nitro? You don't mean… dynamite?"

"What else? That tin mine out by Belsham Manor may be closed, but there's still a few shafts here and there, mouths overgrown with brush, presenting a public hazard. Children, tramps, anyone could stumble upon one and fall inside. The village needs nitro in case of collapse, for the rescue."

"And you don't think keeping *dynamite* separate from live ammunition might be prudent?"

"What, create two hazardous storehouses instead of one?" Gaston chuckled. "Don't go overthinking things, Dr. Bones. Overthinking things never did anyone any good."

"No danger of that on my watch," someone said, loud and hopeful. "Reporting for duty, brigadier!"

"At ease." Gaston didn't turn to look behind him at the young man with limp blond hair, round shoulders, and a half-empty smile.

"Brigadier?" This time Ben couldn't keep a straight face. "It's a courtesy title, Gaston. Why not go right to 'general?'"

"Because modesty is still valued in these parts, I think you'll find." Rising, Gaston buttoned his collar and tightened his tie, reinflating a face already puffed by the heat, tobacco smoke, and stout. "Now if you'll excuse me, I must make my blackout rounds."

"You're Dr. Bones." The young man slid onto the stool the air warden vacated. "I'm Freddy Sparks. Sorry I talk so loud," he practically shouted. "Fell down the stairs and burst my eardrums. Always been unlucky. My mother saw a magpie the day I was born. Just the one. Don't know why she couldn't stay out and wait for a few more."

"Speaking of magpies...." Ben withdrew the chrome Ronson and placed it between them. Freddy's face lit up.

"I lost this months ago! Fell out of my pocket when—" He stopped, goggling at Ben, then took a deep breath and recited carefully, "One for sorrow. Two for joy. Three for a girl, four for a boy. Five for silver, six for gold. Seven for a secret never to be told."

Tipsy already, Ben thought, waiting for Freddy to ask the obvious question, where he'd found it. But the other man said nothing. Was that because he'd lost it at the scene of the accident and didn't dare? Ben signaled Foss, thinking a bit more alcohol would do the trick.

"What are you drinking?" he asked Freddy.

"Scotch. Just a little warm-me-up for the walk here." He patted his jacket pocket where something small and hard, like a hip flask, resided. "It's cold out. A bad winter's coming. Besides, I'm celebrating."

"Scotch for him. One final bitter for me," Ben told Foss. To Freddy, he said, "Celebrating?"

"Right. Came into some money. I mean, it sounds awful, celebrating because an uncle died." Freddy squirmed and flashed his gums. Despite the smile, he looked miserably ill at ease, like a small child in need of the loo. Worse, he stared unblinking into Ben's eyes, broadcasting a desire for connection so intense, it was repellent.

"But I never knew him," Freddy went on. "And he was old. Very old. Past ninety, old. And it's not like the Army would have me. I'm not even good enough to die for my country. So I'll take my money however it comes and be grateful for it." Scooping up the scotch Foss placed before him, Freddy lifted it toward Ben. "Cheers, mate!"

I'm not your mate. This overgrown boy didn't seem capable of squashing a bug, much less cold-bloodedly running down two human beings. Yet there was something off about him, a defect far deeper than poor hearing or missing teeth.

"But I shouldn't have brought up a death in the family," Freddy went on. "You lost your wife. To Mrs. Bones! God rest her soul." He downed half his whiskey.

Ben cringed inside, but no one else in the pub seemed to be paying Freddy any mind. "My wife grew up in Birdswing. Most of the villagers knew her. Did you?"

"Oh! No. I mean, I'd seen her here and there, of course. Pretty as a picture. But she never talked to me. I'd remember that." Down went the rest of the scotch. Cupping his hands around the empty glass, Freddy lapsed into silence, staring straight ahead. Occasionally he smiled to himself, as if replaying an old conversation in his head.

Or rehearsing lies. Ben glanced around the bar again. Edith had not returned. Foss was engrossed in his racing form again. Mr. Dwerryhouse had made noticeable progress in his book but rather less on his drink, which sat forgotten on the table. Blind Bill was refilling his briar pipe as the tall man beside him, dressed in brogues, overalls, and a red tartan mac, expounded on something called Japanese knotweed.

"But how do you explain how it guesses my movements?" the tall man asked. "How it sidles out of one patch and creeps into another, like it's playing hide-and-seek? I'm telling you, this is more than coincidence. It's cunning."

Blind Bill shook his head. The tall man pounded the bar, agitated.

"If birds can have brains, and mice can have brains, and wee insignificant fleas can have brains, why can't plants have brains?"

"Because." Blind Bill held a match to the bowl. "They're plants. That's why."

"That's no logic at all!" Stalking to the nearest dartboard, the tall man yanked a handful of darts out of the wall. "Best two out of three?"

"Aye. Rather play you than talk to you any day," Blind Bill said, joining him.

"I have a notion about women," Freddy announced suddenly. Ben had almost forgotten his existence.

"What's that?"

"They die, leave us, or get sick," he slurred, sounding well and truly drunk. "It's been that way with every woman who's been good to me. My mum died. My best girl left me on account of my ears. And m—m—my word. There's Edith." Grinning, he stumbled off his barstool, eyes on the stairs.

Edith had changed out of her maid's uniform. Now she wore a snowy white frock patterned with red cherries and a pair of black patent heels. Aware of all eyes upon her, she descended slowly, placing each foot with exquisite care and smiling as much at Ben as the rounded-shouldered young man beside him.

"One for sorrow," Freddy began, much too loud. "*Edith* for joy. Three for a girl, *Edith* for a boy…."

"Edith for silver, Edith for gold," she finished, poking Freddy in the chest. "Where you been? I'm bored silly."

"Let me have one more, and I'll be right up."

"See that you are."

As Freddy called for another scotch, Ben watched Edith make a slow circuit through the pub, talking with one man, laughing with another, bumming a light off a third. It didn't surprise Ben to see the world's oldest profession plied in Birdswing, but it was worth noting that Edith hadn't quit her day job. Maybe these fathers and grandfathers too old for conscription were mostly content to remain downstairs, satisfied by flirtatious banter. Did that make Freddy Sparks the only patron to regularly follow her upstairs? If so….

"Are you worried about Edith?" Ben asked Freddy as he finished his drink.

"What? Why?"

"Your notion. Every good woman dies, leaves you, or gets sick."

"Oh. No worries. Edith isn't good." Placing a hand on Ben's shoulder, Freddy rose with exaggerated care.

"She was good enough to deliver your note to me. Or act as lookout while you placed it on my bed."

Freddy jerked his hand away as if scalded. "I never—she never—"

"'Forgive me, it was never meant to be you, just her.'" Ben watched Freddy's face. "What made you run us down? Why did you want Penny dead?"

"I didn't! I never knew her! We never spoke!" Freddy cried. Throughout the Sheared Sheep, all conversation stopped. Men turned on their stools or pushed back their chairs for a better look. Foss, in the midst of drawing another pint, released the lever. A dart thumped against the board, hitting the red bull's-eye, but no one cheered. Even in the far corner, two elderly chess players lifted their heads, peering through thick spectacle lenses at Ben and Freddy.

Ben didn't know what more to say, particularly with half the village listening. He had no evidence, not even circumstantial evidence. Just a gut dislike of Freddy and his clumsy attempts at ingratiation. It wasn't as if Ben could make a citizen's arrest based on the testimony of the Fenton House ghost.

Though if any acting constable on earth would accept such a ludicrous claim, it would be Gaston.

Pale and trembling, Freddy edged backward. His gaze fell on Ben's cane, which was propped beside his stool, and lingered there a bit too long. "I'm sorry about your legs," he said, and hurried away.

"Never mind poor Freddy." Mr. Dwerryhouse had his coat buttoned up and his book tucked beneath one arm. "He's a lost soul. Pity the military couldn't devise some use for him. A man without work is a man without purpose. Will you be driving home?"

"Walking," Ben said, lifting his cane and smiling.

"Brave fellow. Right back up on the horse, eh? And it's no more dangerous than driving without headlamps. If you like, I'll accompany you," Mr. Dwerryhouse said. "I discovered a very interesting paper about novel applications of adrenaline chloride you might like to discuss. And never fear, I'm capable of walking safely back to Birdswing blindfolded. I'll keep you out of the street and away from the ditch."

Ben accepted the stooped little man's offer. As they exited the pub, he pulled the door tight behind him, negating the possibility of light spilling out. As his eyes readjusted, he was grateful for the full moon and those few stars twinkling between the clouds. Hard to believe that just over nine weeks ago, he'd nearly died here, in this crisp darkness smelling of wood smoke, late-blooming sweet pea vines, and, faintly, sheep dung. And moments ago, he'd bought a drink for the man who'd almost certainly sent him an apology for murdering his wife.

Could it be nothing more than a cruel joke? An attempt to pay me back for monopolizing the room Edith usually entertains in?

Mr. Dwerryhouse chatted companionably about adrenal extracts as he led the way, but Ben listened with only half an ear, his thoughts returning to the nursery rhyme every English child learned by heart.

Five for silver, six for gold, seven for a secret, never to be told….

Mrs. Cobblepot had described young Penny as a girl who manipulated her schoolmates by threatening to spread gossip. An amateur blackmailer, paid off in candy and ribbons. Had she continued down that path as an adult, or rediscovered it sometime during their marriage? That letter she'd received not long before their departure, the one that put her in such a foul mood, had been postmarked from the southwest. But who had she kept up with in Birdswing? Who in the village had the resources to pay off a blackmailer, particularly with tastes as refined as Penny's?

Technically, Lady Juliet fit the bill, as did Lady Victoria. But Ben refused to entertain either woman as a suspect. Lady Juliet in particular wasn't one to write check after check to a blackmailer. She was more likely to seize control of the situation by publishing the scandalous news herself, without apology and perhaps accompanied by illustrative photographs. Then she'd drive to the would-be blackmailer's house, hand them a copy hot off the press, and box their ears for good measure. Since Penny hadn't been pummeled by a trouser-clad giantess, Lady Juliet was off the list.

Besides, Penny never did without. Her father kept her supplied with cash. We didn't talk about it, but he must have. My salary wouldn't have covered her summer wardrobe.

And one of the last things Penny ever did was remind him that when she returned to the southeast, it was to Plymouth, not Birdswing.

Walking along Stafford Road reminded Ben of the Hibbets and that long-ago crash in this very spot. If Penny had been discovered with a large bruise across her chest, she'd probably struck the steering wheel on impact. That meant she was the person driving when a deliveryman called John Leighton was killed outside Daley's Co-op. Penny struck and killed by a lorry several years after accidentally killing a lorry driver—was it poetic justice or just a coincidence?

Finally, there was Lucy McGregor. Somehow, she'd provided him with the lighter leading him to Freddy Sparks. But why would Freddy run Penny down? He wasn't the sort she'd have flirted with. Freddy was too low for Penny to even torment. Unemployable, yet capable of purchasing spirits and companionship after coming into some money….

The money means he was paid to do it. But by whom? And why?

He needed to discover which businesses made local deliveries in Birdswing proper and if Freddy had access to those lorries. And it was high time he went through Penny's things: the scant possessions she'd brought to Birdswing by car, even the contents of her handbag, which he hadn't touched since her death. Including that slender volume of Shakespeare's sonnets, the book she'd been reading the day she died.

Chapter 11: Bonfire Day
5 November, 1939

The next few days were busy for Ben. A nasty head cold was moving through the school children, beginning with the older ones and working its way toward the littlest, for whom a high fever could be fatal. Old Mr. Laviolette, father of the widely-derided restaurateur, fell in his bathtub and broke his hip. He was transferred to St. Barnabas, where he was expected to die within a fortnight, like most elderly patients subjected to surgery and hospitalization. And Mrs. Garrigan, barely twenty, was six months pregnant and already showing signs of hypertension. It didn't help that she wept frequently over her husband, off being trained at a location he couldn't disclose, to perform duties he couldn't name. Quite likely the piloting of combat aircraft for the Royal Air Force. She also ate too much salt, drank too much brandy, and worried day and night she would be a widow before she gave birth. Twice Ben was called to her house for false labor, once in the early morning, once in the middle of his supper. Both times he could do little more than sympathize. If only Birdswing had a midwife to help out, preferably a mature woman who'd overseen dozens of births. There was only so much comfort a young, childless male could give.

Attempts to trace a damaged lorry within the village went no better. During his lunch hour, Ben visited three garages, but all the vehicles were intact without a new bonnet or restored grille. One man had sold a lorry three months ago, but through a telephone inquiry, to a lady starting her own delivery service. A third party had picked up that vehicle and driven it away. As for the mechanics, none had worked on a crashed lorry around the time of Ben's injuries and appeared shocked and mildly insulted he would even ask. Acting Constable Gaston might be derelict in maintaining the investigation, but the garage owners insisted they knew vital information when they heard it and would have gone straight to the constabulary, *Birdswing Gazette*, or Ben himself.

Between patients and the lorry search, he sifted through Penny's belongings. The contents of her luggage proved unremarkable, but then it occurred to him to check for hidden compartments. In her valise, he found a pocket unartfully sewn into the original satin liner: Penny was clumsy with a needle and thread, while Ben could make sutures as small and neat as any seamstress. Cutting the pocket open, he found two folded bits of paper. The first was a typed note, unsigned or dated.

This is absolutely the last time we shall communicate in any way. Do not attempt to draw me out by writing letters, making phone calls, or sending third parties. It's done. Do not test me.

The second was a short, handwritten letter from Penny to him. It was dated 29 August 1939, just two days before they'd departed London. Seeing his name in that familiar script, Ben was seized by the temptation to burn it without reading. His breath came faster; his heart thudded against his ribs. But what if it contained the answer? He closed his eyes for a moment, willed himself to remain cold, remain strong. Then he opened it and read.

Ben,

I'd call you darling, but you despise that now. And since I don't suppose you'll ever let me speak to you of Albie, I can only explain in writing. I didn't love him. Didn't even like him. And no, he wasn't better than you, certainly not in bed. He was a toy, love. If you weren't so serious, you'd understand, but I suppose that's asking too much.

I should have told you ages ago about the baby. Did I say the father was a man to be reckoned with? No. He was just one of those fraternity rakes, and would you believe he made a fool of me? It's true. I did everything in my power to bring him to the altar, but he wouldn't have it, and I was desperate. Which brought me to you.

Once you asked me why I chose you. I wish I could take back the lies I told. But you were so close to my darkest secret, that a man broke my heart and left me too far gone for anything but marriage. So I said the worst things I could think of. When the truth was, you had a pretty face and a strong voice and a gentleman's manners. All the raw materials for a good husband, a hundred and eighty degrees from where I'd been. That's why I chose you. Because I foresaw what you would become.

Now you see why I can't stay in London, my dearest, however much you hate me now. Father's money has dried up, and soon I must learn to economize. Why not learn it in Birdswing, since fate seems determined to have her little laugh? If I can make you love me again, it will all be worth it.

Penny

Ben studied the letter for a long time, the well-known pen strokes, the slash across each *t*. Even as his eyes burned, as the words on the page grew watery, he knew it wasn't her apparent tenderness that spurred the tears. Could she have meant it? Had she ever been sincere? Impossible to be sure. And so he never could have found it within himself to love her again, not if they'd stayed married another fifty years. That was why he wept—not because of Penny's words, but his inability to believe them.

Her edition of Shakespeare's sonnets only provoked more questions. On the second page he found an inscription in a man's handwriting:

Dear Penny,

How I enjoyed our talks this weekend! Since you come a virgin to the Bard of Avon, I'll start you gently with pretty verses. But in Hamlet you'll find proof of everything I've said, including a great Englishman's prescient commentary on the troubles of our times. A man deprived of his inheritance may seem pitiless as he pursues justice, but as Hamlet teaches us, "dog will have his day." To the pure of heart, betrayal and cowardice are unforgivable, and without purity, we have nothing. As another great man said, "The broad masses of a population are more amenable to the appeal of rhetoric than to any other force." May the Bard guide you and my fellow Englishmen to right thinking and prevent our nation from making war on those who should be our truest friends.

G.

Ben puzzled over the identity of G. for some time. He'd expected a love note from Albie, not a miniature discourse on Hamlet. Finally he settled on Penny's brother, George Eubanks. The man had never struck Ben as a student of literature, but it seemed worth a phone call.

"Sonnets?" George, also in a reserved occupation—mechanical engineer—sounded harried as the office secretary gave him the phone. "Never had any time for that rot. Neither did Pen. Did you get my wire about insurance money?"

"Yes," Ben said, regretting the call already. "There isn't any."

"Too bad. Dad's in a fix," George said, and rang off.

Within the book, Penny had made little notations in the margins. On page four, she'd written *D. Mail Jackson 3/13*. On page nine, *Olympia photo*. On page twelve, *Times letter Mosley study wall.* On the final page, a list:

1000
1000
3000
1000

He had no idea what it meant, yet his instincts told him the numbers were sums, despite the missing pound signs. And that typed letter had seemed very much like the declaration of a blackmailer's victim:

This is absolutely the last time we shall communicate in any way....

***

In addition to his amateur detective work, Ben kept up his rehabilitation efforts, forcing himself to put on his coat, pick up his cane, and walk the length of the high street twice a day. Only once did he fall, pivoting so quickly to avoid a tomcat that his left knee buckled. As the big, ragged creature darted into an alley, Ben was hauled to his feet by a trio of little old ladies, then questioned by ARP Warden Gaston, who'd burst out of Morton's café when he heard the commotion.

"I'm quite all right. It was only a one-eared cat. Orange, with stripes. Did you think I'd been attacked by German agents?" Ben grumbled, dusting off his trousers.

"I didn't think at all," Gaston said proudly. "In event of emergency I never do. One of my luckier qualities." To the small crowd, he said, "Off with you! Find suitable occupation. That's an order. The poor man's embarrassed enough, making up tales of cats without you lot gawping at him."

"Tales?" Ben peered into the alley, gloomy from the shelter of two overhanging roofs. He thought he saw two yellow eyes glowing back at him from behind the metal rubbish bins. But as soon as he blinked, they were gone.

"I can give you a ride back to Fenton House," Gaston continued, not unkindly. "Or give you my arm and help you there, if you're dead set on walking. Need to speak to Agnes about this Bonfire Day nonsense. I've half a mind to drive up to the manor and tell Lady Juliet I've changed my mind about permitting it."

"Please don't." The village thrummed with anticipation; Ben had heard about little else for weeks. Due to the blackout, Birdswing was forbidden from the usual nighttime festivities for Guy Fawkes Night: roman candles, Catherine wheels, a huge bonfire in the village square. There had been some efforts to convince the vicar to throw a substitute party in the church hall, perhaps with a papier-mâché bonfire, candles, punch, music, and dancing. Having never approved of Guy Fawkes Night, which struck Father Cotterill as practically pagan, he'd refused. But just as the disappointed villagers resigned themselves to 5 November as yet another silent, colorless night, Lady Juliet had appeared on the high street, bursting into shops and salons and restaurants with the news. On the very next Sunday, a daylight version of Bonfire Night would be held at Belsham Manor, and every resident of Birdswing was welcome.

"If you try and shut it down at this point," Ben told Gaston, "you'll likely have a riot on your hands. Besides, your sister isn't home. She's getting her hair done. I've never seen her so excited."

"Excitement breeds disobedience," the air warden muttered. "I can't imagine what's gotten into Lady Juliet. She's never been one for parties. Usually wanders off halfway through or spends the whole night reading a book."

Ben knew what had gotten into her, and while he had his doubts about the scheme's efficacy, he couldn't fault the good intentions behind it. Breathless with enthusiasm, she'd rang him a few days ago, spilling out her thought process before he could even say hello.

"Last night, as I was propped up in bed reading a mystery novel… wait. I just realized I've never asked. Do you enjoy mystery novels? I do, so long as the woman isn't a ninny. Can't abide ninnies. At any rate, I was reading, and thereupon it struck me like Archimedes in his bath: how does one advance a case like Penny's, where there are more suspects than evidence? Eureka! Give a dinner party and invite all the players!"

She paused, both to take a breath and receive praise. Ben knew better than to laugh, though he was glad she'd announced her plan by phone. Had she been able to see his expression, the resultant injuries might have put him back in that ghastly Edwardian wheelchair.

"You mean, actually invite them to Belsham Manor, lock them in your parlor, snuff the lights, and wait to see who turns up dead?"

"No, that's how murders *happen*, not how they're solved," Lady Juliet said patiently. "The idea is to get the liquor flowing, get them chatting and joking and laughing, and just observe. The murderer is sure to be exquisitely uncomfortable under pressure and thus reveal himself. Particularly if it's Freddy Sparks.

"The pretext is simple," she continued. "Guy Fawkes Night during the day. Why moan about not being allowed to burn an effigy when we can do it before sundown? As for our suspects, I doubt I can dig up Mrs. Hibbet, but I'll invite her, just in case. And I'll need to go back to Plymouth to invite Bobby Archer, but that's no sacrifice. I can apologize for accusing him—the better to snare him later, if it comes to it—and purchase a new dress while I'm there."

"New dress?"

"Yes," she barked. "No tartan skirt and no trousers but a proper dress, like Margaret's friends. Perhaps I'll get my hair curled, too, and put on my mother's sapphire earbobs, rendering you and your kind speechless."

He grinned. Any day he could get a rise out of Lady Juliet was a good day. "Ah, but my kind is in short supply. Your table may be overloaded with ladies. How many villagers will you invite?"

"Why, all of them, of course."

"What?"

"It's not so many," Lady Juliet said negligently. "More than a third are headed to France, if not there already. Many won't come. And those mothers with sick children will stay home and tend them, naturally. Leaving Mother and me with three hundred guests, three-fifty at the absolute most."

"Three hundred?" Ben couldn't imagine such an undertaking, particularly on short notice.

"Oh, ye of little faith. Don't forget, this is a fête at Belsham Manor hosted by Lady Victoria Linton, not some slapdash potluck presided over by me. I've never claimed to be brilliant at arranging galas or balls, but Mother was born for that sort of thing. I'm quite serious, *born* for it," Lady Juliet said. "Had a certain summer in her youth taken a slightly different turn, she'd be throwing parties for the PM and His Royal Highness, not Bobby Archer and Freddy Sparks. Ask her someday, and she'll tell you all about the glorious engagement that never quite happened."

"I shall. And… very well, please convey to Lady Victoria how much I appreciate her efforts on my behalf. Just the thought exhausts me." Not wanting to sound ungrateful, Ben was careful to employ his blandest tone as he asked, "How much did you tell her?"

"About our investigation of Penny's murder? Everything." Lady Juliet sounded blithe. "Doctor, please. Don't make that sound."

"What sound?"

"A sort of choked exhalation. Like this—*heh*," she said, imitating it. "I once had a hound that wandered from room to room making that noise. As if to say he was exasperated or ill-used or surrounded by tiresome dogs that weren't quite his sort. We had to have him put down."

Ben swallowed the retort that came to him, caught himself on point of emitting the sound again, and cleared his throat instead. "Is it, er, wise to share so much when we have no proof?"

"Mother is completely reliable and silent as the grave. You'd be better off with her as an investigatory partner, truth be told, if it weren't for her health. Where I'm robust, she's—well. Fragile."

"So you've said. When I met her, I didn't note anything but a bit of breathlessness. I would have thought asthma or even chronic hay fever, but you're not the sort to exaggerate about Lady Victoria's health."

"Her heart is enlarged. Heart failure, Dr. Egon called it, and frightened me half to death, but it still beats, even if the malady's name suggests otherwise. It just performs weakly. He said if she remains calm, eats well, and gets adequate rest, she might live another fifteen years. If she suffers a shock or takes a chill, she might die next week." Before he could frame the proper response, she continued more briskly, "But fear not, Dr. Bones, Mother throws a gala at least once a year, and this one is overdue. Arrive prepared to do some sleuthing; she and I will attend to the rest. Oh, and don't wear top hat and tails. Come dressed for cricket and quoits, and all the usual country pursuits. Some ladies will be dressed to the nines, as is their prerogative, but the war left precious few men in Birdswing and most who remain are men of the soil, as it were. If you wear your best, they might feel ill at ease."

Ben, who'd assumed he must wear his Sunday suit, was impressed by Lady Juliet's thoughtfulness. Penny would have insisted he wear it anyway, the better to emphasize the social distinction between a London-trained physician and the villagers, many of whom had left school barely proficient in reading, writing, and basic maths. "I still don't know what I'm supposed to do if someone makes an incriminating statement."

"What would you do if you heard another doctor made an incriminating statement? Some terrible admission about a patient's death?"

"I'd take it to the hospital administrator."

"Precisely. Mr. Gaston isn't the only authority figure in England. There are plenty of detective constables in Plymouth. All we need do is uncover something compelling enough to secure their interest, and we can step back and let justice take its course."

***

The next morning dawned gray and chilly. Dark clouds brooded overhead, casting a spatter of raindrops here and there. Birds cried in the treetops, toads croaked, and as Ben stepped onto the porch for the day's milk delivery, a grass snake shot across the lawn. He soon glimpsed what had sent it gliding from beneath the hedgerow. A striped orange cat was hunched under the tangled branches, its yellow eyes peering from between ragged brown leaves.

"Not sure that'll keep your fur dry," Ben told the cat. "You'd be better off around Morton's. Or Laviolette's—probably lots of spoilt food in the rubbish bins there."

The cat, almost certainly the tomcat who'd tripped him—the tomcat Gaston had assured him did not exist—pointedly turned his face to the wall. The message was unmistakable: *I do not hear you, human.* Taking the hint, Ben went back inside.

Soon after, lightning flashed, there was a terrific crack of thunder, and the rain came down, strong and steady. When Ben and Mrs. Cobblepot set out for Belsham Manor around noon, it had stopped, but the sky remained an unpromising gray.

"I do hope it clears up," she said as Ben helped her onto the passenger seat. Over her new frock of russet brown grosgrain, she wore a red shawl with a velvet collar. It looked acutely vulnerable to rain, and Ben said as much, but the housekeeper refused to insult the ensemble by covering it with a shapeless mac. She did, however, tie an oilcloth kerchief over her freshly blue-rinsed hair. For his part, Ben took along a large black umbrella.

Old Crow Road's ruts and potholes were full of water, and in low spots the flooding was bad enough Ben was forced to go around. There was also a great deal of traffic for Birdswing: two to three vehicles at least three car lengths apart at all times.

"How tedious, constantly staring up a tailpipe," Mrs. Cobblepot said. "I imagine this is what London is like."

"Slightly less vexing." Ben honked as a wooly ewe wandered between his Austin Ten-Four and the rusty sedan ahead. Looking miffed, the ewe moved on, and they soon trundled within sight of Belsham Manor.

Despite the mid-morning downpour, Lady Victoria had done a remarkable job of transforming the front lawn. Orange, red, and yellow pennons flapped, wet but still cheerful, over a huge white tent. A painted sign above the entrance read CIDER FORTUNES TOFFEE APPLES. Trestle tables were covered with red cloth and brightened by yellow and brown chrysanthemums. White-haired, deaf old Robbie was directing automobiles into the grassy sward near the orchard. A flag clutched in each fist, he herded guests into rows with a concentration and solemnity usually reserved for landing aircraft.

Lady Juliet's estimate of three hundred guests seemed a tad low; villagers were everywhere, sitting on folding chairs, milling about, queuing up for a look inside the big white tent. Beyond the tent, Ben saw the red hair and lithe figure of Rose Jenkins. She was surrounded by at least twenty children, shouting, laughing, and running in circles. On the lawn's opposite end, within the waning garden, he saw the imposing figure of Lady Juliet, topped by a feathered, beribboned hat. Great plumes whipped in the stiff November wind as she walked along a hedgerow, talking over her shoulder as guests trailed behind.

"Oh, dear," Mrs. Cobblepot murmured. "Some women simply aren't meant for hats."

The same could not be said of Lady Victoria, whose hat was pinned at the perfect angle. Greeting Ben and Mrs. Cobblepot beneath a wrought iron arch, she could have been a photo from *Woman's Own*. Instead of a frock, Lady Victoria wore a navy silk jacket that was widely-padded over her shoulders and belted over a matching silk skirt. The effect—a man's suit perfectly adapted to a woman's curves—was one Ben had glimpsed a few times in London. However, the new fashion seemed unfamiliar to the villagers, many of whom gaped in admiration.

"Lady Victoria, you've outdone yourself," Mrs. Cobblepot burbled. "What sort of shoes are those?"

"Dress oxfords with a Cuban heel." Lady Victoria said. "I wasn't quite convinced until I put them on. I thought they might be a little too military, you know. But now I believe they'll be all the rage."

"Oh, I do adore your forehead curls. So feathery." Removing her oilcloth kerchief, Mrs. Cobblepot shook out her bluish-white waves, preening as she was complimented in turn.

"Dr. Bones! Mrs. Cobblepot! Welcome," Lady Juliet called. Her cheeks and forehead were flushed, as if she'd been running. She wore a fluttery-sleeved dress, emerald green and belted across the middle to give the appearance of a waist. Though the dress was lovely, too many gaudy accessories spoiled the effect. Her emerald necklace was ostentatious enough for a coronation; her opera-length white gloves had gold rings and bracelets on top. Her shoes, velvet Mary Janes, were muddy from the rain-soaked lawn, and that hat.… Ben, no fashion critic, didn't know how to describe it. Once while visiting the London Zoo, he'd glimpsed a large bird of prey, dead in its nest. That sight—wings poking up, straw spilling out, the sense of witnessing something best buried and expunged from memory—was what the hat put him in mind of. It, too, was emerald green.

Fortunately, it was also above eye level. "Lady Juliet, we were just telling your mother how lovely she looks," Ben said. "Now that you've arrived, we're at a loss. I mean—who should we compliment first?"

Mrs. Cobblepot nodded vigorously. "Quite right! With you here, the effect is… well. Overwhelming!"

Such verbal gymnastics wouldn't have worked with Penny, who would have instantly demanded explication. If she didn't hear herself called beautiful, slim, stylish, or enviable, preferably a combination of all four, it was back to the wardrobe for another go. But Lady Juliet, perhaps unused to praise—even praise of a plausibly deniable nature—looked overjoyed. "Not even Mother knew about my top secret ensemble until I appeared. I was determined to astonish everyone."

Lady Victoria gazed on her daughter with warm brown eyes. "Well, my dear, you've succeeded. You look beautiful." As far as Ben was concerned, that was the best sort of lie, borne of kindness and unswerving loyalty.

"Mrs. Cobblepot, would you allow me to steal Dr. Bones?" Lady Juliet asked. "There's tea and sherry, and some of the ladies are already playing whist, if you'd like to join them. We shan't light the bonfire and burn Guy Fawkes in effigy till three o'clock."

"Oh, I could never pass up a hand of whist," Mrs. Cobblepot said. On her way toward a table full of ladies, many with hair the exact same shade of blue, she veered for a maid bearing glasses of sherry.

Lady Juliet hooked an arm through Ben's, steering him toward the garden. "I shall begin with a confession. Thus far, events aren't shaping up *precisely* as envisioned."

Ben hazarded a glance at the sky. A trio of black thunderheads was stacked in the west. "I know. Terrible weather for a bonfire."

"Nonsense. It won't rain, it wouldn't dare. Mother's gone to too much trouble. The gloom merely makes it feel like an authentic Bonfire Night. I referred"—Lady Juliet lowered her voice—"to my vision of our suspects locked in the drawing room, metaphorically speaking, with revelations coming fast and thick. Freddy Sparks isn't here. And I simply cannot credit that, as alcohol is being served, and no one will stop him from filling his pockets with custard tarts. For heaven's sake, Edith is here, and that alone should guarantee his presence."

"Could he be avoiding me?"

"I suppose he must. Bobby Archer's missing, too. Another one who can ordinarily be counted upon to turn up the moment a bottle's uncorked. Perhaps he feared a confrontation with the missus. But she's not here, either. The twins are still getting over that vicious head cold, so she stayed home to nurse them. That's our three main suspects, assuming you still count Mrs. Archer as a suspect, missing in action. But in the plus column, Mrs. Edna Hibbet turned up. You remember her, don't you?"

"Mother of Ursula," Ben said. "The girl who died along with John Leighton. The one Penny may have changed places with."

"Yes. I rang up everyone in my book, issuing the invitation through cousins and in-laws, never expecting Mrs. Hibbet to even receive it, much less drive down from Barnstaple. But here she is if you'd care to introduce yourself. Perhaps I can lurk nearby and eavesdrop."

"Which one is she?"

Lady Juliet indicated a white-haired, round-faced woman in a wool dress, smiling amidst several other ladies. They were sipping cups of punch and chuckling. "How do you like her for our murderer?"

"Not at all. In fact, I *hope* she isn't the killer, or I'll be afraid to walk the street in broad daylight. Did you mention Penny?"

"Of course. She professed to be shocked at the news. Vowed to say a prayer for Penny's soul, Sunday next, and told me a long story about the Archbishop of Canterbury and how much she admires him. I think it's all terribly sincere. Either she's a sweet, smiling, spiritual little maniac, or a complete dead end. Now." Lady Juliet glanced about in what she probably thought was a surreptitious manner, but the feathered, beribboned hat made her as conspicuous as a Nazi in the Houses of Parliament. "You might as well know I'm hatching a scheme about Dinah's baby. The prospective mum is a friend of mine. Her husband may prove recalcitrant, so I've a bottle of twelve-year-old Glenfiddich up my sleeve. Not literally, of course. But when the time is right, it shall materialize, and he'll be accorded the lion's share. I intend on placing that little boy in Eunice's arms, and his, too, if the whiskey does its work. With any luck, Baby Mark will be legally adopted by the time these roses bloom again."

"And Dinah gives this scheme her blessing?" Ben had already glimpsed the girl ladling cups of punch near the vast white tent. Some would say she'd forfeited all right to the child she'd abandoned, but Ben remembered the maid's stricken face when he'd questioned her, and the delight Mrs. Locke and her twin victory rolls took in threatening her with farm labor. Besides, during his obstetric training, a stout old midwife had advised, "Never judge a laboring woman or new mum. You don't know. You can't know. And the moment you think you do, you stop being a healer and become just another man."

"Not sure how Dinah feels about it," Lady Juliet admitted. "She says she wants the boy adopted but only when pressed. The rest of the time, she looks wretched, trudging back and forth like a captive. If she truly wants to claim the child, I'll lend a hand, of course. But she knows it will be a grim life for them both."

They'd completed their walk to the summerhouse, a deserted stone shell amidst brown branches and fallen leaves. Thunder rumbled and the wind kicked up, but Lady Juliet appeared not to notice, even as her feathers whipped wildly about. "Well. Much as I'd like to remain in good company, my hostess duties await," she said. "Perhaps Freddy Sparks and Bobby Archer will turn up later. Or Mrs. Hibbet will produce a knife from her handbag and go for someone's throat."

Ben nodded. He had the sensation Lady Juliet was watching him more closely than usual, anticipating some specific reaction, but he couldn't think what. And he was in a hurry to get over to Rose and at least say hello before the skies opened up.

"Well, I suppose I should socialize," he said.

"Yes." The word held a residue of expectation.

"So. Perhaps we'll learn something," Ben said, starting toward Rose. When he glanced over his shoulder, Lady Juliet looked disappointed, prompting him to add, "We can compare notes around the bonfire."

"Of course." Putting on a not-quite-believable smile, she went her own way.

***

Storm clouds or no, the villagers of Birdswing, along with a smattering of guests from Barking and Plymouth, were enjoying themselves. Young ladies emerged from the white tent giggling over their fortunes; apparently, the war would be short and bloodless, at least on the British side, allowing each girl to wed the decorated hero of her dreams. Old men ate tarts, drank cider, and prognosticated about the coming winter, the Fuhrer's stratagems, and future episodes of *It's That Man Again.* Ladies swapped recipes, disciplined children, and discussed their husbands, brothers, and sons in uniform. They sounded so patriotic, and looked so resolved and fearless, Ben almost believed it. Only their eyes gave them away.

Mrs. Cobblepot sat at a card table sipping sherry and playing cards beside Mrs. Hibbet. Was that mere coincidence, Ben wondered, or had his housekeeper taken up amateur sleuthing as well?

ARP Warden Gaston roamed far and wide, sticking his nose into every conversation and threatening to issue citations. He even inspected the bonfire pit, going so far as to restack the cordwood while Old Robbie looked on in dismay. Blind Bill Hancock groaned and shook his head as his tall friend from the Sheared Sheep complained about his croft's cracked foundation.

"I'm telling you, it's the knotweed," the man moaned.

"I said enough with the herbicide. Use fire," Blind Bill told him.

"It knows!" The tall man sounded as agitated as when he'd pounded on the bar. "It hides underground when I come for it and creeps out when the coast is clear!"

On a small bandstand, a brass band with horns, trumpets, and cornets played "Pomp and Circumstance." Screaming and squealing, children darted around the straw effigy of Guy Fawkes, immersed in some savage version of tag.

Rose Jenkins sat watching her charges play. As Ben made for her, hardly needing his cane and eager for her to notice, a heavily accented woman's voice said, "Dr. Bones."

As he turned, Jane Daley darted to him. Hugging him around the waist, she hung there for a moment, then retreated to her mother, attaching herself in similar fashion. Mrs. Daley was dark-skinned, with thick black hair pulled into a bun, making quite a contrast to her little girl's *café au lait* skin and cloud of light brown hair.

"Don't be shy," Mrs. Daley told her daughter, whose expression was both wary and hopeful. "Tell the doctor."

"Thank you," Jane whispered, dark eyes wide. She was one of those children who seemed to absorb the whole world with her gaze, drinking it in, good and bad, wondrous and terrible. "For saving my life."

"My pleasure. How do you feel today?"

She fiddled with the hem of her skirt. Those eyes came up again, fixing on his cane. "Are you crippled?"

"Jane. We don't ask personal questions," Mrs. Daley reproved.

"Only a little," Ben told her and winked.

"Go and play," Mrs. Daley said.

Ben expected Jane to join the youngsters cavorting around Guy Fawkes, but instead she wandered toward the unlit bonfire pit, where a few old men had already claimed the best seats.

"I, too, must thank you," Mrs. Daley said. Tall and shapely, with wide hips and a narrow waist, her face was solemn, eyes heavy-lidded, the corners of her mouth turned down. Amongst all the wool and flannel, her pink summer frock looked out of place, and threadbare, too. She wore no coat. "Mr. Dwerryhouse told me what you did. If not for you, my daughter would have died."

"We don't know that."

"We do. Until my husband returns, Jane is all I have, and I love her more than anything." Despite Mrs. Daley's thick accent, her command of English was smooth and flawless. "I hoped you would come into the co-op so I could tell you. But perhaps that would be too much to ask, so I dared come here to tell you myself."

"Dared?" He glanced at Jane, skipping along the fire pit's edge. Two boys yelled taunts at her, but she ignored them. "I happen to know you were invited. The entire village was."

"Yes, of course," Mrs. Daley said. "That does not mean I was meant to come. It was bad enough before my husband was called to service. Now…." She shook her head. "It doesn't matter. I've wronged you, Dr. Bones. I saw her, but I said nothing. I thought, what do these English care? If I say what I saw, they'll say I'm accusing a white person, a native person, and then it will be worse.

Much, much worse. So I said nothing, and you saved Jane, and now I am ashamed."

"Saw who? My wife Penny?"

Mrs. Daley shook her head.

"Do you mean the lorry? Did you see it run us down?"

"No. It was half an hour before sundown. I'd locked up the co-op's doors and was putting out rubbish. I saw her. The woman on the roof of the Sheared Sheep. She wore a hat and coat, and she was watching me, I thought. I assumed she had something to do with the ARP warden; he's always looking for new ways to fine me. I started to call to out, to tell her I wasn't wasting food, not even spoiled food. But of course, I didn't. I was too afraid. I emptied the rubbish pails and went back inside. Not long after dark, I heard footsteps on the porch."

"That was me."

"Yes, I know that now. At the time, I wasn't sure. When I first came to Birdswing, people used to drive over from Barking just to get a look at me. The men called me exotic and seemed to think—you know. Now that I'm home alone, sometimes I fear...." Mrs. Daley shook her head again. "I went to the attic to have a look, to try and make sure you'd really gone. That's when I saw something glint in the alley beside the Sheared Sheep. And before I knew it, you and your wife were run down."

"I don't understand."

"The lorry must have been parked in that alley," Mrs. Daley said patiently. "I think the woman on top of the pub wasn't watching me. She was watching Stafford Road, waiting for you. She must have taken the fire exit down to the lorry with the intention of killing you."

With an effort, Ben unclenched his hands, which had balled into fists at his sides. "But why didn't you tell me? Or Gaston? Or *someone*?"

She flinched. "I told myself you were nothing to me. And think how it might have gone. Suppose I was obliged to pit my word against hers, this woman in the hat? A colored foreigner against an Englishwoman? Jane is already almost friendless. What would happen to her if no one believed me? She'd be a pariah. Speaking of that, we've stayed long enough. Jane! Come along!"

Groaning, the girl tore herself away from the fire pit and whatever solitary inner game she'd been playing.

"But—you don't have to go." Ben's anger faded as swiftly as it had come. "We haven't even burnt the Guy yet. With that mustache, he looks a lot like Hitler."

Smiling, Mrs. Daley took Jane's hand and turned away, leading her through the villagers in their shifting, commingling clusters. The wives chatting over sherry were momentarily silenced. The older women at the tables, including Mrs. Cobblepot and Mrs. Hibbet, paused in their whist game, following the Daleys' progress with their eyes. Lady Victoria glanced away from ARP Warden Gaston, who was lecturing her about something; even Old Robbie stared as Mrs. Daley and her daughter approached their rusted Aeroford. But it was a pretty little girl with long blonde hair who shrieked "Good riddance!" as the rattletrap car drove away.

***

By the time Ben reached Rose Jenkins, she had that blonde little girl by the arm, whispering something in the child's ear. Stamping her foot, the girl broke away, fleeing toward the knot of sherry-sipping mums. Rose started to follow, then saw Ben approaching. The flush across her cheeks and fire in her eyes made her lovelier than ever as she cast a furious glance toward the women.

"It's that mum who should be ashamed, not me." Rose told Ben. "So why do *I* feel like I'm going to cry?"

"Because you're human. Are you under contract to watch over the children even when school's out?"

"No. Just a habit. All along I hoped someone would come and rescue me."

"Good, because if I stay here another moment, I'm going to give this entire village a piece of my mind." Ben nodded toward the long glass structure attached to Belsham Manor's west wing. "Shall we tour the greenhouse?"

"I'd love to."

After the stiff November wind, the heat felt wonderful, flooding over Ben as he opened the door. Long rectangular panes of glass framed in verdigris-crusted copper formed the walls and ceiling, bathing potted trees and plants in sunlight, at least when the sun deigned to put in an appearance. In addition, a coal-burning furnace squatted beside the tool bench, radiating supplemental warmth.

"Feels sub-tropical in here." Ben eyed a row of dwarf trees. "Is that citrus?"

"Yes. Lady Victoria told me this was originally meant as an orangery. The first Linton had extravagant tastes; citrus at yuletide wasn't enough for him. But Lady Juliet prefers flower gardening. I've tried to ask her about it, to break the ice, but…." Rose shrugged. "She seems determined to dislike my company. Almost as much as she seems determined to monopolize yours."

"I owe her for that," Ben said. "She forced me to leave the Sheared Sheep and begin seeing patients again when I was sunk in gloom, feeling sorry for myself." Smiling, he added, "So much threatening and cajoling creates a bond."

"I'll say. Today was a first. I've never seen her dress so—so extravagantly. Those gloves… that hat…."

It felt disloyal to Ben to criticize a friend behind her back, particularly at her own party, in her own garden. So he said lightly, "I didn't escort you here to talk about Lady Juliet. I confess I scarcely know a violet from a daisy. What is that, do you reckon?" He pointed to a showy bloom with orange petals.

"No idea!" Giggling as if he'd made a joke, Rose slipped an arm through his. Curling a bit of red hair around one finger, she cast down her eyes, showing off the length of those sooty lashes. "I'm sure when it comes to botany, you're far more knowledgeable than me."

From so close, he enjoyed her scent—sandalwood—and could have stroked that hair if he dared. Yes, he was a widower; yes, it was too soon for this, unseemly, certain to make the birds sing in Birdswing. By the same token, those birds seemed well aware that his marriage to Penny had been unhappy. When he tried to remember his arguments against scandalizing his family and colleagues—all those thoughts he'd tortured himself with while traveling to Birdswing—none seemed to apply. *Divorce* maimed a man's character; this was courtship, and merely bad form. If Rose saw no harm in it, why should he?

She's so lovely I can hardly take my eyes off her….

Arm in arm, they toured rows of cascading ferns and pots of thriving herbs. Ben cast as many glances at Rose as he could without seeming like a pervert or, worse, a man unused to the company of beautiful women. Except for giggles, nods, and murmurs of assent, she seemed content to let him talk. And never had he labored so mightily to string together ten words. It wasn't that she left him tongue-tied. It was simply that nothing came to him. He could think of no concern he wanted Rose's opinion on, no topic they might dissect together. The flowers were fragrant, the clouds massing above were black, the hothouse was hot, and that was all. Thank heavens she was so pretty to look at.

When the thunder crashed, echoing off the glass walls around them, the rain came down in sheets, as it seems only to do at garden parties and long-awaited events.

"That's it, then," Ben groaned. "No bonfire. Think the guests will regroup inside the manor?"

"Only to dry off and say goodbye," Rose said. "The villagers took what happened to you and Penny to heart. No one wants to be driving during the blackout, and it's dark out there already. Looks like Lady Juliet's fête is a *fait accompli*."

Ben wasn't quite sure that last remark made sense, at least in the triumphantly negative sense Rose seemed to mean it, but the pretty woman was smiling up at him as if she'd said the wittiest thing in the world. Had she been saving that up all day, waiting for her chance?

Thunder crashed again, a triple rolling boom that rattled the panes overhead, and Rose threw herself in Ben's arms with a squeal, holding him tight. They fit together perfectly. The crown of her head brushed his chin, and his arms automatically slid around her, pulse quickening as he breathed in sandalwood.

Lightning flared behind the clouds, first turning them yellow-gray, then splitting the sky in two. The greenhouse's electric lights flickered out. As Rose lifted her face in the semi-darkness, lightning flashed again. A different sort of electricity coursed through Ben, shooting into dangerous territory down below. He kissed her, not gently, but open-mouthed, hungrily. She pulled him closer, and the kiss deepened as hands travelled and time stopped. Ben had no idea how long they were locked together. He was insensible of anything but Rose until not far away, a generator whined, the electric lights sputtered back to life overhead, and the greenhouse door banged open.

"*Bugger me blind!*" a familiar voice cried, slamming the door hard enough to rattle overhead panes all over again. "*Filthy… stupid… brainless… WOMAN!*"

Ben broke away from Rose as if under enemy fire. More than six feet of fury stood dripping beside a somewhat ironic row of Wellies and macs. For an awful moment Ben thought the torrent of abuse was aimed at Rose, but Lady Juliet saw nothing; her eyes were screwed up tight. As Ben stood frozen, holding Rose a little apart from his body, like a man caught in the act of shoving someone away, Lady Juliet flung her rings and bracelets to the greenhouse floor. Next came the opera gloves, yanked off and cast down. Then, as she began to cry in earnest, the now-sodden hat was pitched. It landed next to his feet, most of the feathers broken, though one was still jaunty if beaded with rain.

"Lady Juliet…."

It was as if he'd slapped her. One moment she was launching into big, ugly wails, the sort of weeping Ben would have signed over his bank account to escape, and the next she was gaping at him and Rose.

"Bugger me blind," Lady Juliet said tonelessly. "I thought I was alone."

"Very nearly. Just we two!" Rose replied brightly. Instead of releasing Ben and stepping away, she seized him in a fresh embrace, arms curling possessively around him.

Lady Juliet stared. "Good God. I've… interrupted something." She looked as horrified as if she'd surprised them in bed together.

"N-nonsense," Ben stammered like an imbecile.

"Not at all," Rose chirruped happily. "Ben squired me inside the greenhouse to admire your plants. When the storm began, the thunder frightened me. Lucky I had this big lug at hand to keep me safe. But oh, Lady Juliet, of course you're upset. The storm is so unlucky. So much hard work ruined."

For a moment Lady Juliet only continued to stare. Then she swiped at her eyes, gave a mighty sniff, and drew herself up to her full height. It was a tall order, exuding aristocratic haughtiness in a sodden cocktail dress and muddy Mary Janes, but she pulled it off. Ben felt the chill from across the room.

"Nonsense, Miss Jenkins. I was momentarily overtaken with concern for my mother, that's all. When the rain began, she went to herd the children inside and was soaked in the process. I was… frustrated that she might catch cold, being in such delicate health after endangering herself in a pursuit best left to younger, stronger women."

"My class!" Rose released Ben, her playful, delicately seductive manner evaporating. "Bloody hell—every last one will have that chest cold after this. Poor Lady Victoria. It's my fault. I should have been with them. Charlie's scared silly of lightning, and Young Frank is probably shivering under a hedgerow, too daft to get himself indoors." She hurried to a door near the potting shed. "Lady Juliet, does this connect to the manor? I need a head count right away."

Lady Juliet nodded.

"It was lovely." Rose gave Ben a peck on the cheek. "I'll be back when I have the class sorted." As Ben watched her exit, he realized she not only meant to count how many children had taken shelter, but to venture after the stragglers herself—into the very storm that had given her spasms of counterfeit terror.

"I don't understand women," he blurted.

"Of course not. You're an idiot." Turning over a large metal pail, Lady Juliet sat on it, shoulders slumped.

"They're so artificial." He was thinking of Penny, of how she'd snared him with a false persona.

"*They*?" Lady Juliet repeated.

He bit back a sigh. "You. I'm sorry. Though if you're a typical woman, you'll find a way to construe my simple remark as an insult."

"A *typical* woman?" Her apathy vanished, along with any lingering trace of tears. "*Typical?*" She surged to her feet, advancing on him and the ruined hat. "If I were a typical woman, I wouldn't have to construe simple remarks as insults, because they wouldn't be insults. If I were a typical woman, I'd be *Miss*"—she stomped on the hat—"*Rose*"—another stomp on the hat—"*Jenkins*!" Panting with rage and exertion, she glared at him as if expecting contradiction. Then she kicked the flattened hat across the floor, where it struck a watering can with a dull *squish*. "Lou Bottley told everyone that in women's clothes I look like a draft horse in a tiara. I heard the old goat say it. Before long they were all laughing, hiding smiles, looking away. You know a cruel joke is the truth when someone like Mrs. Cobblepot puts a hand over her mouth and turns away. I overheard her tell someone, 'The poor thing does her best.' That's the cruelest thing one woman can say about another."

"Mrs. Cobblepot thinks the world of you," Ben said truthfully. "And Lou Bottley has glaucoma. Blind in one eye and can't see out of the other. You know that."

"What did *you* think of my ensemble?" Lady Juliet held his gaze, unflinching.

For a moment he didn't answer. Then, caneless, he limped to the hat, picked it up with two fingers as if it were a dead rat, and dropped it in the rubbish bin. "My wife Penny's greatest virtue was style. She always knew which hat, which scarf, which bit of jewelry. Because she read *Women's Weekly* the way I read *The Lancet.* It wasn't instinct; it was passion and study."

"Ah. So I did look like a draft horse in a tiara. And next time I should let someone who's studied fashion, like Mother, dress me," Lady Juliet said bitterly. "If only I knew when and how to pretend. The trick of cooing one minute and reverting to rational human being the next."

Ben didn't have to ask who that dig was aimed at. "Well, I happen to prefer the rational human being."

"Of course. That's why you kissed her in the dark. Because you found Miss Jenkins's *rationality* irresistible."

Ben's face grew hot. He remembered Rose's laughter, sweet as the tinkling of bells, saw her smiling up at him, hanging on his inconsequential words as if they were pure gold. She'd assured him he knew more about botany than her, squealed over a thunderclap, even called him a "big lug," as if he were a strapping American cinema star like John Wayne. Ben had recognized the absurdity of Lady Juliet's hat and bejeweled opera gloves at once, yet been oblivious to such simple tricks. Would he have made a pass at Rose if she hadn't primed his ego first?

I was attracted to her on sight. Almost any man would be. But still….

"I had no right to say that." Lady Juliet's defiance was gone. She returned to her makeshift seat on the overturned pail, beaten. "I'm a beastly jealous thing and a freak of nature besides. Please forgive me."

"I won't. There's nothing to forgive." Crossing the distance between them, Ben offered her a hand up. "I know you did all this for me."

Her eyes widened, fingers closing over his. "You do?"

"Of course. All the murder suspects locked in the drawing room until someone confesses." He smiled as she rose. "It's not your fault they didn't come. Or that the bonfire was rained out."

"Oh." Disappointment again, radiating in that single word. "Yes, well… Ben. I'm not sure either of us is a very good detective."

"We'll improve. And perhaps I was wrong to pin all my suspicions on Freddy Sparks. I spoke to Mrs. Daley, and she told me—"

The door connecting the greenhouse to the manor banged open. Ben whirled, expecting Rose with some emergency, perhaps a missing child, but it was ARP Warden Gaston. He looked grimly self-important, as usual, but also unhappy, which was less usual.

"Dr. Bones. There's need of you in the village. A man hanged himself."

"Good heavens. Who?" Lady Juliet demanded.

"Who d'ya think? That poor toothless bastard, Freddy Sparks."

Chapter 12: Bonfire Night
5 November, 1939

Juliet tried to take it in, but for a moment she felt nothing but a wave of dreamlike disbelief. Like any village, Birdswing had its share of things the community as a whole pretended not to know about: husbands who drank too much, mothers who beat their children bloody, pensioners lonely enough to stick their heads in the oven and turn on the gas. The petty scandals and occasional tragedies were dealt with individually, each like a shocking aberration. And when the village came together for Christmas or Easter or Bonfire Night, everyone behaved as if Birdswing was the finest village in the world, the cleanest and kindest and best, simply the best. People still clucked over poor Lucy McGregor, dead in her bed, because that had been an accident. They could enjoy the frisson of gossip without being tainted by association. By comparison, the rumor that Penny Bones had been murdered was dicier; it implied a killer in their midst, and as a whole, Birdswing was far more comfortable scanning the horizon for German bombers.

And now this? A suicide? And not by a sickly old person hastening the end of life, but a young man few had tolerated and only a part-time whore had liked. What did this second violent death say about Birdswing?

"Mr. Gaston, are you quite sure?" she heard herself ask.

Usually he was the one who stood smiling benignly while other people lost their patience. This time he scowled. "I've not seen his body yet, Lady Juliet, surely you know that. But his cousin, Luke Hewett, drove here in the blinding rain to say he called at the boarding house and found Freddy with a belt around his neck. You can ask *him* if he's sure—"

"That's enough," Ben cut across him. "She's shocked, and I'm sure you are, too. But you're Acting Constable, meant to set an example. And I'm prepared to assist you in every way I can. Awaiting orders."

Deftly done, Juliet thought, watching Gaston's agitation dissolve as he was reminded of the responsibilities that meant almost as much to him as air warden. Ben had taken control, and she had no doubt he would maintain that control until every detail of Freddy's demise was settled, but he'd done so without shaming the older man.

"We'll need to go right away, rain or no rain. Otherwise we'll have no choice but to overnight at the manor and start out at dawn. And I wouldn't feel right about leaving the boy dead in Martha Kenner's boarding house," Gaston said. "She'll be beside herself until we get the body moved."

Ben nodded. "And for the sake of the inquest, the sooner I examine the remains, the better."

"Inquest? Did I not just say it? The lad hanged himself."

"Any death by violence merits an inquest. I'll not sign the death certificate until I examine Freddy Sparks myself," Ben said firmly. "Just let me find Mrs. Cobblepot and tell her I'll be leaving without her."

"And I'll need half a tick to change out of these wet clothes," Juliet said.

Gaston looked shocked. "Lady Juliet. You don't know what you're saying. Bringing out the dead is no job for a woman."

"Is that so?" Her laugh was genuine. "Then who shall do the laying out? You?"

He didn't answer.

"When my father died," Lady Juliet went on, "Mother was inconsolable. So it was left to me to close his eyes, wash him, dress him in his finest, and comb his hair. Yes, the undertaker came round to fit him for the coffin, and arranged for the gravedigger and the pall bearers, but I did all the rest. Should I have proved unable, I suppose I might have hired the undertaker's wife to do it, since we're all so very modern these days. But either way, laying out has been women's work since the dawn of time. Besides," Lady Juliet said more gently, "Freddy Sparks's mum is dead, and we can't expect poor Edith to act as his wife. Nor should we expect such ministrations of Mrs. Kenner. I'm ready, willing, and able to help."

As Gaston reluctantly agreed, she resisted the impulse to look at Ben. He would already perceive her ulterior motive, a desire to know if Freddy's drastic act had been prompted by guilt. However clumsy and amateurish their joint investigation of Penny's murder, it was still an investigation, and Juliet intended to see it through to the end.

The small number of villagers who owned cars had fled. Those not fast enough to catch a ride now milled about Belsham Manor's main wing, lamenting about the ruined fête while tracking mud on the carpets and dripping all over the furniture. Lady Victoria, who'd already changed into a simple cotton dress, her damp hair covered by a turban, urged everyone to make themselves comfortable.

Watching her mother radiate kindness and solicitude made Juliet feel about as gracious as a head of cabbage and half as sweet. She'd over-dramatized Lady Victoria's role in herding the children for no reason but to wipe the smile off Rose Jenkins' face. Now she saw Rose and Lady Victoria working together, Lady Victoria handing out towels and calling for hot tea, Rose encouraging the tearful children to warm themselves before the hearth's crackling fire.

Why can't I be like Mother and Miss Jenkins? Or, failing that, why can't I give up and be like myself? Today I wanted to be Penny Eubanks, to make Ben see me in a different light. All I did was prove myself an utter fool.

All the way upstairs, Juliet berated herself. For not canceling due to threat of rain; for choosing that hat; for blundering into the greenhouse and revealing how ridiculous she felt to the two people she'd never wanted to know. For allowing Lou Bottley's "draft horse in a tiara" remark to cut her to the bone. Most of all, for forgetting her vow to never again fall for a beautiful man. Because she'd fallen for Ben, as hard or harder than she'd fallen for Ethan Bolivar. And in a tour de force of stupidity and bad luck, she'd intruded on what might have been Ben and Rose's first kiss.

"Let me just clippity-clop over to the wardrobe and choose a new bridle," Juliet muttered, entering her bedroom. At least the maids were too busy changing into dry uniforms and mopping up after dripping guests to follow her up. A generation before, Juliet would have been saddled with a lady's maid, but after the Great War, such vestigial Victorian positions had finally shriveled up and dropped off. It was just as well. Juliet hated primping, found cosmetics bewildering, and saw no reason to subject herself to a girdle. She wasn't fat, just big: broad shoulders, wide hips, thighs and calves as thick and firm as decent logs.

As she stripped, she looked in the oak-framed cheval mirror, just to see what her hair was doing. It was plastered to her skull, the top limp, the ends frizzy. Another reason she desired no lady's maid: so she wouldn't have to endlessly behold herself in a mirror as an employee fought to make her presentable. She did possess the bare minimum of femininity: small firm breasts and enough of a waist to keep from being an utter rectangle. Her still-lawfully-wedded husband, Ethan, had called her brown eyes lively, and her smile beautiful. But Ethan, in the words of the unfailingly sweet Lady Victoria, was a lying son of a bitch.

Leaving her wet clothes in a heap near the fireplace, Juliet selected a fresh white brassiere and knickers. Then a plaid shirt, so large it flapped, and men's trousers she'd purchased by mail order, as only those cut for males ever fit. Wool socks, well-worn brogues, and a dark green mac with flannel lining. Braving the mirror again, she ran a tortoiseshell comb through her hair—three vicious strokes, hard enough to make her wince. There. Now she looked as bad as she usually did, or possibly worse. But a draft horse in its usual harness aroused no special contempt.

On her way out, she looked back over her shoulder at the bedroom she'd once shared with her husband. As a new bride, she'd eliminated every trace of childhood: slingshot, ant farm, beloved storybooks. As a disillusioned wife, she'd purged again: wedding portrait, satin and lace coverlet, once-beloved husband. Now every corner was filled with novels, histories, maps of the world, garden plans, dried flowers, an attar made from her own damask roses. Yet it still felt dominated by the colossal Linton heirloom bed, where she'd slept alone for what felt like ten thousand nights.

Ten thousand and one, on my return, she thought, darting back for a small hand-labeled bottle of attar. *But at least I'll sleep knowing the killer in our midst is no longer at large, and Ben's new life can truly begin.*

***

When Juliet returned to the front parlor, far fewer villagers were in evidence. Rain still beat against the windows, but most guests had nevertheless chosen to say goodbye while an hour or two of weak daylight remained. Not that Lady Victoria would hear of anyone attempting Old Crow Road after sunset without headlamps; she already had maids scurrying up and down the back stairs, opening guest rooms. The mix of those who'd settled themselves with a cup of hot tea or a plateful of nibbles was eclectic. It included Mr. Dwerryhouse, the chemist; Abel, the tall smallholder locked in an endless war with Japanese knotweed; Mrs. Sutton, Birdswing's short-sighted driver; and part-timer Edith, running curious fingers over every embroidered pillow and silk tassel, blissfully unaware of her best customer's demise. Conversation over tomorrow's breakfast table, which might include up to thirty people, was surely not to be missed.

In a far corner, ARP Warden Gaston had put Freddy's cousin, Luke Hewett, still red-eyed and stricken, in an armchair with a glass of whiskey, hovering by his side to ensure he didn't blurt out the ugly news. Near the grand piano, Ben stood beside Lady Victoria, Mrs. Cobblepot, and Rose.

"Lady Juliet, you've changed clothes," Rose said by way of greeting. "You look so—so—"

"Enchanting? Yes, I quite agree," Juliet said lightly, pressing the brown vial in Rose's hand. "For you. A peace offering for my earlier intrusion. And a, well, down payment on amends for all my other rudenesses over the years. Give it a sniff."

Looking the tiniest bit suspicious, Rose uncorked the little bottle. Instantly the heavy natural perfume wafted out.

"You didn't have to—I never—thank you," Rose said, smiling. "It's wonderful. Because of my name, I've always avoided rose fragrances, but this is too good to resist. I've never smelled it on you. Why not?"

Because, brief bouts of madness aside, I know the truth about myself.

"I plan to distill something different for myself. *Eau de* stick insect," Juliet said and was rewarded with a chuckle from Ben. So he remembered the day they'd met—him out of practice as far as civil conversation, her too guarded to accept a polite remark. Though they'd known one another only a short time, he was already a true friend. *And friendship should be enough, shouldn't it?*

"Can't reckon why you lot are standing about grinning," ARP Warden Gaston complained as he came upon them. "It's disrespectful to Luke, not to mention the dead. Dr. Bones, I thought you were impatient to set out."

"So I am," Ben said. He said goodbye to Lady Victoria and Rose—no kiss, even on the cheek, Juliet noted with some relief, but surely it was too soon for such public displays. Then they were on their way, Rose remaining behind and Gaston's sister, Mrs. Cobblepot, insisting on accompanying them.

"I can't leave you alone to manage what's sure to be a grim circumstance," the housekeeper told Juliet, polishing her round spectacles before settling them on her equally round, determined face.

"That's very kind of you, but even alone, this 'poor thing' will do her best." Juliet's exaggerated emphasis was about as subtle as a falling anvil, yet the reference to Mrs. Cobblepot's earlier remark had no effect.

Naturally. She has no guilty conscience because she meant no harm.

Juliet bit back a sigh. It seemed she would never learn, not even that she never learned. Fortunately for her, Freddy Sparks, whether a murderer or just a miserable unfortunate, had presented the perfect opportunity for her to focus on someone else for a change.

***

The trip back to the village went slowly, hampered first by the long line of vehicles trundling along Old Crow Road, then by more rain as they came upon the high street. Ben drove, with Juliet beside him and Gaston and Mrs. Cobblepot following in Gaston's car. She vacillated between wanting to talk, to chatter about anything other than what awaited them, and growing uneasiness as the windshield wipers slapped down and whined up, slapped down, whined up. What had driven Freddy to top himself on a Sunday afternoon? The brooding storm clouds? The prospect of long winter nights marooned by snow and the blackout, alone with his guilt? The obligation to present himself at Belsham Manor and face the man he'd nearly killed?

"Are you certain about this?" Ben asked as he parked by the curb at Martha Kenner's boarding house. "If you faint or fall to pieces, it will only be more work for Gaston and me."

"If I faint or fall to pieces, pinch yourself, because you're dreaming. Of all the ludicrous accusations!" Energized by a surge of righteous indignation, Juliet let herself out of the car, opened her umbrella with a great *whoosh*, and strode up the brick walk, tossing over her shoulder, "When have you ever seen me fall to pieces?"

"About an hour ago," Ben said, limping doggedly behind her as Gaston's car came into sight. "You seemed on the brink of hysteria over a hat."

"That was different. That was fashion, and within fashion lurks the seeds of madness." Reaching the shelter of the two-story house's front porch, Juliet rapped smartly on the door. "This is death. Nothing I haven't dealt with before."

Martha Kenner was the sort of widow one pictured when the phrase "widows and orphans" came up. Unsmiling, white-haired, and sagging all over—pouches beneath her eyes, wattle beneath her chin, round shoulders, drooping breasts. Such was her customary appearance: hands red and cracked, apron gray from want of bleach, stockings falling down. Today she looked even worse, eyes red-rimmed and nose swollen, a gray handkerchief clutched in one hand.

"Mr. Hewett said he'd bring the doctor," she told Juliet accusingly. Even on her best day, Mrs. Kenner's querulous inflection made every statement into a reproach. "Why did you come?"

"I'm here to do the laying out. Dr. Bones is right behind me." Turning to introduce him, Juliet felt a touch guilty for not moving slowly enough to shelter him under her brolly. His hat and upturned coat collar had afforded some protection, but his face glistened with raindrops, trousers wet below the knee.

"Benjamin Bones," he said before she could speak, taking Mrs. Kenner's hand in both of his. They were wet, too, but the old widow seemed too captivated by the handsome young man to notice. "I'm deeply sorry for what transpired under your roof. May I come inside and attend Mr. Sparks?"

"Please," Mrs. Kenner croaked, bursting into fresh tears as she stepped aside to allow them in. Dabbing at her eyes, she managed to tell her story, brief as it was, pausing only to usher Gaston and Mrs. Cobblepot inside as well.

"Begging your pardon about the bonfire, Lady Juliet, but I didn't mean to go. Naught to wear and no petrol in the car besides," Mrs. Kenner explained. "I spent half the morning making bread and pies, the other half raking the back garden. By noon Freddy was still abed, but he came in very late last night, pounding up the stairs like a herd of elephants, so I didn't fret. Thought he was sleeping it off." A sniff and a dab. "I'd just fetched a cuppa and settled by the wireless for *Bandwagon* when Mr. Hewett turned up. I called for Freddy, but he didn't answer. So I took Mr. Hewett up, and—and—" Renewed sobbing.

ARP Warden Gaston cleared his throat, shifting uneasily from foot to foot. He seemed about to pontificate when Ben cut across him.

"That's all we require for now, Mrs. Kenner. Thank you." To Mrs. Cobblepot, he asked, "Would you be willing to put the kettle on for all of us?"

"Of course. Come, Martha." As Mrs. Cobblepot steered the widow toward the kitchen, she glanced back at Juliet, wordlessly inviting her to join in, but Juliet shook her head. Despite her brave words about dealing with death, in truth, she felt a touch uneasy. The only remedy was to march upstairs alongside the men.

Unpleasant odors wafted across the landing like ghosts. Stale vomit, urine, feces. Was there a tinge of something vaguely medicinal, like surgical spirit or strong liquor? Juliet couldn't be sure. Seeing Gaston grimace, she pretended not to smell a thing. Let someone else feel like the weakling for a change.

The door was open, and Freddy Sparks knelt on the floor, trousers soiled, thin vomit down his shirtfront. In death he leaned forward, arms limp at his sides, supported by the leather belt coiled around his neck and fastened to the bedstead. How a wretched soul must hate his life, Juliet thought, to choose such an exit. His face was pale, eyes open and frosted white. What were his final thoughts as he wrapped the belt around his throat, then compressed his windpipe by leaning, leaning, leaning until darkness took him?

"I wouldn't have expected emesis," Ben said, awkwardly leaning closer to the corpse.

"Mrs. Kenner said he was drunk. I suppose sickness comes with the territory." Without bothering to ask, Juliet helped Ben sink with obvious discomfort into a kneeling position.

"That's better. Now I can have a proper look," he said. "And for what it's worth, Mrs. Kenner didn't say he was drunk, she said he came in late and made a deal of noise. Also, that she presumed he was sleeping it off."

"What else?" Gaston sounded annoyed, as if Ben was talking nonsense to obscure some self-evident truth. "The man was down the pub every time he could rub two pennies together."

"Did he often make himself sick with drink?"

"Must've."

"That you witnessed?" Ben asked more sharply. "Occasions you saw him retching in a gutter, et cetera?"

Gaston's attention had gone to a bit of folded paper on the nightstand. "Never mind speculation, doctor. Speculation never helped anyone. Read this and case closed, I reckon."

As Gaston opened the note, Juliet saw a few lines of script, no date, no signature. He read aloud, "'I cannot go on. On 1 September, I drank too much and ran down Penny Eubanks and her husband. In the dark I mistook her for Edith, with whom I'd quarreled. When I saw the truth, I ran away. Soon after, I was discharged from my work, but I'd cleaned the lorry's grille and the owner never guessed. Yet the guilt and the sound of that tire crunching over Penny's skull....'" Gaston stopped and shot a look at Ben, whose face was stone. "Er... 'kept me awake and drove me to send the doctor an apology. But of course he couldn't understand. Let me die for my crime and find peace in the next world.'"

Juliet looked down at Freddy, pathetic in life, pitiable in death. So it had all been a drunken mistake, a momentary rage at Edith, the human contact he purchased once or twice a month?

"Who on earth wrote that?" Mrs. Cobblepot asked from the doorway.

ARP Gaston groaned at his sister. "The dead man himself, you daft old cow. When you find a suicide note beside a fellow who has committed suicide, nine times out of ten, the fellow who committed suicide wrote the note!"

"Then this must be the tenth occasion, you daft old *goat*," Mrs. Cobblepot snapped. "I taught Freddy Sparks, remember? Knew him from primary school on.

He had a trusting nature but a weak head for sums. And he was hopeless at writing."

"You don't think a grown man can have finer penmanship than a wee lad?" Gaston waved the note under his sister's nose.

She snatched it away. "I didn't say he was hopeless at penmanship. I said he couldn't write. He muddled his words and wrote his letters backward. I taught him to read simple stories and words with just a few syllables, but this?" She shook her head. "'*With whom I'd quarreled?*' Bloody hell, if you'd offered him a case of single malt whiskey, he couldn't have coughed up that phrase, much less written it down."

Juliet stared at Mrs. Cobblepot, entranced. Not only had she uttered the words "bloody hell," she'd used them to show her puffed-up brother how ridiculous he was. And just as a low rumbling arose from his diaphragm, threatening to issue from his mouth as a comprehensive tirade, Ben cut across him for the second time.

"I'm glad to hear you say that, Mrs. Cobblepot. I don't think Freddy died by asphyxiation."

"Oh, he didn't, did he?" ARP Warden Gaston bellowed. "What's that around his neck, an Olympic medal? Did he collapse after the long jump?"

"Mr. Gaston," Ben said coolly. "If, with Lady Juliet's help, I stood up, took back my cane, and beat you to death, would it be possible for me to transfer this belt to your neck and position you as if you'd committed suicide?"

What felt like a full minute of ringing silence followed. Juliet exerted a superhuman effort not to laugh or emit even the tiniest squeak, and she sensed Mrs. Cobblepot doing the same.

"Sarcasm." Gaston spoke in a tone usually reserved for estimating tumor size. "There's no call for sarcasm. Sarcasm—"

"Never did anyone any good. Yes, you're probably right," Ben finished for him. "Look. Clarence. Mrs. Cobblepot's information about Freddy is a start, but I still need to examine the body. It would help me a great deal if you took notes. Careful, detailed notes."

Gaston said nothing.

"In that notebook?" Ben's voice crept up an octave. When he wore that half-smile, that hopeful look in his big blue eyes, Juliet could have denied him nothing.

"The notebook labeled 'Official Business,'" she put in helpfully. "I can scarcely imagine business more official than this."

"Oh, aye." With the greatest dignity, Gaston removed the book from his coat, uncapped a pen, licked the tip, and poised the implement over a blank page. "Proceed when ready."

"Lady Juliet, I'd like you to steady the body as I remove the belt. Once I have it off, I need you and Mr. Gaston to transfer Freddy onto the bed."

"Concentrate on your notes, Clarence. I'll help Lady Juliet lift him," Mrs. Cobblepot said, positioning herself on one side of the corpse.

"He's not a big man, but he'll be heavy," Ben warned, gently unfastening the belt. "Dead weight is always—"He broke off as Juliet and Mrs. Cobblepot neatly transferred Freddy onto the bed, the older woman handling her end as easily as Juliet had hers.

"You should see me turn a mattress or wrestle a wet blanket onto a clothesline," Mrs. Cobblepot told Ben. Then she gazed back at Freddy, studying his bent body, stiff with partial rigor, and open, milky eyes. "Poor child spent his whole life trying to get people to pay attention. Now he has what he wanted at long last."

After Juliet and Mrs. Cobblepot undressed Freddy, Ben made his examination, dictating to Gaston and frequently pausing to repeat or spell a medical term. His summation emphasized points Juliet doubted she would have noticed, though once they were pointed out, she had no idea how she'd missed them.

"There are no ligature marks on the neck, nor any abrasions. Subject's loss of body fluids suggests gastrointestinal spasms and violent convulsions. Although subconjunctival hemorrhages could indicate either repeated emesis or asphyxiation, I note there is no froth upon the lips or blood around the nostrils. Lack of such signs, as well as the subject's unmarked neck and intact hyoid bone, cause me to suspect poisoning. Subject will be conveyed to my office for post-mortem. Should I determine further evidence of foul play, I will request confirmation from the pathologist at St. Barnabas hospital."

"Path-*all*...." Gaston prompted.

Ben spelled the term aloud, as he had "hemorrhages" and "asphyxiation." Juliet noted that if he felt any temptation to lord it over the ARP Warden, indicating by look or tone that learned men managed such words with ease, he resisted. Of course, out-spelling Clarence Gaston was no major feat of intellectual prowess. But she didn't think that crossed Ben's mind. He just wasn't the sort who seized opportunities to make others feel inadequate.

Mrs. Kenner fetched up hot water and towels, carrying Freddy's soiled clothes down to the rubbish bin as Juliet and Mrs. Cobblepot bathed the body. It was unpleasant work, less because of those all-too-human sights and smells and more because Freddy was like a ruined church, desecrated and abandoned. Its shape was correct, its once emotionally potent features still recognizable yet degraded beyond all joy and purpose. And Juliet's earlier observation that laying out was women's work still proved true; Ben and Gaston drifted away to review Ben's notes, then prepare a place in Ben's car for Freddy, as if the dead man needed special accommodations in the backseat. Only females, it seemed, had the stomach to wash and dry the corpse, then shroud him in a white cotton bed sheet.

"The thing is, the note made sense," Juliet told Ben as he settled himself behind the wheel. The rain had tapered off, but twilight was upon them, and they needed to get to Fenton House before full dark. "I've seen Freddy get drunk and quarrel with Edith, bawl at her, beg her to marry him. I can't quite imagine him running her down, but heaven knows what a man will do when insensible from drink. For him to mistakenly kill Penny, send you that clumsy note, then top himself out of guilt—it all makes perfect sense. May I examine that handwriting again?"

"Gaston has it." Ben started the engine. "I plan to start on the post-mortem right away. You can read it over again while I go to work. Of course, you'll have all night."

"All night?"

"You'll be my guest at Fenton House. Unless you plan on walking back to Belsham Manor in the black of night."

"Oh. Well. We've a little time left, and I know Old Crow Road better than my own face in the mirror," Juliet said, giving the red and purple sky a nervous glance. "If you'll permit me to borrow this car, I solemnly promise to escort myself safely to—"

"Juliet." Ben's tone was firm. "I won't hear of it. You're my guest till morning."

Attacked by an absurd desire to ask him what Rose would think of that, Juliet bit her tongue till the impulse passed. And luckily it passed swiftly, because they were soon bouncing over fresh ruts, then swerving around potholes, and she talked too much to make do with half a tongue. Why was her heart fluttering in her chest? Ben was merely being decent, not betokening her of his chivalrous love. Besides, her heart wasn't *fluttering*, nothing about her fluttered. Clippity-clopping like the aforementioned horse, more like.

"I agree with you, by the way," Ben said after a moment. "The note made sense, so there's probably some truth to it. But the best lies always contain a kernel of fact. And whoever wrote it must have been desperate to keep the whole truth buried, or he wouldn't have dared enter Mrs. Kenner's in the middle of the night, much less loiter about after Freddy died to make it look like a hanging."

"She," Juliet said.

"What?"

"That handwriting. It was lovely. Perfect. I'd have to look again to be certain, but I believe the note was written by a woman. For decency's sake, I'd like to believe Freddy never brought Edith into Mrs. Kenner's house but perhaps he did. Do you think Edith might have done it? Convinced Freddy to run you down, then killed him when he threatened to tell? Did she have any connection to Pen—"

That last was lost in an explosion so loud, Juliet shrank reflexively, closing her eyes and covering her ears. From behind her eyelids, she saw bursts of illumination, blooming like white dahlias trailing fiery stems. Then hail and rain was pounding down—except the hail was chunks of brick and bits of metal, not ice, and the rain was powder and ash, not water.

"God in heaven!" Juliet cried, throwing open her door in blind panic. She never knew what she meant to do—hurl herself into the thick of it, apparently—but Ben shouted her name and pulled her close. Heart thudding in her throat, in her temples, everywhere but her chest, Juliet clung to him, whimpering as a second, smaller explosion rocked the high street. This time she was cognizant enough to feel the car shudder and heard a *crash* as the windshield shattered.

"It's all right," Ben said, keeping her pressed against him. His voice was calm, but like her, he was trembling all over. "Stay still. Stay still."

Brakes squealed behind them. Too frightened to move and braced for another explosion, for what could only be more German bombs raining down on their heads, Juliet heard a car door open.

Then Gaston, his voice oddly magnified: "Stay in your homes! The zone of greatest safety is nearest the ground! This is your ARP Warden speaking." He must have been using a megaphone. Only Gaston would have had the forethought to stash one in his car, Juliet thought. Yet under the circumstances, such extremes of preparedness no longer seemed so silly. "I repeat, shelter in your homes! Do not attempt to view the skies. Curiosity about the enemy can be deadly!"

"This is real. This war is *real*," Juliet babbled, pulling free of Ben and gaping at the sky over Birdswing, where wisps of smoke still hung in the shape of dahlias.

"Something's real. I'm not sure what. Isn't the constabulary just over there?"

"What?" Braced for another explosion, Juliet could hardly decipher his words, much less reply. Yet when he repeated himself, voice still remarkably composed, she forced herself to focus, first on the words, then on the darkened high street. "You're right. The smoke is rising from the roof. It must have been hit."

"Or the explosion came from inside. Stay here." Ben opened his door.

"No—you can't—" Suddenly she was very aware of the corpse in the backseat, his frosted eyes open beneath a thin cotton sheet.

"I don't hear engines overhead. Either one plane dropped one bomb on a village in the middle of nowhere—sorry—or this is something else." He lurched forward, one hand on the car's bonnet for support.

"Your cane!" Turning to fumble behind the driver's seat, Juliet came face to face with a man-shaped figure swathed in white. For one surreal moment she thought the bombing had claimed a victim, that his shade hung in the smoky air like a flashbulb's afterimage.

And in her moment of terror, of unreasoning belief in the spirit world, a woman's voice seemed to whisper in her ear, "The twins. It's Bonfire Night, after all."

All of Juliet's panic dissolved. The shrouded figure was only Freddy Sparks, his earthly remains awaiting post-mortem. The Germans might bomb her village someday, but tonight the skies were silent and increasingly clear, wind pushing aside clouds to reveal the stars. The constabulary was indeed the only structure affected, and those bright streaks in the sky now reminded her of signal flares.

"This was a prank," she announced, hurrying to Ben's side and pressing the cane in his hand.

"Back in your car until I sound the all clear," Gaston bellowed at them through the megaphone. Juliet and Ben ignored him.

So did Mrs. Cobblepot, who'd emerged from Gaston's vehicle to ask, "Did the constabulary explode?"

"Of course, you daft woman. We've been hit! Are you aiming to get blown to bits like our Paul and Tommy?"

"Gaston! What's happening?" Mr. Laviolette called from his restaurant, where he also resided. A glowing yellow rectangle fell out into the street.

"*DOUSE THAT LIGHT*!"

"The quicker we find Mrs. Archer's boys and force a confession, the better," Juliet told Ben. She didn't question anything, including her sudden calm and soft voice that had not really been a voice, somehow. There were moments of total surety in life; this was one. "Two years ago, Caleb and Micah tried to burn their own Guy Fawkes at the stake. They set fire to an old man's back garden and torched his weeping willow. I remember where their mum found them." She set off at a good clip, still ignoring Gaston's exhortations through the megaphone, strangely invigorated by the tang of what might be gunpowder in the air. Only when she realized Ben was struggling to keep up did she modify her pace.

"I do believe this is what got me in trouble in the first place," he muttered, limping more swiftly than she'd ever seen. "Blundering through the dark in the middle of the road."

"I'm practically inured to the blackout now. And painting the curbs white was a stroke of genius—we should have done it ages ago." Before long, she felt the paving beneath her feet give away to brittle winter grass, as she'd known it must. Around one of the churchyard's trees, a white band had been painted, the bench beneath it also a soft, spectral white.

Are you enjoying all these changes, Lucy? Juliet wondered. *Do you see everything that transpires in Birdswing now, or just bits and pieces?*

She received no answer as St. Mark's loomed before them, nor had she expected one. The moment of connection had been fleeting and might never be repeated.

"Won't the church be locked after hours?" Ben asked.

Juliet laughed. "This isn't London. Besides, in wartime, we have perhaps more cause to pray than previously." Fingers curling around a cold brass door handle, she pushed her way into the vestibule. Unsurprisingly, every last votive candle was lit, small flames dancing inside wells of amber glass. If Mrs. Archer's wayward twin sons had a signature, it was fire.

Two rows of pews stretched toward the old-fashioned wooden pulpit situated on a marble dais, and the altar, dressed in green. Before that altar, Caleb and Micah Archer knelt in conspicuous prayer. Both looked rather worse for wear, shirttails out, hats and coats missing, hair and clothing streaked with soot. Neither turned as Ben closed the door firmly behind him, but Caleb, usually the leader in mischief, lifted his voice so the words practically rang off the rafters.

"… and know the truth of our repentance, and punish us in your own good time…."

"… and protect us from unbelievers," Micah threw in, as if that might help.

"Boys! Your hope for *deus ex machina* is in vain," Juliet called, briskly closing the distance between them.

"Do you know what our Lord said about the Pharisees, praying aloud on street corners?"

"No, Lady Juliet." Caleb leapt up and spun around, presenting wide eyes and singed eyebrows while behind him, Micah sanctimoniously thanked God in advance for services rendered. "But I'll bet he forgave them."

"Forgiveness is a cornerstone of the faith," Juliet agreed. "Alas, confession and contrition come first." Seizing Caleb's ear, she twisted it till he screamed and gave him a swat on the rear. When the boy tried to run, Ben tackled him, bringing him to the tiled floor even as Juliet collared Micah, giving the identical backside an identical blow. "So much for you two being sick. Well enough to slip out, obviously. What in heaven's name were you doing? And be honest, there's a witness. We know it was a Bonfire Night prank."

"We just wanted to set off a flare." Caleb's voice sounded slightly muffled, perhaps because Ben's good knee was hard against the boy's chest, pinning him down. He received rougher treatment from his schoolmates on the cricket pitch every week, yet nevertheless looked on the brink of tears—the gambit of final resort. "We heard where old Gassy kept 'em, and jimmying the lock was easy."

"Proves he needs a better one. He should thank us." Micah tried to pull his hand away. "Let me go, Lady Juliet. Promise not to run."

"I don't believe you," she replied, fighting hard not to smile at the nickname "Old Gassy" as the door banged open.

Speak of the devil, even in church.

"What possessed you to light a flare indoors?" Ben asked the twins as Gaston and Mrs. Cobblepot hurried down the aisle.

"We've done it before," Caleb said contemptuously. "Just a test to make sure they weren't all gone damp or stale before we took 'em out to Pate's field. But Old Gassy must have stored something in there with a bit of a kick—"

"Munitions," Ben cut across him. "A stockpile of bullets and shells."

"What?" Micah looked stunned.

"How's that?" Caleb asked.

Ben nodded silently as the boys exchanged glances.

"*Cor,*" they said in unison.

"I despair of you both," Juliet exclaimed. "ARP Warden Gaston, I fear this is a job for Acting Constable Gaston. Here we have the two miscreants awaiting punishment. They broke into your cache and blew it sky-high."

To say Gaston responded in poor humor would have taken British understatement to extremes even Lady Juliet did not condone. White-faced, he heard the boys' confessions without a word, then left them briefly in Juliet, Ben, and Mrs. Cobblepot's custody. When he returned, soot-stained and smelling of gunpowder, a few minutes later, it was with handcuffs. And leg irons. Only a whispered conference with his sister spared the twins that particular indignity, but another awaited. Transporting them across the village to Mrs. Archer's place was too dangerous during the blackout. There was nothing for it but putting them up overnight in what amounted to jail: Gaston's bungalow.

"It could be worse, boys," Juliet told them as they were frogmarched out of St. Mark's for a short jaunt in Gaston's car. "Dr. Bones has a corpse in the back of his vehicle. A possible murder victim awaiting a post-mortem. Since you two enjoy courting death, we almost decided to let you ride with him."

The handcuffed twins exchanged glances. "Cor," they mouthed to one another, and Juliet swallowed a sigh. It was true; she never learned.

"If it's all right by you, doctor, I'll return to Fenton House tomorrow morning," Mrs. Cobblepot said, seating herself in a pew. "Clarence will be back in a moment, and I thought I'd sit with him until he's quite composed. Then I'll help him sound the all clear and reassure everyone within earshot. I'm sure they're frightened to death."

"We can help, too," Ben said, and despite Juliet's mounting exhaustion after so much excitement—had the disastrous fête really ended only hours ago?—she felt herself nodding.

"You've enough on your plate with poor Freddy," Mrs. Cobblepot said. "I'll see to Clarence. It's just that he—"

She fell silent as ARP Warden Gaston reentered the church. His face was a mask. Eyes focused directly in front of him, he looked at neither Juliet nor Ben, making for his sister and joining her on the pew. A few seconds passed as he sat, back stiff, staring at the altar. Then he slipped to his knees, put his face in his hands, and began to cry.

Ben looked mortified. "What…?"

Putting a finger over her lips, Juliet nodded toward the door. Only when they were out in the cold, smoky November air did she answer.

"He lost both his sons, Paul and Tommy, during the Great War. When he was called up and his wife took ill, they were sent to live with an aunt. Then the zeppelins bombed London...." In the deep darkness, Juliet couldn't see Ben's face clearly, but she heard his intake of breath, and realized he hadn't known. "ARP warden is a big job and mostly thankless. Why do you think he tries so hard to get it right?"

Chapter 13: Post-Mortem
5 November, 1939

Given his preference, Ben would have sent Lady Juliet off with Mrs. Cobblepot for a spot of tea while he threw Freddy's body over one shoulder, single-handedly carrying him into the office. But he couldn't do that with a cane and stiff left leg. Truth be told, he never could have done it, except in his wildest dreams. Besides, Mrs. Cobblepot was going door to door with her brother, and as a free agent, Lady Juliet was typically headstrong. She laughed at the idea of making up her own guest room while Ben devised a makeshift stretcher to drag the corpse inside.

"Don't stand there scowling, the solution is simple. I'll help you carry him in," she announced. "I'll take the head, you take the feet."

Once they had Freddy positioned on the table, Ben removed the sheet and switched on the overhead light. On a sheet of exam paper, blank except for Ben's name, address, and a space for the date, he sketched the body in prone position. After noting a birth mark and a smallpox vaccination scar, he opened Freddy's mouth and made a separate sketch of the missing teeth. Throughout this process, he waited for Lady Juliet to absent herself. Instead, she wandered from corner to corner, peering at bits of medical equipment in a way that grated on his nerves.

"Do you smell that?" she asked suddenly as he struggled to reposition Freddy. "Oh, terribly sorry, let me help." With her assistance, the corpse was rendered face-down, and she sniffed the air. "There it is again."

"I detect more than one odor," Ben agreed, sketching another simplified human outline labeled, "Supine."

"Not Freddy. I hardly notice him now. It's this room." Closing her eyes, Lady Juliet drew in a deep breath and smiled. "Books. Stacks and stacks of old books Lucy collected. They're all in the Birdswing lending library now, but when I shut my eyes, it's like they're still around me."

"I noticed that my first day." Refocusing on the corpse, Ben noted another birthmark, as well as slim white scars stacked on Freddy's upper thighs and buttocks. Although it was nothing Ben hadn't seen before, the sight always sickened him. Clearly, Freddy's parents hadn't spared the rod. Then there were the missing teeth and ruptured ear drums. Ben's groundswell of sympathy was so familiar and automatic, he'd finished his external notes before he remembered.

This man was paid to kill Penny and put me through agony. I might not need the cane forever, but my leg will never be the same.

It was true. Yet his sympathy did not wane. He could want justice for Penny, feel sad and angry as he recalled his weeks of pain, and still view Freddy as an object of pity; a man who'd aspired to only the bare bones of life and been denied them all the same. "I'm not even good enough to die for my country," he'd said. Now here he was, naked under a harsh bulb, dependent on the man he'd almost killed to transcribe and disseminate his final testament, the tale only a dead man could tell. And although many emotions crowded inside Ben, he found he could contain them all without denying any. Maybe he'd never been the sort of musclebound specimen who could heft fourteen stone of dead weight over one shoulder. But he bore the psychological weight of Freddy Sparks all the same.

As Ben gathered his instruments for the internal examination, including scale, scalpel, enterotome, rib cutters, and forceps, Lady Juliet still showed no signs of leaving. After arranging his tray, buttoning his lab coat, and donning rubber gloves, he cleared his throat. Twice.

"Good gracious, doctor. Are you attempting to signal me?"

"I thought you might like to brew us a spot of tea. I'll join you in the kitchen once this is sorted."

"Tea? Tea is commonplace. Witnessing a post-mortem is extraordinary." Lady Juliet's brown eyes sparkled. "I have no intention of leaving this room."

He nearly groaned aloud. "Very well. But if you swoon, don't expect me to catch you or drop what I'm doing to fetch the smelling salts." Ignoring her protestations over the word "swoon," which went on at some length, Ben repositioned Freddy, took up his scalpel, and made the Y-shaped chest incision he'd learned on his first day of medical school.

As he completed the cut, he heard the door between office and living space close, and Lady Juliet called from the other side, "Putting the kettle on!"

Smiling, Ben returned to his work.

***

It was past eleven when Ben entered the kitchen. He'd expected to find nothing but cold tea and perhaps a note from Lady Juliet, explaining that she'd located the guest room and put herself to bed. Instead, he discovered her sitting at the little table, watching a striped orange tabby lap milk from a bowl on the linoleum floor.

"There you are!" She looked up and smiled. "Your rubbish bin was overflowing, so I unlatched the back door to carry it out, and Humphrey ran in. I haven't seen him since Lucy died. Thought the old boy made off for greener pastures."

"He tripped me the other day. Then planted himself under my shrubbery." Ben studied the cat, who spared him one supremely indifferent glance before re-immersing himself in the cream. "Do you suppose he's back for good? As a boy, I had a dog, but I've never been master to a cat."

Lady Juliet laughed. "Obviously not, if you'd dare use the 'm' word so blithely around a member of the feline persuasion." She gestured to the various crocks, boxes, and tins open atop the table. "A lifetime at the manor hasn't rendered me much of a cook, I fear, so rather than desecrate precious foodstuffs in an attempt to make dinner, I raided the larder bachelor-style. We have Stilton, half a coffee cake, stale rolls I presume Mrs. Cobblepot was saving for a meatloaf, and a bit of cold chicken. Oh, and tea, of course. I kept the water simmering. No, no, sit down. You've exerted yourself quite enough tonight. I don't mind serving you. *This once.* Dare I inquire if you uncovered any shocking revelations about Freddy's demise?"

"All I can say for certain is, I still don't believe Freddy asphyxiated himself." Pulling out a chair, Ben sank into it gratefully. It had been a long day. "Finding evidence of poisoning is feast or famine. Either it's unmistakable due to signs like copious vomit and a chemically burned esophagus, or it's so subtle as to be invisible. Fortunately, St. Barnabas has the resources to test Freddy's blood, liver, and spleen. If a toxin killed him, we'll know."

"So you'll be taking him to the hospital tomorrow?"

"Not all of him. Just his blood, liver, and spleen."

Lady Juliet made a little sound in her throat.

"Isn't that the very noise you've accused me of making?"

"No. Yours is pained. Mine is merely contemplative." She placed a cup and saucer before him, then returned to her seat. "When you reduced Freddy to his constituent parts, I'd like to say I wondered where he is at this moment—his essence, I mean. But the sad truth is, I care as little now as I did when he was alive. It's Lucy I can't stop thinking about. Would you believe me if I said I heard her voice earlier tonight?"

"Tell me about it." As Ben listened, he tried again to recall his dream, specific words, specific images. Why had Lucy spoken directly to Lady Juliet, yet given him the magpie lighter? If she could interact with the living so directly, why not both times?

"Oh, my, now you sound like a scientist," Lady Juliet laughed after hearing his questions. "This isn't a laboratory, and if Lucy's become supernatural, you'd do well to recall that word means 'outside the natural.' All over Cornwall, you'll find stories of apparitions bearing messages but rarely do they pull up a spectral chair, as it were, and have a tête-à-tête with the poor soul who stumbled upon them. Usually the living are forced to work a good deal harder. No doubt Lucy could speak to me because I'm, well, exceptional."

Ben snorted.

"A sensitive. A natural sensitive!" Lady Juliet retorted sharply enough to make Humphrey pause in cleaning his whiskers. "I've waited all my life for an encounter with the beyond!"

As Ben fought to contain his mirth, she continued doggedly, "Permit me to educate you, *doctor*, on the well-known behaviors of the ectoplasmic set. It just so happens that dreams are the most common method of communication. Even a rigid, narrow mind may expand sufficiently during sleep to permit contact. And moving objects is also perfectly typical. A possession disappears from one room and reappears in another, begging the question, what needs closer examination? The place? The item? Both together? If Lucy saw Freddy run you down, and then saw his lighter on the street, naturally she might choose to materialize the lighter in this house to lead you to him."

"Naturally." As far as Ben was concerned, Lady Juliet hadn't sufficiently answered any of his questions, but judging by her triumphant expression, she felt vindicated. "Tell me. Do you truly believe in all this?"

"I heard her voice. And what she told me proved accurate," Lady Juliet said. "Besides, if Dr. Carl Jung can believe in a collective unconscious, I can believe in ghosts."

"Fair enough. And I suppose you're right—they do seem to move objects more than they speak. Do you think we should try to contact her? Now, I mean?"

"What did you have in mind?" Lady Juliet collected Humphrey's empty milk bowl, placing it in the sink as the orange cat ran a massive paw under the new stove. When a few swipes failed to produce whatever he sought, he began sniffing beneath the boiler, clearly on a mission.

"My grandmother called this a talking board," Ben said, limping to the living room. He hadn't opened the steamer trunk since the night he'd first become aware of Lucy; perhaps it was time. Pulling out the Ouija board, he studied it more carefully than before. Made of walnut, it looked older than he remembered, and hand-carved: sun on the left, moon on the right, A-Z and 0-9 in the middle, HELLO at the top and GOOD-BYE at the bottom. Across its surface were scratches and deep gouges, as if a séance had gone awry.

"There's no planchette, but perhaps we can devise something. A pencil might work, to point at letters, or a—"

Something skittered across the kitchen's linoleum floor, coming to rest at his feet. He recognized the heart-shaped bit of wood on tiny brass casters at once. The missing planchette, retrieved by Lucy's cat and batted at him right on cue.

Ben stared at it wordlessly for several seconds. He'd only just gotten comfortable again, sleeping in Fenton House, and now this. Humphrey studied him, eyes slitted, feline face inscrutable.

"I'm not too sure about this," Ben admitted, placing the board on the table.

"Neither am I." Lady Juliet ran a finger over the board's many scratches. "It was so strange, the gas leak that killed Lucy. Suppose…. I mean, I don't want to sound hysterical, but perhaps using this board wouldn't be like ringing up Lucy. Rather, suppose it's akin to unlocking your front door and inviting the whole world inside?"

Ben placed the planchette on the board. He preferred not to admit it aloud, but he'd temporarily misplaced his scientific skepticism, just as Lady Juliet seemed to have forgotten her lifelong desire to commune with spirits.

"Before we resort to an actual séance, let's try to solve this case through normal channels," Ben said.

"Penny made some notes in a book that need decoding. I thought I'd start at the village library."

"Oh, no, that will never do. The Birdswing lending library is hopeless for serious inquiry. I should know. I'm its patroness. We offer a wonderful collection of fiction, both classic and modern, but little else. If by research you mean encyclopedias, you'll need to go to Plymouth. If you seek old newspapers on microfilm, scholarly journals, and so on and so forth, we'll have to go to London."

Ben, who was wondering how much community ire he'd incur by closing his office for another day, almost missed the "we" in "we'll."

"You're coming?"

"Naturally." Lady Juliet smiled at Humphrey, who'd sprawled lengthwise beside the boiler as if he owned it. "You'll require assistance with what I suspect may prove the very heart of detective work: perseverance in the face of tedium. Now, if you don't mind, I'm exhausted." As she left the kitchen, she called over her shoulder, "Goodnight! Don't let the tomcat bite."

***

Tedium wasn't too strong a word, at least for the first half of the day. They drove to Plymouth shortly after first light and parked the Austin Ten-Four at the station, taking the train to London and arriving at the British Library on Euston Road around noon. Ben started with the only word in Penny's book of sonnets that stood out to him: the name Mosley. That led to dozens of articles, eventually bringing to mind a certain photograph he'd glimpsed, perhaps coincidentally, perhaps crucially. Taken together, all of them led back to a word Penny had jotted on a different page: Olympia. As Ben looked into that, Lady Juliet discovered, with the help of a patient librarian, the origin of the quote in the front of Penny's book:

"The broad masses of a population are more amenable to the appeal of rhetoric than to any other force."

"This is so exciting," Lady Juliet confided to Ben over sandwiches at a nearby café.

"You think?" He felt slightly dirtied by what they'd uncovered thus far, not to mention the larger implications.

"The librarian was scandalized, absolutely appalled, when I said I needed to see the passage with my own eyes," Lady Juliet continued. "She had the book behind the desk, under lock and key, so only appropriate patrons could get a peek. I asked her why the library didn't just chuck it if they considered it so dangerous. She said a copy needed to be available for criticism from official channels."

"I suppose that means borrowing a copy is out of the question?"

"Afraid so. Plymouth authorities will just have to take our word."

Ben wasn't sure how well that would go, so he returned to his research all the more determined to find additional evidence. Another of Penny's notes led him to microfilm records of the *Daily Mail* on 13 March 1937, when a letter to the editor had been published. The author, as he now expected, was G. Freeman.

***

"I simply cannot fathom it," Lady Juliet said again. The fact that they were in a crowded station awaiting the train back to Plymouth didn't deter her from speaking openly on the topic; indeed, she seemed unable to stop herself. "I've known Gerald for years. Known Margaret since I was a baby. We didn't get on as children, but she improved a great deal with time, or so I believed."

"A year ago, if someone had suggested to me that Penny was a lifelong blackmailer, I would have denied it," Ben said in a low voice, wishing she would follow his example. "We tend to assume the secret conduct of others mirrors our own. That can make us blind to possibilities we consider *verboten*."

"Apt word choice," Lady Juliet said dryly. "But there's another reason Margaret couldn't be involved in Penny and Freddy's murders. She was ill when you and Penny arrived in Birdswing. I'd invited her up to the manor to advise me on the roses—she's a prize-winning gardener, you know—and she had to beg off on account of her skin. The affliction is wretched and quite real, I assure you. When the flare-ups come, she can't bear sunlight and is embarrassed to be seen. She missed my bonfire gala for the same reason, the day Freddy was murdered."

"Speaking of Freddy, I really should ring the pathologist now, or it will have to wait till morning." Ben made the call from a nearby public telephone. He expected a nurse or intern to read Freddy's toxicology results to him. Instead, St. Barnabas's chief pathologist himself came on the line with a pointed question: had Ben treated Freddy Sparks for hypertension or dropsy?

"Neither," Ben said. "I never examined him alive, but except for his childhood injuries, he seemed reasonably well."

"Our records indicate the same," the pathologist said. "Yet he died from an overdose of digitalis."

Ben returned to Lady Juliet, seated on a red-lacquered bench and still visibly stewing over the Freemans, and said, "Freddy was poisoned. Perhaps by prescription medication, perhaps by a plant called foxglove. Tell me more about this illness of Mrs. Freeman's."

It was long past full dark when they arrived in Plymouth. Neither had expected to be in London so long—Lady Juliet had only her handbag, Ben his black doctor's bag—yet circumstances demanded they rent rooms for the night. A policeman escorted them to the nearest hotel, which mercifully had not only vacancies but a restaurant. Over dinner, Ben outlined what he saw as the best way to proceed.

"But I feel I should be there when you confront them!" Lady Juliet cried, once again louder than necessary. "I'm outraged by Gerald's conduct, and Margaret's beggars belief. I want to look her in the eye and hear what she has to say for herself."

"Do you expect to be swayed by it?" Ben asked. He'd ordered steak and kidney pie, but his stomach was so tense, each mouthful was a burden.

"Of course not. I only plan on inviting her to explain so I can tell her how very wrong she is." Lady Juliet pushed her fish aside. "I can't swallow another bite. If it weren't for the blackout, I'd march up to her door this instant."

"Then the blackout has finally done me a favor. *Juliet*," Ben said, deliberately omitting the honorific to be sure he had her attention. "Beyond this point, you shouldn't be involved. I understand you feel as if you know the Freemans, but if we're correct, you never knew them at all. Beneath the surface, they're dangerous people. Turning up at their house hurling accusations isn't smart. Or safe. Tomorrow, I'll go to Plymouth CID and tell them everything. True, there are a few missing pieces, but with any luck, they'll listen anyway. If you ring the manor first thing tomorrow, Old Robbie can come collect you, and you'll be safely back in Birdswing when the police apprehend the Freemans."

Lady Juliet said nothing.

"Are we agreed?" Ben prodded.

She took a deep breath. "Oh, very well. I suppose I'll have one more bite of fish."

Chapter 14: Chain Home
7 November, 1939

Now this, Juliet thought, *is terribly clever. Ben will be so impressed.*

Of course, she'd pretended to ring Belsham Manor for Old Robbie, but that was just a white lie. After Ben set off in his car, bound for the police station, Juliet engaged a cab to take her to Margaret Freeman's house.

She wasn't being foolish. She was utilizing her insider knowledge of the enemy's movements. On Tuesdays, Margaret chaired a breakfast meeting of the Compassionate Ladies, a charity she'd founded after every Plymouth organization of good repute refused her application to join. While Margaret presided over her group, Gerald would be at the office. On Tuesdays, he habitually left around half-past eleven, which meant he and Margaret would both arrive home at noon. They spent every Tuesday afternoon together, reserving that time for the two of them, something Juliet always kept in mind when scheduling luncheons with Margaret. This Tuesday afternoon, their usual tryst would be interrupted by Plymouth CID. And as it was now nine o'clock, Juliet had nearly three hours to comb the Freeman property and dig up some crucial bits of damning evidence.

"Good morning, Bertha. Those spots are clearing up," Juliet greeted the maid who opened the door. Bertha, young, nervous, and usually spotty, seemed about to launch into an apology when Juliet swept past her into the hall. "Never mind that, I know Margaret's not at home, she's never at home Tuesday mornings. I'm in Plymouth for the morning and simply cannot delay. I require clippings from her garden and a book from Gerald's study, I saw just the thing last week at the party, surely you remember?" Juliet tried to speak faster than she estimated Bertha's mind could process data. It seemed to work; the girl nodded dully.

"Now, ordinarily, I'd sit down, have a cup of tea, and await my dear friend Margaret, but I'm terribly busy, you understand, terribly busy, and I've no wish to disrupt this home's domestic routine," Juliet continued even faster. "So pretend I'm not here, Bertha dear, and don't trouble Mrs. Nash with my presence, either. I'll collect what I need, write Margaret and Gerald a heartfelt note of thanks, ring up a cab, and be on my way."

Or stroll down the block, lurk in the shrubbery, and pop up as Margaret and Gerald are led away in handcuffs, Juliet added mentally. It was a fantasy she'd enjoyed three times since breakfast. She hadn't yet decided if crying "*J'accuse*!" was fitting or slightly over the top.

Leaving Bertha, still nodding uncertainly, in her wake, Juliet went first to the garden. As she expected, the foxgloves were past blooming but still alive. She cut a few pieces for evidence, tucked them in her handbag, and carried one of the pots to a dark corner behind a wheelbarrow. Suppose the police questioned Margaret and Gerald before thoroughly searching the house? She might dispatch a maid to destroy all evidence the medicinal plant was ever grown in her garden, and Juliet couldn't permit that.

Smiling to herself, she made her way back into the house through the back parlor's french doors. She half expected Bertha to reappear, dull wits in need of another verbal drubbing, but no servants turned up or asked any questions. She was inside Gerald's study in a minute flat.

And there it was on the wall, displayed in Gerald's inner sanctum: that photograph of him beside Lord Oswald Mosley, founder of the BUF, or British United

Fascists. Juliet had seen it many times but taken no notice; Lord Mosley, after all, looked like just another blandly handsome aristocrat, the sort who generally cared more for his horse and hound than his fellow man. But Lord Mosley had at least one personal detail in common with Gerald Freeman—he, too, had married his mistress. In Mosley's case, he'd wed Lady Diana in secret at the home of Joseph Goebbels, with a guest list that included Adolph Hitler.

A clock ticked loudly on the desk. Compulsively, Juliet checked, but it was barely half-past nine. She had plenty of time to rifle Gerald's desk in search of damning evidence. Clearly, Penny and Margaret had kept up their friendship over the years, and at some point Penny had seen or heard enough in the Freeman house to realize where Gerald's political sympathies lay. In terms of simple blackmail, it didn't matter if the British government considered Gerald's association with Mosely, his pro-Nazi letter to the *Daily Mail's* editor, and his presence at the BUF's violent Olympia rally to be high treason. If Penny had spread the news, Plymouth society—English society—would have washed their hands of Gerald, his shipping business would have failed, and he and Margaret would have lost everything.

And right now that's all Ben has, evidence of social crimes, not literal crimes, Juliet thought, opening the top drawer and pulling out a handful of papers. *He can tell the police Mrs. Daley saw a woman on the Sheared Sheep's roof, but we have no proof it was Margaret. He can say Lucy's ghost led us to Freddy, but that road goes straight to a padded room. He can present all our circumstantial findings, including the numbers Penny jotted in her book, and say it's logical to conclude she blackmailed the Freemans till they killed her. That might be enough for an arrest, but suppose counsel gets Margaret and Gerald off? I need to find something solid, something undeniable, something—*

"Just what do you think you're doing?"

At the sound of Margaret's voice, Juliet looked up. Freezing behind Gerald's desk, a pile of letters and memorandums spread across the green leather blotter, Juliet tried to speak, but for once in her life, no words came out. Margaret's disheveled hair and silk wrapper revealed that she'd been home all along, and sleeping late, apparently. It was a fact Bertha might have managed to pass along to Juliet, had she paused long enough to allow it.

"Margaret. I—well. The plain truth is, we—that is to say, I—happen to know—"

Margaret closed the library door. And before Juliet could get around the massive desk, the key turned in the lock and was withdrawn with an audible scrape, leaving Juliet alone with no way out.

And suddenly she didn't feel so terribly clever after all.

***

The study had no window, alternate door, or telephone, and Margaret and her staff proved deaf to shouts and pounding on the walls, so Juliet sat down behind the desk and waited. And waited. And waited. Around ten o'clock, she gave up trying to concoct a clever excuse for her snooping and started going through Gerald's papers again. As noon approached, she gave up, infuriated to have uncovered nothing significant. Yes, before the declaration of war, he'd done extensive business with Germany, Russia, and Spain, but that was public knowledge. And if he possessed specifically incriminating documents, such as proof of ongoing communication with Reich Minister of Propaganda Goebbels, he kept them elsewhere.

Margaret must be waiting for Gerald to come home, Juliet thought. *Then they'll march in and confront me, perhaps with a policeman to charge me with trespassing. I've made a complete and utter fool of myself, and Ben will never speak to me again.*

Around half-past twelve, her prediction came true for the most part. A key turned in the lock, the study door opened, and Margaret and Gerald entered. Margaret looked coldly composed, if a touch overdone; she wore hat, gloves, and a warm woolen dress. Gerald, attired for business as always, looked as gray as his pinstriped suit. It was the first time he'd ever greeted Juliet without that genial smile on his face.

"What's all this, then?" he asked.

Rising, Juliet made an effort to stand tall, despite the fact her knees were shaking. This confrontation would end with her being tossed out on her ear, of course, but the powers of speech had returned to her, and she was determined to have her say.

"I know about you, Gerald. That's Lord Mosley you're standing beside." She indicted the framed photo. "I saw a newspaper picture of you at the Olympia rally, the one where some poor soul lost an eye. And I found that reprehensible letter you wrote the editor of the *Daily Mail* linking *Hamlet* to Hitler, of all things. And while I shudder to imagine Penny was cleverer than I, the truth is, she worked it out years ago, didn't she? Pretended to be on your side. And once you gave her that book of sonnets, including the quotation straight out of *Mein Kampf*—which a rather scandalized librarian was kind enough to show me—Penny had proof enough to begin blackmailing you."

Gerald gave a shaky laugh. "Do you think I'd leave that picture hanging up , even in a room that's intended for friends and family, if admiring Lord Mosley was a crime? I'm hardly alone in believing this phony war is the worst possible course for our country. And as an Englishman—a *patriot*—I have not only the right but the duty to express my views. The voice of the loyal opposition must be heard."

"If you've done nothing but criticize the war without the bounds of legal propriety," Juliet asked, "why pay off Penny? A thousand pounds here, a thousand pounds there … I know you're well-off, Gerald, but those are sizable sums. And if you couldn't afford to go on, why not allow her to do her worst? Why hire Freddy Sparks to run her down after dark?"

"For God's sake, Ju, this is nonsense!" Margaret burst out. "Penny's death was an accident. Freddy's was suicide. What's more…." She pushed up one sleeve, revealing an arm covered with half-healed welts and angry red boils. "I missed your catastrophe of a fête because of my skin condition, remember? Shall I strip naked, *detective*, and show you why I haven't left the house for a week?"

"I'm grateful for your garden mentorship," Lady Juliet went on, enjoying the sight of high color marring Margaret's usually flawless completion. "You've won so many cups. But you never told me your ranunculuses had a secret purpose."

"I have no idea what you mean." Margaret's tone indicated just the opposite.

"It's a medieval beggar's trick, smearing ranunculus oil on the skin to produce sores. Greater sympathy means additional alms. Whenever you need an excuse or an alibi, you use that oil to create 'flare-ups,' don't you? And they look so painful, no one suspects it's self-inflicted."

Margaret let her sleeve fall. "You've been talking to that doctor. I pity you, Ju. You had one chance at happiness with Ethan, and you botched it. Now all you can do is spin fantasies and retreat into madness."

"We're willing to reconsider going to the police," Gerald announced, doing his best to look severe, but his face was still gray. "Lady Juliet, I'm sure you wouldn't want this written about in the papers or gossiped about in Birdswing. You've always been considered lightly-balanced, perhaps intellectually deficient—"

"How *dare* you?" Fists clenched, Juliet started around the desk. Gerald stopped her with an upraised hand.

"Let me put it differently. You often behave in a manner that suggests intellectual deficiency. Why else break into our house, root around our garden, and rifle my private papers with Margaret upstairs the entire time? After this, even Lady Victoria might agree you need confinement in a sanatorium. But if you give me your word, your absolute word, that you'll abandon these notions and seek the attentions of a physician—"

"Not that man you're obsessed with but a qualified physician," Margaret broke in.

"—and we'll permit you to leave. If you refuse, I have no choice but to inform not only the police but the press."

Juliet was too angry to be frightened by their threats. Gerald's words were insulting enough, but Margaret's taunt about Ben was unbearable.

"There were witnesses!" she cried. "One saw Freddy Sparks behind the wheel of the lorry. The other saw Margaret on the roof of the Sheared Sheep just before Penny was killed."

Gerald sucked in his breath. He fumbled in his breast pocket, coming up with a small bottle of pills, but Margaret elbowed him in the ribs and he put it away.

"What witnesses?" she asked coldly.

Juliet smiled. She knew Gerald was a hypochondriac, that his nitroglycerin was probably just a placebo, but seeing him so gravely frightened made her more certain than ever.

"With regards to the lorry," she said slowly, determined to watch them sweat, "many inquiries were made. You purchased it from a Birdswing garage, didn't you, Margaret? Probably claimed it was for a delivery service. I can't pinpoint its location now, since you must have hidden it once it served its purpose, but I expect when the police question your staff, someone will sing. Doubtless it's parked in Gerald's shipyard or down by the docks."

"I don't believe there are witnesses," Margaret said. "Not even people you've recruited to tell lies. If there were, you'd name them and be done with it."

"The witness who saw Freddy behind the wheel won't be coming forward," Juliet said. "But she found Freddy's magpie cigarette lighter at the scene. I'm keeping it somewhere safe, Margaret. It's another link in what's growing to be a very long chain of evidence. And the person who saw you atop the Sheared Sheep, dressed in a hat and coat and watching Stafford Road, *will* testify, rest assured."

"Who? One of those drunks at the pub? That little whore Edith?"

"Mrs. Daley," Juliet said.

Margaret and Gerald exchanged glances. She put a hand on his arm, just lightly, before giving Juliet a dazzling smile.

"Oh, my! The word of a colored gal from Golliwog-land verses a native Englishwoman of means. How much did she charge to lie for you? Testimony from her sort probably comes at a bargain. You're better off with the imaginary witness who saw Freddy behind the wheel, so long as that imaginary witness is white." She laughed, and even Gerald managed what sounded like a pained chuckle.

Lady Juliet stared at her. "I'm ashamed I ever called you friend."

"Well, if it's any consolation, Ju, old girl, I've enjoyed you very much. You were always good for a laugh," Margaret said. "Even now, when you've clearly gone round the bend, I'm more amused than angry. Go on, spread lies about my skin condition. The rest is utter rot. Of course someone found Freddy's lighter at the scene. Before Freddy did himself in, he confessed to killing Penny in writing—"

"Freddy could barely write his own name," Juliet cut across her. "Careless of you to miss that detail. You're only a few years older than Freddy. I remember how he used to follow you around. I'll bet he adored you. I'll bet you were the first girl he ever loved. How could you forget what Mrs. Cobblepot, Luke Hewitt, and surely Edith will swear to in court: Freddy couldn't write anything, even a one-line note begging forgiveness, without resorting to clipping words from a newspaper. Besides"—Juliet paused to savor her triumph—"Acting Constable Gaston has said nothing publicly about Freddy's death. How do you know a confession was found beside Freddy's corpse unless you wrote that letter yourself?"

Gerald reached deeper into his coat pocket, but this time he didn't bring out the nitroglycerine. He brought out a gun.

"I do wish you listened more and talked less," he said, hand trembling as he pointed it at her.

For the second time that day, Juliet found herself momentarily speechless. It was hard to locate even simple words when staring down a revolver.

"Don't… don't make this worse for yourselves," she began, fighting to keep her voice steady. "If you shoot me, you'll… you'll…."

"We'll what, Ju, dear? Be hanged a second time for your murder after we swing for Penny and Freddy?" Margaret's color was back to normal, her tone calm and resolved. "I'm rather relieved you caught me out. It makes this so much simpler. After I locked you in the study, I told Bertha you'd had a nervous breakdown, and I was off to find a doctor. Instead, I drove to Gerald's office to make arrangements. We've always said if things go wrong, we'll liquidate the business and sail for Spain. We hoped we wouldn't be obliged to smuggle ourselves in the cargo hold of one of Gerald's freighters, but…." She shrugged. "We returned here hoping to convince you to say nothing, at least for a day or two, so we'd have time to get safely away. Naturally, you wouldn't have it."

Softly but distinctly, the front doorbell rang. Juliet, whose world had narrowed to a pinhole the moment she saw that gun, suddenly remembered why she and Ben had parted that morning: to tell Plymouth CID everything.

"Margaret," Gerald said nervously.

"I told the staff to admit no one. Absolutely no one. We are not at home." Margaret still sounded calm.

"I don't understand," Juliet said wildly. All she could do now was stall them, encourage them to talk, distract them in case rescue really was on the doorstep. "How can you abandon your country?"

"Spain will be temporary. We'll return when things are different," Margaret said. She glanced at her husband, but his attention remained fixed on Juliet even as perspiration stood out on his forehead. "I've told you, we're patriots. We love the English. Not dirty immigrants with their hands out, not those disease-ridden warrens in London, not interlopers like Mrs. Daley and her mongrel child, but England. The true England of Alfred the Great, of Shakespeare, of Lord Nelson. Whatever mistakes the Germans have made, they were driven to it after Versailles. And their vision for the Thousand Year Reich will save the Anglo-Saxon race before it's diluted beyond recognition."

"And what about Freddy? I know Penny was greedy. I know you must have felt trapped by her demands, and if Freddy adored you half as much now as he did before…."

"He did." Margaret's eyes shone with a curious pleasure. "Freddy lived a few houses down from my mother's. He wasn't always so sad to look at. On rainy days, when I was twelve and he was eight, we played together in Mum's parlor. Before I had my looks, before I had my wealth, before I had my sex appeal, I had Freddy. He worshipped me. He would have done anything for me, absolutely anything."

"And was that reciprocated?" Juliet asked. "I seem to recall him tagging after you much later, when you were seeing Mitchell Watkins and Freddy's eardrums were still intact. He picked wildflower posies for you. You flung them in the rubbish bin and told everyone you were his maths tutor. But he was your creature, wasn't he, even if you wouldn't claim him. How far did you go to keep him ensnared?"

"Not as far as poor Ethan went to ensnare you," Margaret snapped. "But when it comes to sex, it's easier for a man to stall a woman than the other way round. So I turned to ranunculus oil. It creates a very convenient escape from obligations, and Freddy always said he understood."

"You know, when Freddy was drunk, he told me he had a theory about women." Ben Bones appeared in the study's open doorway. His black doctor's bag was in his left hand, his cane was in his right, and Bertha the maid stood beside him, cringing.

"You did say you wanted a doctor, Mrs. Freeman," the girl quavered.

What happened next went so fast, Juliet failed to act, though perhaps she might have. Gerald gasped, flinching from obvious chest pain, and Margaret snatched the gun from his hand. In the blink of an eye, she was beside Juliet, pointing that black revolver at her face. From this close, Juliet could see it was cocked and ready to fire.

"Gerald, get hold of yourself! I have this under control!" Margaret barked, a steeliness in her voice Juliet had never heard before. "Ju, I don't want to kill you. I'd rather take you to Spain. A hostage is better than a corpse. And who knows, if you behave yourself, we might even drop you off at an embassy after things settle down. But if you test me, if you put one toe out of line, I'll pull the trigger, I swear it." Without taking her eyes off Juliet,

Margaret added, “Gerald, Dr. Bones is a cripple. See to him.”

There came a thump, a clatter, and a man cried out. Juliet saw everything that transpired, but Margaret, still staring fixedly at her, did not. Only when she took a step backward did she dare look across the study.

Bertha was running away, rapid footsteps echoing down the corridor. Ben, who’d dropped his bag and cane, held a shiny hypodermic needle. Gerald, one hand clapped to his neck, wore a look of astonished horror as he sank to his knees.

“What have you done to my husband?” Margaret demanded.

“Give the drug a minute to circulate through his bloodstream and you’ll see,” Ben said calmly. “And keep in mind, you’d better not shoot me if you want an antidote.” He cast a significant glance toward his black bag before fixing his gaze on Margaret. “Put the gun down.”

“I’ll shoot Juliet!” Margaret sounded uncertain. “I’ll shoot you, too!”

“Then your husband will die. How are you feeling, Gerald?”

“My heart,” he gasped, pressing both hands to his chest. “Beating fast… so fast….” His face was turning red, beads of sweat rolling off his forehead. “Was it cyanide?”

“Hardly. Adrenaline chloride. Very bad for a man with a delicate system. But I have just the thing to reverse it, if you let Lady Juliet go.”

“Margaret, make him help me,” Gerald pleaded. “Use the gun….”

The moment Margaret swiveled the revolver toward Ben, Juliet sprang at her. Seizing the smaller woman's wrist, she jerked away the gun, which went off with a deafening bang. Plaster dust drifted from the ceiling, an acrid smell hung between them, and Juliet was so shocked and infuriated, she let her fists do the talking, felling Margaret with a right cross.

"Now," Juliet declared, placing the revolver on the desk and looming menacingly over her erstwhile friend. Margaret lay on the floor, hat off, nose pouring blood, and it took all of Juliet's self-control not to kick her for good measure. "Let's hear it! All of it."

"Help me...." Gerald moaned.

"If you want help, do as the lady asks," Ben said. "As I mentioned, when Freddy was drunk, he had a theory about women. He said the best ones die, leave, or get sick. His mum died, and his best girl left. If Edith hadn't interrupted, he would have named you, Mrs. Freeman, as the woman who kept getting sick. And that's why he had to die, wasn't it? Because he couldn't keep a secret?"

"Yes." Margaret's voice sounded odd now, as if coming through a broken nose.

"Did he have a particular grudge against Penny?" Ben looked Gerald up and down. "I don't like your husband's color, Mrs. Freeman. Tell me precisely how you did it and leave nothing out."

"Penny was nothing to Freddy." Margaret made no effort to sit up, though she kept her eyes on her husband, speaking rapidly for his sake. "He didn't want to shoot her, and strangling was out. But running her down on Stafford Road, where everyone knows she killed that deliveryman years ago, that suited him fine. By then, Penny wanted another thousand, and I knew she'd arrive in Birdswing the evening of September first. Around four o'clock, I climbed the fire escape to the Sheared Sheep's roof and waited. We thought it would happen in daylight, and Freddy would have to blame glare from the sun or falling asleep behind the wheel, but instead you arrived at twilight. That was a gift.

"I climbed down and told Freddy. He roared out of the alley the moment you rejoined Penny on the street, Dr. Bones. Hit you both, then backed up and ran Penny down a second time, just to be sure."

"How did he get away?"

"It was easy in the blackout. Down Stafford Road he stashed the lorry in some trees. Walked back to Birdswing with no one the wiser. But the memory of crushing Penny's skull seemed to haunt him. Running you down bothered him, too. When he told me you'd accused him of leaving that ridiculous note, I realized he had to go."

"Margaret, hurry." Gerald had begun to hyperventilate.

"Freddy's vital organs were analyzed yesterday by the chief pathologist at St. Barnabas," Ben said. "In life, he never would have spoken against you. In death, he told the truth. Poisoning by digitalis. A drug derived from a very pretty flower called a foxglove."

"I accompanied him up to his room. Put it in his whiskey," Margaret said. "I thought a belt around his neck, not to mention the written confession, would be enough. Now please, doctor, help my husband! Your part in all this was mere coincidence, and you were injured, I'll admit that. You're right to expect compensation. Money, favors… surely we can come to some agreement. But first give Gerald the antidote!"

"You're in no position to give money or favors," Ben said, still in that unruffled tone Juliet found remarkable, considering the bullet hole in the ceiling and the sweating, writhing man at his feet. "I spent the better part of this morning trying to convince Plymouth CID of everything you just admitted to. I'm sorry to say they didn't take me very seriously. All I had were theories and bits of circumstantial evidence, and they wanted something concrete. That's why you took matters into your own hands, isn't it, Lady Juliet?"

"I'm so very sorry," Juliet said.

"Quite all right." Ben smiled at her. "By the end of the interview, I was grasping at straws. Describing the guests at the Freemans' luncheon, hoping one might be important. I mentioned the fellow with the red nose, the one suffering from that peculiar sneeze." Slowly, he knelt beside his doctor's bag, opening it wide. "He said the name of the ship was Chain Home. That he had the information from Lady Diana. Mr. Freeman, would that be Lady Diana Mosley?"

Gerald, still looking to the black leather bag for his deliverance, nodded desperately.

"The funny thing is, no one will tell me what Chain Home is. If it's a British ship or a German U-boat, or code for something else altogether. But I know the Plymouth chief of police rang up Scotland Yard. And when they come for you today, they won't only charge Mrs. Freeman for murder. They'll arrest you, Mr. Freeman, for espionage."

"Yes, yes, it's all true. It doesn't matter now," Gerald cried. "Give me the antidote!"

Ben made a show of looking in the bag. "Well . . . I did imply I carried it with me, but that's not strictly true. However, it's easily obtained. Something I prescribe to many patients, especially those with nervous conditions. Tincture of time."

"W-what?" Gerald gaped at him.

"Tincture of time," Ben repeated. "I carry adrenalin chloride in case of acute allergic reactions. It's a chemical your body produces naturally—fight or flight. For certain patients, it's therapeutic. For someone like you, who's prone to exaggerated complaints, it produces a racing heartbeat, flushed skin, and copious perspiration. But it does no harm and should wear off entirely before long."

Gerald looked appalled. "But this is real! You've poisoned me. I'm dying!"

"Suit yourself," Ben said, rising. "You don't have to believe me. Just wait. You should be feeling better right about the time the police turn up. And I should thank Mrs. Freeman for tipping me off about your hypochondria," he added. "I've no doubt your wife loves you dearly and would have killed Lady Juliet and me to keep you safe. But if she'd been able to resist teasing you in public, I never would have known."

***

"I do hope they let me attend the hanging," Lady Juliet said. Plymouth CID had ordered them to wait in the Freeman's living room until officers could interview them. A long night stretched ahead, and now that the crisis was past, she felt as shaky as Gerald in the throes of his panic.

"Fairly certain executions are no longer a spectator sport," Ben said.

"I know that. We receive news of the outside world in Birdswing, thank you very much." She rubbed her knuckles, which were sore. "By the way. Thank you very much."

"You've said that," Ben said lightly. But he, too, sat very straight, hands clasped rigidly, and she suspected he felt just as inwardly disturbed.

"How did you know where I'd gone?"

"I didn't. When the chief excused himself to ring Scotland Yard, I begged leave to call Lady Victoria. I was worried you might not have listened to me—imagine that—so I wanted to find out when Old Robbie was dispatched to collect you. Your mother said she hadn't heard from you yet. Then I rang up the Freemans, and Bertha answered. I identified myself as Dr. Bones, and before I could ask if you were there, she said, 'Are you the doctor who's coming for Lady Juliet? She had a nervous breakdown.'"

Juliet laughed to conceal her mortification. "Not my finest hour."

"No, indeed. It wasn't till I turned up at the door that she told me you'd been locked in the study all morning. I did a bit of thinking on my feet, drew up a syringe of adrenaline chloride, put it in my vest pocket, and told Bertha to lead me to the patient."

"That settles it. I'm offering Bertha a position at Belsham Manor," Lady Juliet declared. "And if she prefers to remain in Plymouth, I'll find some other way to reward her. If she weren't so gullible, I might be on my way to Spain right now. By the way, I rather enjoyed the trick you played on Gerald. Though I wonder if it pained your conscience, given that oath doctors swear."

"Strictly speaking, I didn't break it," Ben said. "I promised to do no harm, not to refrain from giving the *impression* I'd done harm. But whether or not a jury of my peers would exonerate me for frightening a man suffering from angina pectoris...." He shrugged. "He was threatening your life. Still, I'd appreciate it if you didn't disseminate that part of today's events to the rest of Birdswing."

"And have your patients worry you'd sworn a Hypocritical Oath? Never." Juliet smiled. "Do you suppose we'll ever discover what Chain Home is?"

"I don't know. After the war, perhaps. As long as the Germans don't find out, that's good enough for me."

There was a moment's silence. Then Juliet forced herself to say, "I do feel I ought to explain why I went snooping. If only Margaret hadn't given up on that charity of hers, or at least told me it was dead. Because except for her being at home when I thought she was away, and except for Gerald not actually keeping incriminating papers in his desk, it was really terribly clever of me…."

He made that sound again, the pained one she found so annoying. But Juliet, overcome with gratitude for the man beside her, pretended not to hear.

Epilogue
22 November, 1939

Ben was exiting St. Mark's church by the vestry door when a familiar voice called, "Doctor! You've gone off and forgotten your cane again."

He waited until Lady Juliet crossed the high street. She'd been preparing more of Belsham Manor's garden for winter from the look of it, and had raided Old Robbie's wardrobe in the process. He checked her hair for stick-insects and was rather disappointed to find none.

"I didn't forget my cane. Just left it at the office." Lifting his black doctor's bag, Ben added, "Baby Mark has a cold. I came to check him again before he spends the weekend in Plymouth."

"And he received your blessing?"

"Wholeheartedly."

"That's a relief. I do hope Eunice's trial run convinces her husband. They desperately need this child in their lives."

"How's Dinah holding up?" Ben asked, easily matching Lady Juliet's pace. These days his limp was hardly noticeable, except when it rained. "No more crying jags?"

"None. She knows this is for the best. And I'm really quite proud of her. Dinah's still half a child herself. It isn't easy for her to know right from wrong. She's never had what you'd call a role model."

"She does now." Ben let his fondness for Lady Juliet creep into his voice, but instead of seeming pleased, she looked away.

"Any disturbances in Fenton House? Things going bump in the night?"

"No. Mind you, no one's died in Birdswing, either, so perhaps Lucy can rest comfortably for a time. Why, are you ready to try that talking board?"

"Not until we must. Oh! There's Rose Jenkins. I can practically smell my own damask roses from two hundred yards away." Lady Juliet waved at the petite redhead, who waved back. "Will you be taking her to the church hall dance, Sunday next?"

"I doubt it."

"Why not?"

"Because I took her out last week. And I'm in no hurry for matters to progress any quicker than that. My first experience with matrimony had a rather chilling effect."

"As did mine, Dr. Bones," Lady Juliet said solemnly, but she was smiling, smiling as if they were discussing the happiest topic in the world. "So I won't see you at the dance?"

"Of course you will. Just not with Rose. Care for some lunch?"

"Yes, indeed. I'm famished."

"Good. I've decided to try Laviolette's. Enough of these rumors. I prefer to experience things for myself." As Ben hoped, this declaration proved too much for Lady Juliet. He loved the look of horror in her eyes when she didn't quite realize she was being teased.

"Dr. Bones, I forbid it! I have it on good authority Mr. Laviolette purchases third rate flour and unsound beef. Once he served horse meat from a knackery!"

Ben laughed. "I thought you said you never spoke ill of your fellow villagers to an outsider."

Slipping her arm through his, Lady Juliet steered him toward Morton's café. "Ah, but you're not an outsider any more, Dr. Bones. You're one of us, and Birdswing is your home."

THE END

From the Author

I hope you've enjoyed book one of my new series, the Dr. Benjamin Bones Mysteries. In case you're wondering, "Chain Home" was the code name of Britain's first coastal radar system, a major breakthrough in defending the country against enemy aircraft. Thanks to Chain Home, it was no longer a sad truth that "the bomber always gets through."

For those who've enjoyed my Lord & Lady Hetheridge mystery series, I want to assure you it will continue. I have no desire to end it, I simply wanted to start a new series set during World War II. During the "War at Home," the heroism and daily sacrifices of ordinary British citizens was quite extraordinary, and I decided to celebrate it in this small way. (Throwing in some mystery, some romance, and a touch of the supernatural at the same time!)

So thank you for reading. As I continue working on my next Hetheridge book, BLACK & BLUE, I'll be thinking about the next Bones novel. Its working title is DIVORCE CAN BE DEADLY, and I have a very strong feeling that bounder Ethan Bolivar will show his face at last.

Cheers!
Emma Jameson
November 2014

Acknowledgements

The author would like to thank her expert early readers, Kate Aaron and J. David Peterson, for their help with countless small details. It is a truth universally acknowledged that no matter how many history books you read, or how many times you turn to Google, there's no substitute for a conversation with an expert. In the event that errors, like bombers, still got through, those errors belong to me alone.

The author would also like to thank the following priceless early readers, most of whom are published authors as well: Shéa MacLeod, Karin Cox, Alisa Tangredi, Leslea Tash, Tara West, CD Reiss, and Mary Ellen Wofford. Thanks also to Theo Fenraven, Jenx Byron, and Bonnie Toering. I'm so grateful to you all!